FOR[...]
& AL[...]

M.E. Brady is originally from Rockaway Beach, NY. She currently resides in Delray Beach, Florida with her husband of 39 years. She loves writing romances and creating characters her readers easily fall in love with. Her family, friends and fans have always encouraged her to keep that dream alive. She is grateful to have such a supportive team around her.

Dedication

"I know you're gone but I wasn't ready to say good-bye."
This book is dedicated to all those we loved and lost too soon.

Lori you will never be forgotten.

Kevin, we have that special kind of love and I'm always grateful
I have you in my life. To my children Jennifer,
Katelyn and Kevin love you forever.

Thank you to Mom, Katie, Neil, Rosa, and Kathy (Grammy)
for helping to make this project the best it could be.

To Mom and Dad a love story in itself.

A special shout out to Steven for all your help,
much appreciated.

Chapter One

Morgan stared out at the distant horizon from the balcony of her hotel room, entranced by the calming scenery the California ocean landscape had afforded her. *How could loving my beautiful little boy so intensely become the catalyst, the reason I lost my life-partner, my lover and my best friend?* She had been warned by many that this might happen but she was too consumed by grief to see it coming. She had spent the last six months in California; it was just what she needed to help her put the last year into perspective. She needed this solitude, being away from her family, to allow her time to reflect on the decisions she had made over the past year and address the grief that led to those poor decisions. She needed some space, to get away from any of her well-meaning but overbearing siblings and she took advantage of the opportunity she was offered. She spent her time wisely, keeping busy on the set, working on the adaptation of her latest romance novel into a movie and it came at the perfect time. Her life was in shambles and she needed to focus on herself for once. She knew it was time to work through her emotions to finally get the help she dreadfully needed. Perhaps her therapist had hit on something when she asked her if there was a chance that she blamed herself for Michael's death and wanted to put herself through an emotional wringer for being alive without him. She hadn't realized how badly she needed the therapy until she began to open up to a professional. It took the better part of these last few months to come to terms with Michael's loss, to be able to say the words out aloud; it was a major step in the right direction for her. But once the flood gate was opened, she felt a giant weight slowly being lifted off her shoulders as the wall she had created to keep herself numb came crashing down. It was difficult to admit that Michael was gone, that she was left behind to go on without him. Her life would never be the same without her beautiful son but she realized she owed it to Michael's memory to go on with her life and stop blaming herself for something she'd had no control over.

She had spent the last few weeks reflecting on the choices of the past year, choices she made out of fear, which ultimately impacted not only her life but Gage's life as well and not all for good. She and Gage both mourned the loss of their son together but each handled the loss very differently. Every time she looked at Gage, she saw Michael's face; it left her breathless and in tears. He was a constant reminder of the son she thought she couldn't live without.

She didn't want to feel anything after his death so the offer of running from the familiar seemed like a gift. She wanted to forget the horrible truth and shield herself from reality. California seemed as good a place as any to relocate.

It took many months of therapy but she was finally at a point where she didn't blame herself for Michael's death. He was gone for over a year now and he wasn't coming back. She accepted the realization that his death wasn't her fault or Gage's. Her little seven-year old boy was dead. Running from that truth, rather than dealing with it and going through the grieving process, wasn't good for her or her state of mind. The marriage she valued had also suffered very much.

She recalled the first day she arrived in Los Angeles. Her agent, Michele Ruggerio, saw to it that she was set up in a beautiful apartment overlooking the ocean. Her workday had started out normally, she was looking forward to going back to work again.

On her first free day that week, she decided to explore her new neighborhood with a morning run. Everything was uneventful until she met Martha. After running a few miles she stopped at a local vendor to pick up a bottle of water. She spotted a bench across the street that was vacant and looked directly out to the ocean. The view was magnificent. After her run it was truly relaxing. Martha had joined her on the bench shortly thereafter. They spoke about the little things in life for a while and Martha began to open up to her. She told her a story that had left Morgan speechless.

"I wasn't always alone. I had a family. My husband and I lived here in Oak Knoll with our two children, Max and Sofia. We were happy for a long time. Our life was perfect, until the fire." She began to tear up as she pointed to a lovely home across the street. If the fire had occurred there, it had certainly been meticulously restored. It was a beautiful home, obviously reconstructed with care to model the home that stood once before. But it didn't seem as if anyone lived there now. *"My family was wiped out in less than one day. I never recovered from that loss. I have spent the past twenty-five years praying I could have my old life back, but it never happened. One day, when the pain was just too much for me, I tried to take my own life but I didn't succeed. I ended up in the hospital. As soon as I was fit enough to leave, my attorney saw to it that I was committed to the best psychiatric facility money could buy. I began to get the help I should've gotten a long time ago. Perhaps, if I had, I could've have met someone instead of being all alone today. I might've had a chance at starting a new life. My husband, Kevin, and our kids Sofia and Max would've wanted me to be happy, even if it meant going on without them."* Morgan never forgot what the woman divulged to her that day. Although she was curious, she never saw her again. She often wondered if Martha was really an angel sent to her to give her a message. She tried to stop by the home to visit Martha on several occasions but was always told the lady of the house was not available for visitors. She never saw her again but was thankful for the day that Martha came into her life because everything changed for her because of that encounter.

She entered into therapy the very next day and it finally felt good to remember Michael with a smile, instead of the intense sadness she had been become accustomed to experiencing over the past year. There were days she would wake up and feel such overwhelming sadness that she didn't think she could go on. No parent should ever have to feel such loss. *You should never outlive your children.* She often thought that suicide might end the pain but then she remembered Martha and the wise words she had shared with her. Besides, she couldn't bear the thought of what her death would do to all the people she loved. Her family had suffered enough at the loss of Michael. She missed him. Even though her new normal would be different, she knew she was getting stronger each day and she was ready to enter the world of the living once again. She owed Michael and his memory that much.

She didn't know why she was blessed to have finally reached this point in her recovery when it was so difficult for so many in her grieving parents group. Group therapy was working for many of them but they still hadn't reached that point in the grieving process that would allow them to move forward. Each time she attended the group, the sadness she witnessed was heartbreaking. She felt such camaraderie with these people. Accidental deaths, health issues, murder, suicide, it was all so horrendous. Everyone had a different story to tell. The therapist said they would all surmount different stages in the grieving process at different times but she promised them healing would come in time. *For some, it will take longer than for others, if ever,* Morgan thought to herself.

She had spent six months in therapy, thanks to Martha. After many bouts of anger, tears and sessions of intense emotional pain, she had finally made a breakthrough. She knew she had to stop blaming herself. There was nothing she could've done to move his name up on the transplant list. He didn't have a heart condition because of anything she or Gage did or didn't do. They had both suffered a lot as they watched their little boy wither away; in the end, she and Gage had to find the courage to let him go. She realized now that the time she spent recapturing the salient segments of her life was all part of the normal grieving process. She had just needed the help of a professional to get her through it. She decided rather quickly that the life she walked away from with Gage, when she ran from the pain of the loss of their child, had been a mistake. She wondered if it was already too late to go back and try to fix things with him.

Will Gage still want me in his life after the horrific year I had just forced upon him? I should have been there for him while he was suffering. Together we could have dealt with Michael's passing. Instead, I ran away from the one person I should've been running towards.

She stood in her pink silk nightgown stretching her neck up to the heavens, allowing the sun's heat to sooth her with its unbridled warmth as she thought about Gage. Even the sound of the surf was relaxing to her as it whipped lively against the rock wall jetty below. The sight of the seagulls as they skimmed across the ocean's surface searching for food brought comfort to her tired soul as well. Morgan would never grow weary of the ocean and its entire splendor. She found serenity and contentment being near any ocean, the Atlantic or the Pacific.

Memories of Michael skipping in the sand and building army forts with his father unexpectedly came flooding back as she stared out at the surf. Now, recalling those precious moments spent with her family, she smiled. They were happy times, when life couldn't have been any more perfect for them.

It was amazing how, in the blink of an eye, the security and contentment she felt with her little family had been ripped away. At times, her religious beliefs were called into question. *How could my God take my innocent little boy from me like that? If He had to take someone, why couldn't it have been me?* She knew that the answer to that question was something she would have to wait to understand. God didn't want her to suffer. One day she would understand why her cherished little boy was called home so soon. Her faith was being tested. During moments like this she would ponder the meaning of life.

Suddenly, Morgan snapped out of her musings as she took notice of the tourists in her line of vision. They were frolicking in the waves and had little or no indication that their vacations were about to be ruined by Mother Nature. She could tell that a storm was brewing on the horizon and it would probably arrive soon. Raised at a beach community, she had become accustomed to being able to recognize the early signs of an impending storm by watching the ocean; it spoke to anyone who would listen. For the first time in a long time she fondly remembered the rainy days of summer spent with her friends on the beach in Rockaway as a teen. *How crazy we were back then. We would stay on that beach as it down-poured all around us without any protection from the storm except makeshift tents we would build with blankets and beach chairs, as if they would protect us.* She smiled remembering her friends, it was crazy, but they all thought they were invincible. Lightening was a different story. They always stayed on the beach until the first sign of lightening, seeking shelter in nearby homes. The visitors down for the day, the DFD's (down for the day) as they were referred to by the locals would scramble to trains and buses that had taken them to the beach earlier in the day.

Rockaway had a lot of large homes that were used for summer rentals, huge homes that housed families from other places. Most of the families stayed for the entire summer; many lifelong friendships developed from those days. The end of summer was depressing, each of those friends would pack up, leaving the seven mile stretch of beach she and the other locals had called home. As time went by, the need for summer rental opportunities dwindled and the locals began to turn them into large single-family homes. These memories were guarded with affection; up until now she hadn't thought about them in a very long time. It was time to remember her past experiences with pleasure, something she hadn't felt or thought about in over a year. Perhaps, it was even time to reconnect with old friends.

It had been many months since she'd visited Rockaway, her home before and after she married Gage. Being in Rockaway only bought back memories of Gage and the life they shared together with Michael. Until now, she wasn't able to face the darkness those memories conjured up.

Her family was large, an Irish Catholic family well known on the Rockaway Peninsula. It was hard not to bump into at least one of the McCleary's at some point during a stroll on the boardwalk or the boulevard. When they were younger, the McCleary brothers; John, Jake, Logan and Alex were a force to be reckoned with; they were always in some sort of trouble. There were times she thought her mother would single-handedly kill one of her brothers for the grief they put her through. But Morgan knew her mother better than anyone and knew she wouldn't trade any of them or the experiences she went through because of them. As time went by they grew up and worshiped the matriarch of the family, though they often teased her about how mean they thought she'd been to them. Her brothers would do anything for the mother they shared so many stories and memories with. Her sister, Patti, didn't cause as much havoc as her brothers but she was a handful in her own right. She was a pro at sneaking out of the house and would walk in the house at all hours of the morning as if she had just stepped out for air a few minutes before. Morgan doubted that her parents were ever fooled by her siblings and their shenanigans. According to her mom, her Mom chose her battles carefully and it seemed to work for them. They all turned out pretty well considering all the havoc they had caused over the years.

By the time Morgan was of age to cause any havoc, she refrained from mischief-making. She had always been the one with larger than life dreams; she wanted off the peninsula. She wasn't about to allow anything or anyone to sway her from her goals. Going to school and staying out of trouble became a priority for her.

Another delightful memory surfaced as she thought about her family. They all gathered as a family at their parent's home for the usual Sunday ritual when they were in town. It always turned into a big party. She yearned for those times spent with her family. She wondered if Gage still attended family night, even without her. There was always the possibility that he had wiped her family out of his life, just as easily as he had discarded her.

John, Patti and Logan still called Rockaway home after all these years and Jake, currently serving in the military overseas, still came back when he was home on leave. Alex was the only one who lived in Manhattan. He felt he needed to be closer to work. She and Gage had a house on the beach block in Neponsit. Their house looked directly out toward the ocean. She missed everyone and she knew they were probably all wasting time worrying about her at their weekly gatherings. She was sure she was the topic of frequent discussion.

No one knew how or when their Sunday family gatherings began but it's been a family custom they all enjoyed and it brought a smile to their mother's face each time they came home. Her Mom loved preparing a big meal for them and having them at home. *It's time to go home.*

She'd had sporadic visits from her siblings while living in New York City, during the six months of her separation from Gage, and then during her stay in California. The visits were few and far between at her coaxing. At first she made excuses because she did not want to alarm them, but when she reached California she wanted to spend time focused on fixing herself. She convinced them not to come as often as they would've liked because she didn't have the time to spend with them during filming; for a time it worked. She didn't want them to know that she had reached rock bottom and had finally gone for the help she needed. She wanted to face her demons on her own. They would find out soon enough that she was a much healthier person now than when she'd left.

In the past, she had always thought she resented them meddling in her life but even though she hated to admit it, she missed their interfering and prying ways. Most of all, she realized just how empty her life was without Gage and her family.

Morgan decided to stay at a hotel during the final week of filming while the movie was wrapping up and to have all of her belongings boxed and shipped back east by truck before her arrival home. It was one less thing for her to think about while getting ready to return to her family. The movie was coming to a close any day so unless she was going to extend the lease for another six months, she would have to vacate the house. One of the actresses she had befriended on the set, Rachael, had offered her a place to stay but Morgan decided a hotel would be the best place for her right now so that she could be alone with her thoughts.

Her brother, Logan, had also called her earlier in the week and offered to fly out to stay with her this last week but she assured him she was more than capable of handling her exit on her own. The last thing she needed was for Logan to show up on set and mention anything about Gage or Michael to her new friends. They were oblivious to the fact that she was married or had had a child and it just made it easier not to have to explain her circumstances to anyone. She often felt a little guilt for that deceptive omission. She decided to meet with Rachael privately and explain why she had kept her past a secret. Of all the people she had met since arriving, Rachael was special. They had become friends and she wanted her to know just how much she cherished their friendship. It was refreshing to know that Rachael was such a down-to-earth person even though she was a superstar.

Morgan thought of her family again and was grateful for the closeness they shared; very few families were as close as they were to each other. It was often difficult, growing up in this family dynamic, to find any place to be alone with your thoughts. But on a whole, it was great growing up with such a crazy cast of characters. She wondered if they would they all be friends if they hadn't been born to the same parents. They were all so different from each other. *It often influenced what I wrote about,* she thought, laughing. *I could write numerous stories about my brothers. I never lacked for new ideas being around them, for sure.* Her brothers were always around, not because there weren't enough rooms in their home, there were plenty. The McCleary family believed it was their right to know what was going on in each other's lives all the time and any kind of isolation, even if it were self-inflicted, was simply unacceptable. That closeness and the need to know each other's business followed them into adulthood. It was amazing to Morgan that she had actually found the time to write her first novel without having one of her family members close by to offer suggestions or advice. She remembered a conversation she'd once had with Logan. Logan came into her room with her manuscript in hand, a manuscript he had no right to read. "Morgan, who the hell is Charlie, you can't trust this guy. He's a joke." He kept talking while Morgan ripped the manuscript from his hands.

"Logan, what are you doing? You had no right to read this."

Logan could see that she was upset, knowing that he had taken it upon himself to read her manuscript. It was a spur of the moment decision when he saw it on her desk and was heading to the bathroom. Reading material was his excuse. He didn't know if it was true, that authors sometimes wrote from experience. But if it was true, someone named Charlie was in trouble. He needed to find out who Charlie was. What was Charlie's real name and did he really sing to Morgan from the window of a building? How lame is that? This guy was singing about how he woke up with love this morning. Logan was afraid for his naïve teenage sister. It was obvious that she was taken in by this jerk, based on what she wrote.

"Who is he?" he asked her again.

Morgan remembered their conversation and smiled. Charlie had been a three day romance, a young man who had a crush on her and the feeling mutual, although fleeting.

The moment he began singing out his window to her, they were finished. To Morgan, that was just too weird for the young teen. She broke up with him three days after he'd asked her out. That was how they did things back in the day. It was innocent, one minute you had a boyfriend and the next you didn't. She laughed wondering what Logan might have had in mind for Charlie. They had barely kissed but Logan was convinced he had to protect her virtue. She and Logan were close and still were today. He was the one she shared most of her secrets with. But her writing was hers and she wasn't ready to share her love of writing with anyone. She recalled how difficult it was to find a place in the house to hide from her family in order to allow her thoughts to flourish. Quiet walks on the beach became a must.

The McCleary's were a tough bunch they didn't condone self-pity and they saw what she was doing to herself after Michael's death. They wanted to intervene but their mother had forbidden it. She knew Morgan needed time and she asked them all to give it to her. The five siblings had been truly concerned. They had been circling Morgan since she had left Gage. Her mom and dad called a family meeting to address the issue but there was one problem, Morgan wasn't having any of it. She made it perfectly clear that her personal life was none of her family's business; that they needed to stay out of it. They needed to let her deal with Michael's death and her marriage on her own, without their help. Her brothers' constant hovering and trips to her office at work and to her apartment was part of the reason why she ran.

Morgan recalled the day she decided to leave Gage to get her own place. She simply couldn't be reminded of Michael every moment of the day. Gage was a constant reminder of the son they lost. She thought her Mother would choke when she called to let her in on her plans. That call led to many others and that led to yet another surprise family meeting. This time the meeting excluded her. The McCleary's weren't exactly known for keeping secrets from one another. Her decision to split from Gage shocked and disappointed the entire family. Word spread like wildfire once the first call was made but the admission disappointed and distressed her brother Jake very much. He and Gage were best friends; they became more like brothers even before she and Gage became a couple. Jake saw their breakup as a mark against Gage's friendship. Morgan was not shocked when she received an overseas call from Jake, who was in Middle East. It was the first of many overseas calls regarding her relationship with Gage. Jake was worried about her. She'd had no idea where Lt. Col. Jake McCleary was stationed at that moment but she knew wherever he was there was enough danger to go around. Knowing Jake's background, if there was a mission that needed to be completed, his team would be the first to be called upon. No matter the extent or the danger they would encounter, they handled the job flawlessly as they had so many times before. *"What Jake doesn't need right now is to lose focus on his assignment worrying about me",* she had remembered thinking.

Another one of her brothers, John, wanted to know if there was anything he could do to help her. Being F.B.I. trained, Morgan was afraid to ask what he'd meant by that. John had taken a long time to warm up to Gage and it was apparent that he still didn't trust him. He often said repeatedly, *how can you trust a man who lives such a cloak and dagger lifestyle, always pretending to be someone else?* The answer was simple she loved Gage with all her heart and she trusted him. Her sister, Patti, loved Gage as well but she was loyal to Morgan, she immediately offered her husband Bill's legal services to her should there be a divorce in their future and Logan, who ranked third in the birth order, was a bar and restaurant proprietor and he made the best offer of all, his booze and a shoulder to soften the blow, free of charge. Logan hated to take sides in the separation since he had developed strong feelings for Gage as well, but blood was thicker than water and he owed his sister his loyalty, at least until they could make sense of it all.

Her younger brother, Alex, was finding the separation extremely difficult and trying to deal with it. Since college, Alex worked for Gage's construction company and had been with him ever since, learning all he could from Gage. She knew he had grown to love Gage as a brother, as had Logan and Jake. The separation was putting Alex and the others in a very complicated situation. They couldn't turn their backs on their brother by marriage. Therefore, since Alex had to work with Gage and see him every day, he chose to stay neutral. Morgan reassured him that she understood and respected him for his decision. Since she had split with Gage, there seemed to be something that Alex was keeping from her. Something he knew that no one else was privy to. Personally, she wished that the whole family had stayed out of her personal life because if they had, she wouldn't have had to admit to any of them that it was *her decision to move out of the house. She hadn't given Gage a chance to fight for them.* Truth be told, had it been up to Gage, they would still be together and be working on fixing whatever it was she perceived had gone wrong with their relationship.

Morgan glanced once again to the beach below, allowing the breeze to whip through her hair. She recalled her morning walks at home; walking on the beach was the only time she had found clarity and peace of mind. She loved the serene feeling the beach had always given her. She had never been a sun worshiper, like the tourists she found herself observing at the moment. She was one of those rare beach dwellers who hated lying around, baking in the sun and Gage had always felt the same way, or so she thought. She remembered walking with Gage along the water's edge at twilight or riding their bikes on the boardwalk whenever they had a free moment to spare in their hectic lives.

It wasn't until years into their marriage that Gage admitted that he did whatever he could to be near her because he loved her so completely. He loved the beach and swimming and surfing and any other sport that involved the ocean.

Chapter Two

Gage had been a trained killer and loved the danger and the high his job gave him. His dauntless personality came from all the time he had spent in Special Forces and then the C.I.A. Slowing down and becoming accustomed to civilian life was difficult for him at first. Morgan appreciated his willingness to change his lifestyle for her so that they could build a life together and have a family. She couldn't picture them having a family while still living the life he had within the C.I.A.

Recalling the first time she met Gage made her smile. She remembered Gage sharing some very intimate details with her. Gage and Jake were part of the elite Special Forces Team at the time. Gage was Jake's commanding officer, over time they had become great friends. They stayed friends even after Gage was recruited by the C.I.A. Jake invited Gage home with him on numerous occasions. Morgan, a young woman barely out of her teens, was out of town during most of his visits in the early days.

On one occasion, Jake invited him home after meeting up with him in Afghanistan while Gage was there on C.I.A. business and Jake was there on a mission of his own. He insisted that Gage looked as though he needed to take a break and spend some time with the crazy McCleary brothers. Gage agreed without much persuading and thought maybe some time away from all the darkness was just what he needed.

GAGE

Gage found himself thinking about the past. He recalled the darkest moment of his life when he felt all was lost. There was a time that he believed he could help make this world a safer place; but he was losing faith. The world had become a dark and dangerous place and there were many who hated America and their presence in the Middle East and changing that mindset was becoming more difficult. It was his job to get into these places and get information that not only would bring security to his part of the world but would open a dialogue for peace. His missions were becoming darker and more dangerous as Isis continued to expand.

Gage couldn't stop thinking about the McCleary family as a whole or Morgan McCleary. Perhaps he needed to start over. He knew Jake was in the region. There wasn't much that went on in this part of the world that he didn't know about. He would make an accidental meeting with Jake a reality. He used his resources and made it happen. Jake and his unit were thought to be in the mountains of Afghanistan near the Pakistani border. But Gage knew they were gathering information in Syria and he would hook up with Jake there.

Gage thought about Rockaway Beach. It was definitely his kind of town. The people were friendly enough and at times Gage wondered if they ever strayed further than the two bridges leading to their town. He had the feeling they all talked about it. Other than the occasional vacation, he didn't get the impression they drifted too far. After spending some time in Rockaway, Gage found himself wanting to stay and lay down roots. His cohorts found it hard to believe that the infamous Gage Delaney would ever settle in small town America. But he proclaimed that he was taken in by the place just as the dwellers before him had. He often wondered; what is it that draws people to this town?

Even though Gage was very interested in Jake's younger sister, Morgan, almost immediately after meeting her, he didn't let Jake know just how attracted he was to her. This situation was just too crazy; she wasn't even twenty-one yet. She was off limits as far as he was concerned and it was just as well, considering his bond with Jake. This was the first time in a very long time that he actually allowed himself to get close to someone and he and Jake had become more like brothers than friends. Although, he had secrets he hadn't even shared with Jake and that was for his own protection.

He found Morgan to be amusing at first. He admired her tenacity and the way she handled herself with her older more worldly brothers. She was a force to be reckoned with for sure and he knew he should've been ashamed for the thoughts he was having regarding her, but he wasn't. He needed to keep his thoughts to himself, until the right time. His attraction to her was actually surprising since the women he had been attracted to in the past were just the opposite of Morgan McCleary. He remembered thinking that he would find a way to keep in touch with Jake and after some time had passed he would find a way to get himself invited back to the McCleary compound. It was that promise to him that had kept him alive during those days. He convinced himself that he and Morgan McCleary had unfinished business.

Gage made good on his promise and jumped at the invitation from Jake to go to Rockaway for a few weeks that one summer. Jake and his unit were going to be overseas for an extended period of time in the near future and he took advantage of the time between missions to request a furlough for him and his unit to spend some time with their families before going on the next tour. It would be a dangerous mission, one that Jake didn't think all his men would survive. The next mission would keep them in Syria. Syria was not a very friendly place for Americans and Jake and his team were being sent there to find out as much as they could about the whereabouts of Isis and a way to remove the problem. Jake worked hand in hand with the C.I.A. throughout the early days of Isis and it was during that time that he met up with his former leader and brother, Gage Delaney.

Gage was C.I.A. and went by the name, Alex Summer. Not many people were privy to that information and it was kept that way for Gage's own safety. His cloak and dagger life put him in a lot of danger. There was a target on the chest of the man known only as *the Ghost* and it was a tough job for Alex Summer to keep one step ahead of the many groups who wanted him dead and to keep his real name from their lips. Terrorists from around the world all knew of the *Ghost* but couldn't put a face or name to the man they all wanted dead; the bounty on his head grew with each passing day. American soldiers, especially the men of the elite units serving in the Middle East, admired the man who was known only as the *Ghost* by so many; they were in awe of him. Some who served under his command knew that Gage Delaney was Alex Summer, and they guarded his secret with their lives.

Alex Summer ruined many would-be plans with the Intel he was able to extract on his lone missions. Those missions always took him to places he despised. He had a handler but usually he was alone and made decisions and choices that were too dark to even talk about to anyone.

When Jake invited him to Rockaway, it came at a time when Gage was falling into a black hole, living as Alex Summer, something he was growing tired of. He was beginning to believe that there would never be a light at the end of the tunnel for him until Jake's invitation reminded him of the beautiful young Morgan McCleary. She was like a ray of sunshine slicing through the darkness he lived within. She was his unfinished business, his chance at a future that didn't include death, torture and deception.

It took a lot of convincing on his part to get Morgan to accept his offer of a first date that summer. Even though she didn't think they could be any more different in personality, she could hardly deny her attraction to him. It wasn't long before they were inseparable and in spite of Jake's concerns to the contrary, their relationship actually worked. Jake was apprehensive and he believed that Gage, without meaning to, would hurt Morgan. But Gage had other ideas in mind and convinced Jake to trust him and the friendship they shared, that he would never betray him. He told Jake that, Morgan was a lifeline he could hold on to and he needed him to trust him.

MORGAN

Morgan often wondered if Gage would have taken her out on a second or third date if Jake had asked him not to that summer. Somehow, she suspected that the man she had come to know would have left New York immediately and gone back to Syria regardless of how he felt about her. Gage respected Jake and was loyal to the friendship they shared, that was the type of man he was. This was the man she married. He admitted to Morgan many years later that he would've liked to believe that had Jake asked him to stay away from her that he would have, but he had to admit that he didn't know if he would've been strong enough to walk away from her. He teased her, often telling her that was how deeply he was attracted to her.

 He and Jake seemed to have similar schedules over the next year because they often had furloughs at the same time. Jake knew Gage was making sure his free time coincided purposely with his so that he could see Morgan. Gage had a way of finding out when Jake was going on a furlough. It wasn't a coincidence that he made time to join Jake and Jake wasn't a fool to believe otherwise. Gage shocked the entire family when he proposed to Morgan. After all, Gage Delaney wasn't the marrying type. He was a confirmed bachelor of sorts; that was what everyone who came in contact with him believed. He even went as far as following custom in the McCleary family and met with Joe McCleary to ask for his blessing to marry his daughter. It wasn't until years into their marriage that Morgan learned that Gage had approached Jake before going to her dad to get Jake's permission as well. Gage didn't want Jake to feel he had gone behind his back in any way. The other siblings were shocked to hear how easily their father acquiesced. It wasn't like Joe McCleary to be so easy but he saw something in Gage Delaney that really impressed him. Gage had a plan for his future and he knew how to convince Joe McCleary to give his blessing. It took a little persuading at first and Gage understood his reservations. After all, Morgan was her father's little girl and Gage couldn't blame him for wanting to protect her from someone like him. He knew his little girl had so much potential and a gift she had yet to realize. He didn't want *any* young man interrupting the future he had envisioned for her. But if there was one quality Gage possessed more than any other, it was the art of negotiation and Joe McCleary listened intently.

 Gage had to convince Joe McCleary that he had a plan. Morgan recalled the conversation as told to her by Gage. He had to convince her father that he had a future all mapped out for the two of them. The one obstacle Joe McCleary realized was that he didn't want his daughter being saddled with a husband who lived such a clandestine life-style. But Gage had a plan for that too. He understood Mr. McCleary's fear and told him he would leave the C.I.A. after completing his latest mission and he promised to start a construction company with money he had put away over the years. He had given it a lot of thought since he met Morgan and it was time he left that life behind. He had saved quite a lot of money over the years and he began to set his plan in motion. Gage had always believed, since the first day he entered Annapolis, that his future was set, making his service to the military a lifelong career, but then along came the C.I.A. He enjoyed the danger and the risks involved but that world was not one that included a wife and a family. Of course he hadn't planned on falling in love with Morgan but that was the perfect example of how easily your life could change. He hoped he could adjust to civilian life and with Morgan at his side, he knew he could. He agreed wholeheartedly that he didn't want his wife spending her life worrying about whether he would come home from his latest assignment or if she and her children were in any danger as well because of his career choice. Very few active agents of his caliber were married. It was almost impossible to remain married and stay alive in this business. There were too many unknowns and he didn't want Morgan to ever have to deal with any of the issues that could and would arise. He knew that the longer he stayed in the C.I.A.; the possibility that he would put both their lives in jeopardy became exponential. His life was complicated enough without worrying whether his activity was putting her in danger. He and Jake both took a lot of risks but they were necessary risks in order to keep the world safe from terrorists.

Morgan wrote to him as often as possible when they first became a couple but his letters to her were few and far between; he was always on a mission and he rarely had time to check in. He lived among the enemy most of the time. Gage didn't keep the life he led in the C.I.A. a secret from her but he did keep the details from her for her own safety. They agreed not to talk about it and she and her family would never know the danger he lived with every day. John and Jake were the only family members who were aware of the danger he faced on a daily basis. There was a time when he believed that his future was a star on the wall at C.I.A. headquarters, a star for the men and women who served their country and died doing it. His missions were getting more and more dangerous as time went on. As Alex Summer, he was able to infiltrate places the C.I.A. had never gone before and it was best for everyone that Morgan was kept completely in the dark about them. He had made the decision to leave the life for her sake. His exit would not be easy but he couldn't live this life any longer if he chose a life with her.

Gage tried to convince Morgan that she should date other men while he was away. Morgan disagreed but she did go out with other male friends on occasion at her siblings' insistence. She never told Gage about those outings because there was nothing to tell. To her, each of her dates was with friends. She couldn't wait to be reunited with Gage.

Six months later, at the end of his latest mission in Syria, Gage announced to Jake and the family that he had made the move to leave the C.I.A. The time had come sooner than he anticipated; his identity as Alex Summer had been leaked by someone at the White House and his life was in more danger than ever before. With his identity compromised even slightly, he could not move around as easily as he had before.

Gage let Jake in on what he'd been thinking, letting him know that he had been exploring a civilian career for some time and had already begun to take steps. Though Jake was happy, he hoped that Gage knew what he was doing. Jake wondered if civilian life would be enough for him. He knew that Gage craved danger as much as he did and he hoped that he wouldn't regret his decision to walk away from the career he was trained to do.

Morgan recalled those early days of their relationship with fondness. She was glad to have found Gage so soon in her life. It hadn't been an instant attraction but the more she was around him the harder it was to ignore his advances. He reminded her often that she was a little too stuck up for her own good. Gage grew up in a rough neighborhood in Chicago and he had a very hard way about him which Morgan was able to break through without knowing it. She had broken through the wall he had created to keep himself from ever getting hurt and she did it with ease. Gage had admitted to her that he had become a product of his environment and in his haste to save himself and leave that life behind; he chose a career in the military. He was good at his job and moved through the ranks rather quickly.

Gage fell fast and hard in love with Morgan and did so unconditionally. It was difficult finding time alone in a family that big and at times, proved to be rather formidable. You didn't date one McCleary without dealing with the rest of them. In time, Gage grew to love her family and they became the family he never had. It was easy to fit in with them but it was difficult to have a romantic relationship with her when her older brothers were so protective, overbearing and ever present.

Gage Delaney had a presence all his own, when he walked into a room he commanded the attention of everyone and they gave it to him willingly. Men and women flocked to be engaged in conversation with him. Besides being alluring to the women he met, because he was so mysterious and strikingly attractive, he commanded the attention of men as well. He had seen so much in his young life that people found conversation with him engaging. His knowledge on just about every subject caused men and women to become completely intrigued.

Gage possessed a sense of humor and he projected that sense of humor on to the people around him. Morgan first saw that side of him at a street block party in Rockaway. Gage and Jake and the other men of their unit crashed the party while on a short furlough. She had wavered on whether she wanted to continue the conversation he initiated with her that evening. Even back then, she knew that she needed to be wary of him. Even though he was a friend of Jake's, it would be rude to walk away from him, but she was unsure about what to make of him.

That crazy beginning was a first for the aloof Gage Delaney. He was being shot down by a woman, not just any woman, only the one woman he secretly wanted most to impress. She was the first woman to ever turn him down and he was not having it. He decided to pull out all the stops and go for her comedic side, even though he knew she kept this side of her personality hidden deeply. Her family thought she was always very serious and tough but he witnessed her sly humorous side when she thought no one was looking or listening. He studied her in great detail before he approached her. Jake had wanted the men of their unit to enjoy some down time at the block party but Gage had other plans. He offered her a ride home later that evening after he overheard her say to a friend that she was leaving the block party early because she had to get up the next morning for work. Morgan looked at her friends and then to the other soldiers; who were daring her to take their commander up on his offer and she reluctantly agreed. She didn't want anyone to think that the infamous Gage Delaney frightened her in any way. The only person who seemed remotely alarmed by Gage's advances toward Morgan had been her brother, Jake. Gage knelt down on his knee and told her in front of the crowd that had gathered to hop up on his shoulders. Morgan regretted her decision to bate him and couldn't believe his audacity. They were embattled in a game of dare and he held the upper hand. His friends were obviously in on the joke; they were aware that he didn't have a car. Her friends were outwardly appalled and shocked by the soldiers' behavior. They were also intrigued, wondering what their usually serious friend would do next.

Morgan had only seconds to decide what to do. She chose to piggyback on his shoulders and have him carry her home rather than get teased by his friends. *It serves him right, she thought.* She was Gage Delaney's opposite in every way. She was very serious and lacked a sense of humor while he was outgoing, commanding and somewhat amusing. They didn't belong together and the sooner he realized that fact the better it would be for them both. The moment that she agreed to get up on his shoulders went against everything expected of her but Morgan had a stubborn side too and she knew he wasn't about to get the better of her. It was a mistake, she realized, to allow him to provoke her and if she was wise she would grab her bag and walk away from him, alone. She had goals for her future and any kind of relationship with this rogue, Gage Delaney, would push those goals further away if she let herself get swept up by him. Foolishly, Morgan took the bait he set and as the night progressed, she became captivated by the man. Soon, she found it difficult to avoid getting involved with him; it all happened in a blink of an eye. She had let her guard down.

As her musing came to an end, Morgan took in a deep breath of salty air blowing off the Pacific and smiled as she relived those unforgettable first moments. She wondered if she would ever find peace with her decision to leave Gage and the marriage she thought would last forever. When she decided to leave, she did so because she felt as though she was drowning in grief and she knew if she had stayed with him any longer she would have lost herself completely. She had to make herself whole again before continuing their marriage. If leaving Gage would help her achieve that, she had to try. Gage thought that if they both kept busy and worked, it would make the pain go away, but it didn't. They had become successful workaholics and it did make it easier for her because the alternative was to fight with Gage about going to therapy. Alas, working nonstop and not talking only allowed the wall forming between them to become harder to climb and they simply avoided each other. They were working long hours and his small business was growing into quite an empire. They were spending so much time away from each other that they were fast becoming strangers while occupying the same house.

Morgan thought about the first time Gage walked into her office and suggested they go for help. She was lost in thought while she stared out the window in her office and hadn't noticed as he came up behind her and wrapped his arms around her, holding her as if his life depended on this feeling of closeness. She remembered with sadness the exchange that occurred next.

"Morgan, we need help. We can't go on like this. This isn't living, babe. I've been seeing the pastor at church and he gave me the name of a therapist. I've been seeing him myself for some time but I think we should both go. I think it's time. There's also a group that meets once a week at the church, a support group for grieving parents." Gage could feel her body as it tensed beneath his arms.

She became angry knowing that he would even suggest that they go for help to forget about Michael. "You do what you need to! I don't need to hear other parents tell me their sad stories. I have my own issues and I can't handle anything else right now. I can't, I'm sorry, Gage. I want you to continue going if you think it's helping you." Her response was that simple and she voiced it without once turning to look into his eyes.

"You can't even say it, can you? Look at me, Morgan." He turned her body to face him and said what he thought needed to be said rather forcefully. *"Michael is dead. He isn't coming back to us and pretending it didn't happen is not going to change the fact that he's gone.* Damn it, Morgan, you can't even look at me. You won't even let me pack away the things in his room. It's like a shrine in there. It's not healthy for either of us. I can't walk past that room anymore. It hurts too much. I need us to move on. *We need to move on,*" he repeated. He pointed to her and then himself and then he punched a hole in the wall when he realized he wasn't getting anywhere with her.

"Go ahead and go on with your life, Gage. Forget that Michael ever existed. Do what *you think you need to do.*" Morgan couldn't believe the vile words spewing from her mouth. She hadn't meant any of it but she wasn't able to deal with Michael's death just yet. It was all too much for her. She wasn't as strong as Gage.

"That's not fair. I loved Michael too. But this thing we're doing, it's not living. We can't keep going on like this." Morgan said nothing in response and after waiting for any kind of response from her, and getting nothing, Gage stormed out of the room.

GAGE

It became easier to work longer hours and avoid each other at the office. It wasn't long before they became strangers to each other at home as well. They no longer talked to each other or spent any quality time together. Any time they did speak it had to do with business. She had officially shut him out and he didn't know what to do about it. He was surprised and hurt when she decided to move out of their house a few months later, into her own apartment. He thought it would be a temporary move and he decided against his better judgment to let her go without a fight. Six months later they were still apart and her brother, Alex, informed him that she was leaving for California to be on the set of the adaptation of her book into a movie and would be gone for at least another six months. It had already been six months since she left him and it hadn't become any easier, not for either of them. There was still an emptiness that only she could fill in his life and he was sure it was the same for her.

There was a time during those first months that she found herself talking to Michael as if he was there in the room with her. It offered her a glimpse of sanity in the jumble of chaos she felt when no one was around. There was no one to judge her when she talked to him. She took out a plastic bag; she had kept it hidden from everyone, locked in a draw. She had kept the pajamas Michael wore on the night he'd passed away; they were in that bag locked away just to keep his scent trapped within it. On the nights when she didn't think she could handle the pain anymore, she would take out that bag, open it and press her face into the softness of his clothes just so she could smell the scent of him. She would cry for the son she couldn't hold in her arms any longer. What if's often rushed through her head on nights like this, his first big game, his graduation, his first car, his first girlfriend or the special mother and son dance at his wedding when he knew he'd found the girl of his dreams. The girl he would never find now. *Why was life this cruel?*

She and Gage had waited so long to have a baby. They tried for several years and nothing happened. They had almost given up hope when finally, after five years, she found out that she was pregnant. Everyone thought it was by choice that they didn't have children. When Michael arrived, they were ecstatic, a happy family for next few years. If they were never blessed with another child, they would be content. They had Michael and he was everything to them. But, then something changed. During a routine office visit with his pediatrician, Morgan mentioned that Michael seemed to tire easily. He seemed unable to do anything strenuous without getting tired. Dr. Kaylan was openly concerned and ordered a few tests after listening to Michael's heart. She told her to try not to worry and said they would talk more after all the tests came back.

It was difficult to wait but when the results came, Morgan almost wished they hadn't. Michael's heart was damaged and very weak. He was a very sick little boy and he would need to see a few different specialists over the coming days and weeks. All of the doctors came back with the same diagnosis. They didn't know what caused Michael's condition but Michael needed a heart transplant, the sooner the better. He would need to be put on a transplant list immediately. Morgan never realized the importance of organ donation until that moment. It saddened her when she was told that in order for Michael to get a heart, a child would have to die. She couldn't imagine making the decision to donate your child's organs while he or she is on life support when you're going through the worst period of your life. She prayed that someone would be brave enough to be able to make that decision. It was the only way Michael would live a long life.

She and Gage were heart broken but they needed to let the rest of the family know without upsetting Michael. As soon as the family gathered and were told the situation, each of her siblings asked what they could do to help. Prayer chains began and masses were being offered at the local church for Michael on a daily basis. All Michael knew was that he was sick; it was too soon to tell him much more than that.

Morgan tried to keep Michael's life as normal as possible but before long it became impossible for them to keep him in the dark. Two years had passed and still no donor match had been found. Michael was becoming weaker with each passing day and his situation was becoming very bleak. It was a miracle that he had made it this far. To their surprise, Michael knew a lot more than he let on. He told Gage that he figured out how bad things were when he had to wear a mask to go outside. "Dad, you and Mom always smile and laugh when you're around me but when you think I'm sleeping I hear you both crying. I know you don't want me to know what's going on but I have to wear this mask all the time, I know it's to protect me from getting sick but I need you to stop protecting me and talk to me. Tell me the truth." It broke Gage's heart to witness his son's bravery. He was his tough little soldier. That was what he always called him. He should be able to protect his son from all this heartache but he couldn't so he decided to tell him the truth. It was difficult to get through the conversation but in the end he was glad he had the strength to complete it. Michael was less afraid when he understood the situation he was in.

Their trips to the hospital became more frequent and after a while the time came when Michael couldn't leave the hospital. It hurt to the core to witness what was happening to his son but Gage was worried about what it was doing to Morgan. He saw the toll Michael's illness was taking on her and knew the worst was yet to come. He had seen death enough to know that Michael was running out of time. Morgan, on the other hand, was always hoping for a miracle. She was becoming fragile; he wasn't sure if she could handle the inevitable. They took turns sleeping at the hospital, every night she prayed a heart would be available the next day. Michael was never left alone. One member of the family was always there with him. They patiently waited and prayed. Michael died while Gage held him in his arms. Morgan had just returned after a quick run home to shower and change. She stood at the door as Gage held Michael's worn out body in his arms. To this day, Morgan relives that scene over and over again in her mind.

Through tears, Gage told his son it was okay to go with the angels. "It's safe for you to go with the angels, Michael. Mommy and I will see you again one day, I promise. You don't have to be my tough soldier anymore. I know you're tired. I promise I will see you every time I look at the sky. Don't be afraid, son, spread your wings and fly. I love you, Michael." Gage looked up and saw Morgan standing there. He pleaded with her to tell Michael the words he needed to hear her say, that it was okay to let go. They both knew by the look on their son's face that he wouldn't give up until Morgan gave him her approval. It was true what people said, the dying tend to hang on until the living are ready to let them go.

Morgan remembered how physically ill she felt at the time and prayed for the strength to do what her husband was pleading with his eyes. She reached over Gage's shoulder and brushed the hairs that had fallen in Michael's eye. With all the strength she could muster, she kissed him on the forehead and as he took his last breath she told him not to be afraid. "Fly with the angels my sweet boy. Don't be afraid," she whispered in his ear and added, "I'll love you forever," through her tears and with that, her baby boy was gone.

Chapter Three

Morgan found herself buying business magazines and cheesy tabloids this past year just to catch a glimpse of Gage in the background. His company was growing quickly and everyone wanted to find out more about the man behind creating the successful company. It was always Alex who stood upfront and on the covers of magazines. But even turned away in the background Morgan could see Gage always close by to support Alex. On occasion Gage could be seen walking away. She knew Gage kept out of the spotlight so he wouldn't bring danger to any member of the family. Alex, her brother, was the acting CEO of Paragon International. The letterheads and documents all listed Alex as CEO and only shareholder but she knew Gage employed Alex and hid his identity so well that only a professional forensic audit would ever find his identity. Alex Summer had a bounty on his head all over the world. The bounty had even grown over the years. Perhaps his enemies had long memories and held even longer grudges. Alex Summer had to remain a mystery man and Gage had to do everything he could to make sure that happened.

Morgan was bothered knowing that Gage had found it so easy to move on with his life and without her. On more than one occasion she questioned whether he would ever want her in his life again. He hadn't waited for her as she had thought he would and it seemed as though he was enjoying his new single life. Though he did shy away from the tabloids, she could see the occasional woman in the background.

Gage had made Alex into a superstar of sorts. Every newspaper wanted to interview the notorious Alex McCleary but he rarely gave interviews, if at all. According to the magazines, Alex had a Howard Hughes personality because of his unwillingness to be photographed, which only intrigued the tabloids even more. It appeared at least on paper that Alex McCleary was among the one per centers in the financial world. There were all kinds of women vying for his attention. They never knew that it was Gage's company, not Alex's.

The tabloids implied that the company's second in command was the brains behind the success of the company but the rumor faded as soon as it was in print. Gage saw to that. He couldn't have any speculation about him with curious minds diving into their business to find out the truth. Gage worked hard to build the company and had his connections in the C.I.A. to keep him informed if someone was asking about him. Those same connections made sure that any curiosity about the second in command of his company was buried as soon as it surfaced.

Morgan felt as if he'd been cheated because he couldn't publicly acknowledge what he had accomplished. But she knew Gage preferred it this way. When Gage established the business years earlier it never occurred to them that it would grow into the empire it was or that there would be such an interest in its CEO. But Gage took the necessary precautions to remain hidden. He had always thought two steps ahead of everyone else which was why he had been so successful in the C.I.A.

Why, Morgan wondered, was she having so much trouble believing that Gage would go on without her? She was so deep in thought that she hadn't paid much attention to the light flashing on the telephone. She knew she had to get to the studio this morning and she was already late. With a definitive gaze, she opted to ignore the recording; she would listen to it once she arrived back at the hotel that night. It's probably a family member *since it's our wedding anniversary. They would think today would be a tough day for me.* Her siblings would find it impossible to resist intruding on her solitude to make sure she was dealing with the day without any issues. *Who could not love them for that,* she reminded herself.

Morgan patiently sat in the backseat of the car that was sent to take her to the studio and thought about how she had arrived at this point in her life. She tried to dismiss her latest thoughts of Gage as melancholic. Sadness and regret came easy in the days leading up to their anniversary when everything that surrounded her reminded her of Gage, even her latest manuscript she had been working on. The main character was reminiscent of Gage, certainly his charm and behavior. It was difficult to put the words down on paper without having her personal feelings or experiences come through in her writing. It was problematic for her to write having the hero and heroine live happily ever after when her own life was in such shambles. She found herself wondering about what things could have been like had she not made the choice to walk out of Gage's life that afternoon. She knew in her heart of hearts that it was the right choice for her at the time.

She knew she was suffocating from her grief. At first, working long hours in Gage's business helped her forget. It was easy to pretend it never happened and fantasize that Michael was home with a sitter. She knew, by ignoring the issue completely, she was chipping away at pieces of herself each and every day that slipped by. It wasn't working; she knew she had to do something, anything to address the emptiness she felt. Gage hadn't put up a fight when she announced that she was moving out. He didn't fight to save their marriage and that left Morgan feeling as though she had made the right choice. He accepted her decision without a single word of regret or argument. Perhaps, in his own way, he had been searching for a way out, too.

Morgan recalled the day she began to work on the manuscript, right after Michael's death. She hadn't even told Gage what she was doing. She just decided to take out her laptop and see where it took her. She put in a lot of late nights working on that romance. Her goal was to become a published writer and someday, she had promised herself, she would accomplish that task. She tried to write every chance she could but they each were focused on building up Gage's company. There was hardly any time to devote to writing. She'd made a promise to herself that she would commit a certain amount of time each day to her writing. The more she wrote, the more pieces of herself she found, things that had been buried began to surface once again.

She was nervous and excited the day she completed the manuscript. Good, bad or indifferent, she was ready to put herself out there and hear what a publisher thought of her story. She only hoped that it wouldn't sit on some slush pile for too long. It would take a miracle to get someone to read her work, especially since she was an unknown writer, but it was worth the risk.

Barbara Moore, an assistant editor with Evergreen Publications, happened upon her manuscript when she needed something to read on a long business flight to Los Angles. As they say in the movies, the rest was history. Three months after sending her manuscript to various publishers, Morgan was contacted by Barbara. She seemed genuinely interested and offered advice about fixing it before final submission. She was a wealth of information and although she had never given so much input in the past, Barbara told Morgan she had a good feeling about her and wanted to help her out any way she could.

She and Barbara now find themselves laughing at how easily their friendship blossomed and how that never would have happened had it not been for fate. Barbara remembered the cover letter attached as if it was yesterday. She had regrettably convinced herself that the manuscript would just be another daring attempt at writing from a well-meaning housewife. Barbara was pleasantly surprised to find just the opposite to be true and had wondered why Morgan had kept her talent to tell stories to herself for so long.

Barbara and Morgan often talked about her original impression. She had found herself so engrossed in the characters of Morgan's manuscript during her flight that she wasn't able to put the manuscript down. Morgan Delaney would be going places, especially if this was just an early attempt at a manuscript. She had almost finished reading the manuscript in its entirety when she was taken back by how fast the time on the plane had passed. The stewardess announced the plane would be landing shortly and she would have to put the manuscript away and prepare to land. Barbara didn't want the flight to end; she wasn't finished and was unable to put it down. She had been inspired for the first time in a long time and couldn't wait to deliver the news to her senior editor.

That fateful event happened a little more than a year ago, Morgan had shared four more romances with Barbara. With the support of an agent recommended by Barbara, her dreams were all falling into place. The agent was Michele Ruggerio. She called her immediately after Barbara gave her Michele's name and number. After meeting with her and talking about goals for the future, Michele agreed to do the final edit. A contract was signed at the same time. Evergreen approved the edit, published the book and had it on shelves in major bookstores shortly thereafter. It wasn't long before Morgan had received another phone call from Michele with an offer to buy her first book to adapt into a screenplay. Part of the deal negotiated was that Morgan be on the set to offer advice on re-writes for a fee since the book was being adapted into a full-length motion picture. It was unheard of to make such demands, Michele had explained to Morgan but it would offer great exposure for Morgan and any future books she would write. Morgan was scared to death at first, overwhelmed by how fast her career had taken off but Michele assured her that she would be able to handle everything coming her way. Michele agreed to always be available if she was needed. The first phone call she made once the deal was sealed was to Barbara to tell her the news. Although she and Barbara had become great friends, she had never shared her history about Gage, until recently. Barbara had the feeling that there was more to Morgan's story and she always felt Morgan's detachment had something to do with a man. Even though she had never met the man, she speculated that Gage and Morgan still had some unfinished business.

Morgan arrived on the set a little late that morning. In spite of the way she was feeling, she continued to work and was happy with the way the film was turning out. The director and actors were true to the body of her work as she intended and felt a sense of satisfaction to see the characters she had developed come to life before her eyes. Rachael was the perfect actress for the lead. The director certainly knew what he was doing. Morgan was thrilled with Rachael's performance. She hoped, once the film wrapped up and it was debuted, that the audience would feel the same sense of fulfillment and excitement she had this day.

Suddenly, she felt an overwhelming sense of loss now that it was over. She would no longer have a place to go to and she would have to return to New York and face the inevitable, the realization that her marriage to Gage was wrapped up as well. Morgan decided to opt out of the after-party and try to arrange an earlier flight home. She would call Joe Kirby, her neighbor and best friend, after she landed and ask him if he wanted to meet for dinner, just so she wouldn't have to spend any part of the day alone. There was three hours difference between California and New York City and by the time she landed at JFK International airport it would be dinner time.

She could have called any of her brothers or her sister; they would have run to her but she didn't want them to know the extent of the regret she was feeling. If she had called any one of her brothers, they would have felt it their duty to confront Gage and let him know what their sister was going through because of the feelings she still harbored for him. Her brother, Alex in particular, would feel obligated to tell Gage how he was hurting her and Gage would feel responsible to make that hurt go away. That was the kind of response that had its own problems. She had to face this situation on her own because this was the future she had chosen for herself.

Joe Kirby wasn't shocked to hear Morgan's voice on the phone. He had noted the date on his calendar months ago. He had warned Neil, Joe's partner, earlier in the day that he needed to make himself available for Morgan in case she called. Neil wanted to help out in any way that he could. If that meant not seeing Joe tonight so that he could be there for her, so be it.

"I'm glad to hear from you Morgan. I was worried about you, baby girl." She and Joe shared a little small talk and then Joe informed her of the delivery that had arrived earlier in the day for her. "Listen, when the car drops you off tonight, don't go straight to your apartment. Come to my place first, there's something I want to talk to you about."

"Joe, what's going on? What are you hiding from me? What was delivered and why can't you tell me over the phone?" Morgan asked, getting a little nervous waiting to hear his response.

Joe said nothing at first and then, in just a whisper, he said something that left her feeling worse than she had earlier in the day. "It's just better if I show you in person."

Morgan agreed after being denied the answers she was seeking. She didn't like being kept in the dark and was concerned about the reason for his secrecy. She and Joe became instant friends when she had moved into the apartment next door. His sexual orientation was never an issue, though it did surprise him when she began to share stories about her husband and her family. He was pleasantly surprised to be so easily accepted by her but he wondered what her macho four brothers would think. Joe and Morgan talked, laughed and joked together for months; their relationship was like nothing either of them had experienced before. Life drew them together at a time when they were vulnerable and they needed each other. Each welcomed the other into their private lives and let the future be their guide, it works for them. Joe helped her through a pretty rough year; in the process, they had become even closer than either of them ever anticipated.

Joe was an international investment banker and a pretty successful one. He moved into his apartment a month before Morgan moved into hers and what was supposed to be a temporary move turned into something much different. He didn't want to lose her friendship and though the penthouse had long been ready for his return, he just couldn't seem to pull the trigger. He enjoyed their late night talks and even though he suggested she move into the penthouse, he knew she would never accept his offer. Joe continued to rent the apartment next to hers on a month to month basis, putting off the move to his luxury penthouse until he could prepare himself to go without her. Morgan selfishly hoped that day would never come, though she knew as his friend she should encourage him to move. She knew how much she would miss him when he did take her advice.

The ride home from the airport was uneventful; it gave Morgan time to think about the only man who occupied her mind these days. She recalled the night she told Gage she had heard from a publisher; that her book would be in print soon. Gage was shocked and disappointed, realizing that she had written a full manuscript, sent it to a publisher and had gotten an agent, all without his knowledge. This was such an important event in her life and he felt he should have been a part of it, every step of the way. He had had no idea that his wife, the woman he loved with all his heart, had been writing anything at the time, let alone a novel. He seemed perplexed that Morgan's life had taken such a meaningful turn totally without him. He was beyond proud of her but saddened knowing that all this time she had spent working at their company she had this separate, secret life, one that he knew nothing about.

Morgan vividly recalled the day she told Gage she was moving out of the house. She said it had taken a lot of soul-searching to come to that decision. It was even harder to admit it out loud but she needed to be on her own for awhile. She tried to convince him she wanted to explore this new life being offered to her and that her leaving had nothing to do with Michael's death or him, that it had more to do with her being able to find herself again. At first he was angry, angrier than she had ever seen him; more than that, he said he felt betrayed by the one person he thought incapable of betraying him. He wanted to make things right between them but he didn't have a clue about how to accomplish that. She knew what he what he was thinking, with all his worldly knowledge he was stumped as to why he couldn't fix this. He repeated that he felt like a stranger within his own marriage. Gage said he knew her better than anyone and that he still believed her leaving had nothing to do with her wanting to be on her own to explore her new career; that it had everything to do with running from Michael's death. He said she needed to face Michael's death and that she should go for help with him. He didn't have the words to talk to her anymore, this whole situation felt very wrong. He had always had answers and strategies for every situation he'd found himself in but with Morgan he had none. Morgan was his Achilles' heel. He left the room angry and frustrated but alone, he needed to retreat to his office to think more clearly. When he came back to the house later on that night; he said that after much thought and contemplation, he knew he had to let her go. She had asked him for time and he would give it to her. He couldn't blame her for the way she was feeling he'd said. He'd been absent from their marriage frequently. They both lived at the office to try to forget their grief and when they weren't at the office they were avoiding each other. He had given up trying to get her to go for help. He became so busy with his own life that he had inadvertently left her behind and now he was paying the price for that oversight. He told her as calmly as he could that he was sorry for the place they found themselves in, that he still had faith in them as a couple and wished that she had that same faith. He didn't want what they had to end, not without a good fight. If she needed a little time he would give it to her and try to go on without her for as much time as she needed but he didn't agree that it was the best way to deal with what was haunting her.

Morgan tried to restate her case; that she needed time separate from them so that she could feel whole again. Gage heard the words as they passed her lips but all he *really heard was that she was falling out of love* with him and it was ripping him apart. He couldn't believe that she had gone through the grieving process through her writing and that she was moving on without him. He was confused. He congratulated her on her book deal, kissed her forehead and hugged her briefly before walking over to the door. He had always been the unfeeling, aloof soldier who kept his cool under dire terrifying conditions, but his feelings about Morgan made him a different man than the commander and agent he had been trained to be. Using all of his agent's training, he turned to her and said, without showing the extent of his feelings, words that tormented her for months after she'd left.

"I'm not capable of falling out of love with you Morgan. I wouldn't know how or where to begin. I believed we were each other's forever and always." As he stormed out of the door, he knew he would have to make sure that he was nowhere in sight when she moved her things out. That was the last time they saw each other in almost a year.

Morgan thought about what he had said that last day, about loving her, but his actions of late told quite a different story. Even though a year had passed, it hadn't made it any easier to deal with the failure and collapse of their illusion, their *good marriage. Maybe Michael's death was just too much for either of us.* Her career was flourishing and she was doing what she always wanted to do but this journey to find herself had been a painful one. In the end, she knew that being Gage's wife was exactly where she wanted to be all along. Instantly, she remembered one of her favorite quotes from George Moore; *"A man travels the world over in search of what he needs to return home to find it."* She had given up her life with Gage to find herself and become whole again. Even though she had felt what she wanted was still out there waiting for her, now she wasn't so sure that decision had ever been the correct one. She didn't run to try to find herself, she ran to avoid her life and having to face her son's death. Searching for what she thought she needed, she might have lost what she needed most in her life, Gage.

The journey she had taken with Gage hadn't allowed her the time she needed to grow into becoming the woman she was meant to be; that was her fault. She believed they needed to concentrate on his business while raising Michael. It had been her decision and Gage had gone along with it. Putting her writing career on hold was what she thought was good for them both. It never occurred to her to talk to him about doing anything differently. Michael's death and leaving Gage had shaped the woman she had become. The car was pulling up to the curb when Morgan noticed Joe looking out the window of his apartment. *What could he think is so important that he felt the need to watch for my arrival?*

Morgan noticed how troubled and nervous Joe had become as soon as she stepped inside. He started to speak and then decided to let the note that arrived with the boxes this morning do the talking for him. Morgan stared at the note and knew immediately that it had come from Gage. She felt a flutter of nervous apprehension as she held the letter in her hand. *Is this the letter notifying me that divorce papers will follow?* If it is, his timing stunk. She took a deep breath and looked up at Joe. With tears threatening, she nervously opened the note and read aloud what could be the end of their marriage.

Dear Morgan,

It's been a long time since we've talked and that fact alone saddens me. I can't tell you enough how proud I am of you and all you've accomplished in such a short time. I feel much regret for having kept you from your dreams. In my ignorance, I always thought that there would be time for your writing and I selfishly believed that concentrating on our business and family should have been our first concern. I realize what a mistake that was as I see your books on display in the windows at a local book store. I hear that your novel is being turned into a movie and it just proves how wrong I was. What, I ask myself time and time again, what might have been lost to your fans because of my goals?

I'm sending these boxes to you because once you left the house I couldn't stay there without you, too many memories of you and Michael and our life together. I had all our things packed and put into storage with the exception of these few boxes. Since I'm moving into my own apartment, I'm leaving these boxes in Joe's care so that you can decide what to do with them. I did keep a few mementos of my own, I hope you don't mind.

I hope that when you recall the memories of the time we shared together, you will do so with pleasure. I want to believe that our marriage was basically a good one. I don't know where I lost sight of your personal dreams and that will always be my biggest regret. It will always haunt me. I'm sure, in my grief, I wasn't thinking clearly at all. That's not an excuse and I'm sorry for the hurt I caused you. I hope someday you'll forgive me and maybe we can be friends, if nothing else. I always thought we would be running after a little girl by now, one who looked just like her mother. But I see now that my dreams were not yours. I see your brothers often enough and sometimes I think each one of them would like to kill me. I doubt they would ever say so out loud. It's hard to face your dad when I drop by and visit your parents now and again. I let him down and I'm sorry for that. I sometimes wonder if your father regrets the day Jake introduced us. I pray and hope that Jake is safe in the Middle East. I think about him a lot these days with all that is happening but I'm sure he's fine. He's great at his job, who would know that better than me. Try not to worry about him. I would trust him with my life. That is the kind of soldier he is.

I know that I'm not part of your family any longer and I know you're just as saddened by the situation as I am. Again, I apologize for any hurt I've caused you and wish you luck with your new career; you deserve to reap all the benefits you have sown. I don't want to be the one to hold you back. So go and be happy and know that you're free of me, to be able to discover the part of your life you thought was missing. Do what you want with the boxes. I just don't know what to do with this stuff. I think of you often and I want you to believe me when I say that I want you to be happy, Morgan.

Gage

Chapter Four

As Morgan finished reading the second page, she looked up at Joe with tears staining her cheeks, and she asked about the boxes. *So like Gage to send the boxes over on their wedding anniversary. Like he hasn't hurt me enough* by flashing different women on his arm; now he sends me this note today, of all days. Joe took his spare key, showed Morgan back to her own apartment and opened the door. She was shocked at the number of boxes that had marked their time together. He did say he put most of them in storage. She sat down on the floor staring at the boxes, trying to take in what it all meant. Joe hurried into the recently stocked kitchen and poured them both a much needed beer before joining her on the floor.

"Do you want to do this alone?" he asked, handing her a beer. He was glad he had her place cleaned earlier in the day; and did a little shopping for her too. It was easy to pick up groceries for her since he knew what she preferred.

"I'm not sure I want to do this at all. This is all that's left of my marriage, Joe," she said, pointing to the boxes strewn on the floor. Morgan flipped open a box and the first thing she happened upon was a delicate block of glass with a pen as its main decal, a beautiful inscription of words of encouragement and pride etched on the glass. Suddenly, Morgan remembered that Gage had had the plaque made for her. He had given it to her along with a laptop for no reason at all, except to let her know that he believed in her, knowing that one day she would be published. He wanted to be the first to encourage her to pursue her passion.

Joe watched as the memory of that moment grabbed Morgan. He knew that the rest of the boxes held more of the same. In order for her to get past this point in her life and move forward, she would have to feel the pain of going through each and every box. All he could do was to be there for her if she needed him. After an hour of regret and reliving memories, most of which were good, Morgan decided she was just too wiped out to continue. She knew it wasn't fair to Joe to have to witness her emotional ups and downs and all the tears.

"Lets order in and get drunk together," Joe said jokingly. "You're long overdue for a girl's night out but you'll have to settle for me," he added flippantly. Morgan laughed at Joe's rendition of the gay flamboyant friend as he handed her another beer. He always knew how to pick up her spirits when they were down, tonight was no exception. Joe Kirby was hardly the stereotypical gay man. Or the look perceived by the ignorant. Joe was every bit a man's man with one exception, he preferred men romantically.

Joe knew that Morgan was hurting, by the expression on her face. He knew she was feeling worse on the inside. *I could kill Gage Delaney with my bare hands for what he is doing to my very best friend in the world.* Then he began to wonder if Gage had done this purposefully today. Every instinct told him that his knowledge of her husband, based on information from her and her family, included these facts, Gage was a smart man; he was loyal and shrewd and he thought carefully before he ever acted. Gage Delaney was an enigma, of sorts. Joe decided he would try to find out what the infamous Gage Delaney was indeed up to.

"Joe, I can't thank you enough for this. I really needed you today," she added hugging him. She could see by his expression that he had just remembered something.

"Hey, when I brought the boxes into your apartment, your phone was ringing. I think someone left a message; the light was blinking when I left," he added as he sat on the couch and flung his arms over the top of the sofa.

Morgan suddenly recalled another blinking light, the one at the hotel. She had also received a message this morning but forgot to listen to it in her haste to return home. *Maybe it was a message from the same person.* She wandered into the bedroom to listen to the message privately. She stared down at the recorder and listened to a voice she hadn't heard in a year. She had never forgotten how the sound of Gage's voice made her shiver with excitement, regretfully, it still did. He wanted to be sure that she had received the boxes and he wanted to know if there was any way they could meet this week and talk and maybe have dinner together, or something. Joe stood in the frame of the doorway as his friend stared at the machine that was repeating the same message from her husband. At that moment, Gage was reminding her of his cell number in case she had forgotten it.

"Are you alright?" He didn't know how she would feel about hearing her husband's voice again, but naturally he wanted to be there for her if she needed him. He noticed pictures of Gage Delaney around the apartment and he had to admit the girl had good taste. If Gage was gay, Joe would have vied for his attention, he had teased her often enough. *Whatever possessed the man?* Gage's letter and his voice message certainly sounded as if he was still in love Morgan.

Before Morgan could answer him, the next message played. It was from Barbara. She wanted to invite her to a gala at the museum. Apparently, Darien Preston, CEO of Evergreen Publications, was going to announce the acquisition of Stardust Publications. It was a big deal and Barbara would be getting a promotion out of the merger. She wanted her friend to be there to help celebrate. Joe placed his hand under her chin and tilted her to face to him. "It will take your mind off things," Joe added softly, staring at the answering machine.

She knew he meant well but nothing was going to help her feel any better. Maybe Joe was right; perhaps it was time to get on with her life, attending the gala with Barbara might be a first step in that direction. "I guess I could, I would have to go shopping tomorrow for something to wear. Would you be interested in helping me shop? We could do lunch afterwards," she added, as if lunch would somehow entice him.

"Why do straight people always think gay men love to shop and do lunch?"

"…Because most do. I just happen to be friends with the only gay man in New York who hates to shop. I don't know why, you have excellent taste and besides you would tell me what looks good on me and what doesn't. A salesperson won't tell me the truth. A salesperson will only tell me what they think I want to hear," she said before adding, "Besides, I don't want to do this alone."

She and Joe made plans to meet in the morning and Morgan promised Joe she would leave the rest of the boxes for another day. It was getting late, Joe told her he needed to leave because he had promised Neil he would call him tonight and tell him how she was doing. He knew if he wanted to see Morgan tomorrow morning, he would have to make it right with Neil tonight with at least a call.

"Neil is in Chicago at a medical conference and I promised to call tonight. If you need me, I'm right next door," he said before leaving and before giving her a hug of encouragement. "But if you want me to stay, I will."

Morgan closed the door behind Joe after convincing him to leave; she leaned back against it and sighed. She knew there was no hiding from the boxes. She decided that she would take a long hot bath and then rifle through more of them to see what, if anything, she wanted to keep. She would put aside what she wanted to keep and toss the rest. *I can do this, I have to.* This was the only way she was going to purge herself of the past and move forward. She needed to put her marriage behind her once and for all. It seemed Gage had found moving on a lot easier; somehow, she had to find a way to arrive at that same place.

The bath felt great, it was relaxing to say the least. After the long plane trip and arriving home to be accosted with boxes from Gage, a bath was just what she needed to lift her spirits. After drying, Morgan threw on a pair of shorts and a T-shirt and pulled her still damp hair into a pony tail and walked down the hall to the kitchen to grab a drink and turn on some music. Morgan glanced at the boxes with confidence. She dropped to the floor and started tearing at one of the boxes. This last year had been traumatic for her but, like her husband, she needed to adjust to being single again. Gage had already moved on without her. She had to accept it and realize that they were finished. They would always share Michael; maybe someday his memory would make it easier for them to be friends. *When the divorce papers are finally delivered, I have to be able to sign them without feeling as if my world is coming to an end.*

Her hands were shaking as she reached into the box and pulled out another memento of their time together. It was the photo album from their honeymoon. *How could he dispose of our keepsakes so casually?* Didn't he cherish those happier times we spent together as much as I did? Morgan tried to understand Gage's reasoning for giving up all of photos of their happier times together but she realized it wouldn't help her in any way to dwell on it. Why was he able to move past what they had together so easily and why was she having such a difficult time letting go, she didn't know the answer. She didn't think she would ever understand. Theirs had always been that once in a lifetime kind of love story. A kind of love, few couples ever experienced, accepting that it had run its course was difficult for her.

Morgan poured herself a cold glass of beer and walked over to the window, photo album in hand. She was feeling guilty about not telling her family she was back. She thought she should probably let someone in the family know she had left the hotel early and was already home. She placed the beer and photo album on the table before calling her parents. They would tell the entire family she was home. Before she picked up the phone, she glanced down at the overflowing album in her hands. Morgan could recall each photo and where it was taken. She laughed and cried as she recalled each of the moments they shared together as it was caught on film. She had never imagined that this day would come. She had always thought that she and Gage would reconcile and have the houseful of kids. It never occurred to her that he wouldn't want the same things she wanted.

She dialed her parent's home and spoke to her mom to let her know she was back, assuring her that she was alright and didn't need anyone's company just right now.

"Mom, I'm fine. I'm tired from the flight and want nothing more than to curl up in my own bed and sleep." It took her quite a while to convince her mother of that fact. In the end she thought her mother was satisfied, that she was beginning to sound like her old self. Her mother promised not to tell the others that she was back until the morning so that she could rest.

Morgan was setting the last of the boxes to the side when her phone began to ring. Her body was still on California time so she was wide awake but whoever was calling obviously didn't know that. Morgan decided that she would let it go straight to the answering machine hoping that whoever it was would just leave a message.

She was a little startled to hear Matt Hastings' voice on the answering machine. He was the actor who played the male lead in the movie adaptation of her book. He had been hitting on her for months during filming but she was able to fend him off. At the time she had thought Matt was looking for a diversion, someone to spend time with to keep him from getting bored. There were plenty of willing women on the set, but he seemed to have focused his attention on her. Hearing his voice, when she was actually feeling more vulnerable, was shocking. It was also an indicator that she wasn't ready to move on quite yet. If she had made the choice to move on while she was in California, Matt had made it clear that all she had to do was to take that first step.

Morgan smiled as she went to bed feeling better than she had before she'd walked into her apartment. As she started to drift off to sleep, her phone began to ring again. I bet that's Matt again. She decided to ignore the call as reached over and unplugged her bedroom phone so that she could get some sleep. She had a lot to do tomorrow and she knew Joe would be knocking on her door first thing in the morning.

Chapter Five

Morgan pulled her shirt over her head and studied her reflection in the mirror as she rushed to get ready to spend the day with Joe. She had overslept and Joe was due to arrive at any minute. She was far from ready and didn't think she'd have time to finish dressing before he arrived. She must have been dreaming heavily last night because she kept hearing Gage's voice off in the distance. At one point his voice seemed almost terrified. She didn't have time to analyze her dreams but she was sure Joe would say something knowing that she had the dream on the night that would have been their anniversary. He would probably tell her that her subconscious was trying to tell her something.

Satisfied that she had done the best she could, she put on her sweater and reached for her purse just as the phone began to ring. One of her family members obviously had heard she was back in town and she knew if she didn't answer they would be worried sick.

It was Alex; he sounded frantic. "Where have you been? Don't you ever answer your phone?"

Before he could say another word, the doorbell rang. She told Joe that she would be right there as she turned her attention back to her youngest brother. "Alex, I'm on my way out and I really don't have time to talk, Joe is at the door. I got in late last night and I wanted to sleep so I unplugged the phone in my bedroom. I also told Mom to hold off telling anyone I was back until this morning. Is everything all right with you? You sound funny," she added with concern.

Alex said nothing; she knew he wanted to say so much more but something or someone was holding him back. There was a slight pause before he spoke again.

"Everything is fine. I just wanted to check on you and make sure you were alright. I called last night but there was no answer so I got a little worried," he said reluctantly. Morgan knew that Alex was probably at work and that meant that Gage was probably nearby. Gage could've been too close for him to talk freely and for all she knew he would be listening to every word her brother spoke. Alex had been working for Gage's construction company for years and he felt a strong bond to Gage. They were like brothers. He went to work for Gage right after college and learned the operations of the company rather quickly. Though it didn't surprise her, after all, he had Gage mentoring him all the way. She worried about Alex often because she knew their situation left him in an awkward position.

She was sure that Gage would do everything in his power to help Alex adjust and move forward with his career regardless of whatever happened between them. He would never put Alex in a situation where he would have to choose between them but it didn't make Alex feel any less uneasy about the situation.

"I don't have time to talk right now Alex, can I call you later?" she asked knowing Joe would want to leave, to get their shopping trip over with.

"You don't have to call me later. If you get a chance, I'll be in and out of the office, so call my cell phone. I just wanted to make sure that everything was good with you and now that I know you're good, I can wait to catch up. Congratulations on the movie by the way. I can't wait to see my big sister's book played out on the big screen. I'll have to drop your name when I'm out trying to impress. It won't hurt with the ladies when I take them to a romantic movie that my sister wrote. We're proud of you Morgan. Really, this is so great." he added, before telling her he had to get back to work. He said they had a big job that needed to be finished and Gage had all the tradesmen working seven days a week to get it done. The guys on the job didn't minded since overtime for union workers was an added bonus during these tough times. They ended their conversation on a happy note but Morgan couldn't shake the feeling that Alex was holding something back. Morgan unlocked the door and let Joe in. Before she had a chance to tell him about her weird dream from the night before the phone rang a second time.

"You might as well answer it. You're going to go crazy wondering who it is if you don't. Besides, I'm sure it's one of your crazy siblings. I'll wait the extra ten minutes," Joe said as he plopped himself down on to the sofa.

Morgan was glad she decided to answer the phone, when she did it was Barbara. She was calling to give her the information about the event for later that evening. Barbara asked how she made out last night since she knew it would be a tough night for her emotionally. Morgan found herself wanting to tell someone else about the weird dreams she had but she knew she and Joe were pressed for time. She told Barbara they would talk at the dinner party and thanked her for the invitation. She was looking forward to getting out.

She was sure her family and friends would be calling and looking in on her over the next few days to make sure she wasn't falling apart. She was stronger now than they gave her credit for but how would they know that since they hadn't seen her in six months.

As she began venting her frustration to Joe, he tried ushering her out the door by pushing her forward. "Your family and friends love you Morgan. You should be glad to have people in your life who care so much about you. They aren't aware that you went for help. Right now, they are probably thinking you're one step closer to jumping off a bridge," he told her, knowing that had to be able to understand how the family felt.

He once believed that he had what she had but that life seemed so far away. It had ended with just a few words from his father many years ago. "Do you know that besides you and Neil, I don't have anyone who I could say really cares for me the way your family cares for you? I have plenty of people in my life but they're in my life because of what I can offer them. I never told anyone this before, other than Neil, but I am an only child and as soon as my loving parents found out that their prodigal son was gay, they asked me politely to leave their home and I haven't heard from them since. They gave up on developing any kind of relationship with me as soon as they realized being gay was who I was, not a stage I was going through. I regret to admit even to you that I didn't try very hard to convince them that my sexual orientation shouldn't matter to them. I was young and I rebelled the only way I knew how, by making sure that I was the best at my job and that I climbed the corporate ladder as quickly as possible. I knew everything about the company and before long I took it over. It was easy to ignore my family in the beginning, when I let my career guide my life's path. I was determined to show my parents how successful I could be without them in my life. It wasn't long before I became CEO and majority shareholder of the company."

He hesitated but decided he might as well finish his train of thought. "When you put your career first, you might rise to the top quickly but there's a high price to pay for that struggle. For the first time in my adult life, I'm actually rethinking some of the choices I made in the beginning and I'm thinking about my future. You've changed me, Morgan Delaney. I'm thinking about taking time off to have a personal life. I think you should start thinking about doing the same." He pressed his finger lovingly against her nose and smiled.

As she thought about his comment she hesitated. She hadn't thought much about what he was saying and how it pertained to her own life until she tried to answer him. *Did I do that this past year?* In my grief, didn't I walk away from our marriage to help me forget? Maybe there could have been a happy medium for Gage and me but instead I walked away completely and became involved in my own career to the point of leaving him behind. Gage hadn't left her behind as he had alluded to in his letter. She had left him and at the time she didn't give him a chance to change her mind. *Joe is always insightful, making me stop and think* with his thoughtful words.

The more she thought about it, the more she realized she didn't like the answers she was coming up with. She had never given Gage the opportunity to help her find a way that would make it feasible to keep their marriage together. She had made the decision to end things without consulting Gage at all. Perhaps together she and Gage could have come up with a solution that would have worked for them both.

Did Joe tell me his story on purpose? He was a very intelligent man and he also had the uncanny ability to see things in people that they couldn't, or otherwise wouldn't take the time to see in themselves. Had she given up more than she should have by leaving? Was having a career something she wanted to be able to mask her pain? Perhaps she should have had a discussion like this with Gage a long time ago. The fault of their marriage falling apart lay at her feet, she realized. Gage must have asked himself these same questions over and over. It was something to think about but right now she had to think about Joe and focus on what he had revealed to her.

"You deserve to be happy, Joe. At this point in your career you can make changes and it won't hurt you. I say you should go for it," wrapping her arm around his. "You certainly have enough money to call the shots in your life. You don't need to worry about what you'd do if your career suddenly took a nose dive. I think you're the golden boy, isn't that what they call you in your world? Besides, I'm beginning to think that the ruthless Joe Kirby, the man I keep hearing about, doesn't exist at all. The Joe that I see before me now is the real Joe," she added as they continued. With Joe on her arm, Morgan knew she was going to be fine today and, like Scarlet, she would worry about tomorrow another day.

They shopped for hours and Joe tried to be as honest as he could as she tried on every different style of dress. He gave her his truthful opinion on her fashion sense and what he liked and didn't until they both agreed that they had found a winner. Morgan came out of the dressing room sparkling with confidence, dressed in her latest find. She settled on an emerald green satin dress. It clung to her body like a veil of silk. It didn't hurt that she had lost weight since she and Gage split because the dress didn't allow for any flaws. It clung to every inch of her body.

"Beautiful!" Joe said, staring in awe at the girl next door. There were millions of gorgeous women in the world and he could appreciate a beautiful woman when he saw one. Morgan looked dazzling in this emerald number. "There's no doubt that this is the one," he said having her do a twirl so he could admire her from all angles. Morgan knew that Joe appreciated expensive things and had impeccable taste so she felt more than satisfied.

Morgan took the green dress and the shoes she had picked out to match to the register and paid for them as Joe answered a call on his cell. After her purchase was made they opted for lunch at an outdoor cafe along one of the side streets. While they ate lunch, Joe received another call and it seemed to rattle his cage a bit more than she expected. He excused himself and headed for the sidewalk to talk to whoever it was with more privacy. Joe seemed visibly shaken by the call. When he came back to the table, Joe asked if she minded if he left. Apparently his father had taken ill and he was asking to see his only child.

"I can't believe that after all these years my stoic father is asking to see me." But it was his mother who had made the call to him on his father's behalf. By the sound of her voice, her immediate plea didn't seem unfounded. Joe left Morgan at the café and told her he would call her as soon as he returned home and would let her know what happened with his parents.

Once Joe was out of sight, Morgan was left alone with her own thoughts to keep her company. Placing her purchases on the floor next to her she decided to go ahead and order lunch. She ordered her favorite, grilled chicken Caesar salad and raspberry ice tea, and dialed Barbara. She wanted to assure her friend that she would be attending the gala with her this evening and that she had found the perfect dress. She and Barbara were so engrossed in conversation that she almost didn't see him; suddenly she wished she hadn't. Why she had chosen that moment to look up from her phone she didn't know. Directly across the street, she witnessed Gage, dressed in one of the Italian silk suits she had chosen for him. Perched on his arm was a tall, beautiful brunette. Without warning she was overcome with anxiety and found it difficult to breath. Actually, seeing Gage with another woman was just too much for her and after making excuses to Barbara she turned the phone off. She reached for her drink but her hands were trembling badly, she tried to steady them but she spilt her drink. She tried to sip from the glass again and as she did she watched her husband with an unhealthy curiosity. *He's ripping my heart apart while he's smiling fondly into the eyes of another woman!*

Matt Hastings glanced from Morgan to the object of her attention; what he saw was a great-looking couple directly across the street. *Whoever he is, he's obviously left the ice queen distraught.* Matt couldn't help but wonder who that guy was. "So… you have a heart after all," Matt said to Morgan as he tried to force her attention in a different direction.

"Matt, what are you doing here in New York?"

"I'm in New York to attend a meeting with my agent about my next film. I was going to look you up while I was here. It's funny, but the last thing I expected was to bump into you on the street my first day here." Matt hesitated, and then decided he'd ask because he was curious, "Who is he?" he asked as he tilted his head in Gage's direction.

Before she could answer he rested his hand over hers and he added, "Don't say he's no one of importance. If you saw what I saw when you noticed them together, you would be hoping that he didn't witness the same thing. So fess up, who is he?" he asked again.

Morgan sat up straight and considered what Matt had just said, hoping that Gage hadn't seen her. "I don't think you have the right to ask me such a personal question," she said as Matt took the seat opposite her. It didn't take long for passersby to recognize the man sitting across from her. Within minutes, they were being crowded by young women who wanted his autograph and a picture with him. Morgan could only smile at the young women, hoping that Matt would get bored with her and leave with one of his many admirers. When he didn't, she tried to escape while he was preoccupied, only to be followed by Matt and his adoring fans as well. He kept after her as she walked down the street pleading with her to allow him to take her out. He asked his fans for help but they only pleaded for themselves. "Come on, after one date, if you don't want to see me again, I will leave you alone. You don't want to turn me down in front of all the cameras, do you?" he pleaded with a demure smile.

His fans were shouting from every direction, that if Morgan turned him down, each one of them would gladly take her place. He smiled and pleaded his case again.

"I know you might find this hard to believe, Matt, but like a book I once read, I'm just not that into you. I wish I could give you the answer you want, but I can't. If you must know, that man, *he was my husband; well I guess he's still my husband, in title only.* Now, do you think you could leave me alone?" she asked as she continued to walk away from him.

Matt stood silently for a moment, shocked at her admission. He had never heard anything on the set about her having a husband. He was genuinely interested in Morgan Delaney but he didn't want to come between a man and his wife. People could say what they wanted about him in the tabloids but he did have some scruples and this was one line he would never cross. It was obvious that her husband didn't realize how lucky he was. *Morgan is a good person and she deserves to be treated like the lady she is.* What he had just witnessed was cruelty in its worst form. He was shocked that Morgan would accept this kind of womanizing from any man. The lady he had gotten to know in the last six months was strong willed and a little on the icy side when it came to the opposite sex. Perhaps her husband's behavior explained a lot about that side of her.

Matt thought it was him she had a total disdain for but it was obvious that Morgan didn't seem interested *in any other man besides the one across the street.* At least that was the way it looked to him. He stopped Morgan and told her that he would back off, but he only wanted to talk to her first. He stood before her for a few seconds and waited for his fans to move along before saying what he wanted to for her ears alone.

"Look, I apologize for my behavior. I had no idea you were married. If I had, I would never have hit on you in the first place. Don't let this get out but that's one line I don't cross," he teased. "My parents have been married fifty years, my sister Meg for ten years and my other sister, Ginny, over nine years. The Hastings family takes marriage *very seriously*. Judging by what I saw today and I don't mean to be disrespectful to you in any way, your husband doesn't take his vows all that seriously," he added with a gentle simper.

She didn't know what to say to Matt. He was correct in his assumptions about Gage's behavior. Right now she was at a loss to explain why her husband had been strutting around in her town with another woman on his arm while still being married to her. Though, who could blame him, she had been gone for such a long time.

"Matt, I can appreciate what you're trying to say but this is really none of your business and I don't want to talk about it. As for my husband's behavior and I'm not offering excuses for him, we have been separated for a long time. Even so, I don't believe I owe you an explanation. Go back to your hotel or have one of your fans show you around the city, but don't include me in your plans. I'm not interested in spending any time with *you*," *she added with note sarcasm,* but once it escaped her mouth she regretted saying it. Matt was just trying to be honorable and she had lashed out by being short with him when it was Gage who should have been on the receiving end of her anger.

Morgan couldn't help reliving the last few moments, seeing Gage with another woman on his arm; all the while smiling at whatever it was the woman was saying to him. She thought about it over and over again as she continued to walk down the street, heading toward her apartment. With her purchases in hand, she continued to walk, hoping that Matt wouldn't follow her. She couldn't believe her luck, the very first time she saw Gage with another woman Matt Hastings would-bear witness to that act of betrayal and *if it had to be someone, why Matt? Why couldn't it have been Joe with me today, as planned?* Suddenly, the agony she felt while recalling her own situation seemed trivial and narcissistic as she remembered Joe and all he was going through.

She remembered with sadness that he had rushed off to see his sick father for the first time in many years and here she was, thinking about her own issues. *Perhaps his visit to the hospital will bring them one step closer to reconciliation.* He had obviously missed his family if his admission this morning was anything to go by. It seemed that Joe was ready to take that next step at this point in his life and she hoped that the call from his mother was some kind of confirmation that they had arrived at the same place. Life was too short to cut the people you love out of your life, only to realize the gravity of the mistake when it's too late. She didn't want Joe to be without his family any more than she wanted to be without hers.

She was so enshrouded by her own thoughts that Morgan hadn't taken notice that her cell phone had been ringing. It wasn't until she had almost reached her doorstep that a stranger pointed it out to her. Barbara was frantic, she was sure that Darien Preston was going to change his mind before tonight's gala. Morgan had to convince her that Darien Preston was a professional; he wasn't about to change his mind. He had promised to make the announcement tonight, that he would be making changes as they merged the two publishing houses together. Morgan assured Barbara he would be adding her to his list of senior editors and that he would not go back on his word. Barbara was nervous about the evening ahead, she hoped that by filling up the table with friends and family, she would feel a little less stressed than she did at the moment.

In the meantime, Barbara neglected to tell Morgan that she had her own agenda planned for this evening, regarding Morgan, and she hoped it wouldn't backfire. Barbara reminded her once again that she would meet her there. She also told her the time she and her husband, Marty, arrive. It was going to be a fun-filled night with plenty of surprises, she added before disconnecting the call to take care of some last minute things.

Morgan smiled and threw the phone in her purse. That was the first time she had seen Barbara so anxious about anything. She entered her building with her key and pushed the button for the elevator. *I wonder if Joe has any news about his dad.* She hoped his father was going to recover and that somehow their relationship would be renewed. She couldn't fathom why people who loved each other would find it so difficult to accept the lifestyles of another family member even if it was different from their own. She couldn't imagine anyone in the McCleary family going years without speaking to one another, regardless of the issue. She knew sexual orientation would never be the catalyst to begin that trend. *My mom would never allow it.* She would call one of her family meetings and make sure that, by the time each one of them left the table, they were in agreement and would never allow any member of the family to be shunned by the others. *I am lucky to have a family like that.* Her family, though overbearing to a fault and in each other's faces most of the time, was always there for her when it mattered. That was the way they were with each other and it made her feel secure, even though there were times when she wished they would go away for a just a little while.

Before she got to her door, she checked Joe's apartment to see if he was back from his visit. He hadn't yet returned just as Morgan suspected; he had only left her an hour ago. She decided not to call him on his cell in case things were going well. She didn't want to interrupt the family reunion. She knew this was going to be a life-changing event for Joe and she wanted to be there for him, either way.

It was amazing how early events in a person's life can shape who they become. She was sure that the business side of Joe Kirby was molded out of necessity. He was known in his financial circles as a man who would do anything to rise to the top; that included crushing anyone who got in his way. The real man, the one she had come to know, was not that man at all.

There was a softer gentler side to Joe; that was the man she knew. Sure he was stubborn and a born leader but he was also a family man. He loved being included in the McCleary gatherings. The first time she brought him to a family function, she was shocked at the outcome. It was like he had adopted her family immediately and they adopted him. Joe had turned a corner in his life, after that first family meeting, and Morgan was there to witness it. He began to think about what was missing in his life. Neil was thrilled at the transformation.

Morgan turned the key in the lock, immediately grabbed a piece of paper and a pen and scribbled a note to leave on Joe's door. She expected to check up on him before she left, but if he still hadn't arrived home she wanted to make sure he knew that, no matter where she was, he could call her if he needed her.

Chapter Six

As Morgan's cab arrived, she looked around for any sighting of Barbara and her husband. She spotted them exactly where Barbara said they would be, standing with some other members of her family. After paying the cabdriver, she walked over to join them. As Barbara motioned her over, Morgan was shocked to see Matt Hastings standing there. He had no business at this function but she was going to find out how he managed to glom an invitation to the gala. It came as no surprise to her. When she whispered her objection into Barbara's ear, she found out that Barbara had set it up. She was disappointed in her friend's decision to play matchmaker, but she knew that she had done it out of love. As everyone was taking their seats, she was not at all shocked to find herself sitting opposite Matt.

"Look, I know this makes you uncomfortable. I would never have accepted the invitation had your friend extended the invite more recently, like today. Morgan, your friend called me last week and since I was interested in looking you up when I got here, I thought, why not? I was going to be in New York this week anyway and since I was genuinely interested in pursuing you, I took her up on her offer. What do you say we make the most of the night? Friends, nothing more," he promised as he raised his brow and pleaded with her to relax. "You don't want to ruin the night for your friend, do you? I promise we'll start fresh, no pressure, just two friends out for a casual night," Matt added with a smile. At that moment, she realized this was *the smile women couldn't resist.*

"Your right Matt, I apologize for my behavior this afternoon. Let's start over. My name is Morgan Delaney," she said, offering her hand to Matt.

"Matt Hastings," he said, taking her hand in his, raising it to his lips and gently kissing it. "It's a pleasure to meet you, Miss Delaney. I've heard nothing but nice things about you since my arrival. May I order you a drink?" as he motioned for a waiter.

"You're too kind; I'd like a cosmopolitan, if you don't mind."

"The lady would like a cosmopolitan and I'd like a scotch, neat."

Morgan smiled, she was surprised as they continued their conversation, at the unforeseen pleasure she was experiencing while spending time with him. She found that once she let her guard down she was actually enjoying herself. After all the announcements and speeches were completed, Darien Preston announced that the dance floor would be open for all to enjoy. He introduced the entertainment for the night. After hearing the first song, Morgan and Matt both admitted they were glad they had attended the gala. The people, the food and the entertainment made the night worth it. In the end, they found each other's company to be another added bonus.

"Would you like to dance, Morgan?"

"Sure," she said as he eased her chair out for her and led her on to the crowded dance floor. It was a slow song, as he held her in his arms he told her about his latest audition and the role he was expected to play. He was going to play an undercover agent whose sole purpose was to immerse him in the world of Washington D.C. lobbyists to find out what dirty dealings, if any, went on with the special interest groups in order to get bills passed. Hollywood wanted the film to hit the screens as soon as possible because it explained the problems that led to the failure of the financial system as we know it today and where the blame should ultimately fall. The movie teetered on the edge, just how far will these special interest groups go? Secretly, murder and bribery are some options opened to them, at least in the movie version. Matt would play Jax Grogan. His presence in Washington would lead to the uncovering of many dirty secrets. Politicians won't be happy with Jax Grogan so Jax will have to fight to stay alive.

"Sounds like an interesting plot, very James Bond-like. Don't tell me anymore, I don't want you to ruin the movie should I get to see it. You must love your work, getting to be someone else each time you take a role in a film."

"It's no different than what you do, except that I'm in front of the camera playing the part. Screenwriters, make the character come alive by taking the story you wrote and bringing it to film. You, as the writer get to decide what happens to me. By doing so, you live a different life every time you pick up your pen; living through the characters you create. But you get to change the outcome if you don't like the way a chapter is going." They continued to dance and make small talk. Though Joe was not far from her thoughts, she found herself having a good time with her new, but unlikely friend. Until, they went outside to get some much needed fresh air.

Matt had enjoyed himself tonight and Morgan hadn't been bad company either, in spite of the way she originally felt about spending time with him. The night was turning out to be a pleasant surprise for them both. He had found a new friend and he hoped she felt the same way about him. It would be great to know he had a friend in New York when he came to town, not someone pretending to be his friend. Many of the people who surrounded him these days did that. They were enjoying a conversation about Morgan's latest book when Matt spotted the man; he was directly in his sight. Matt thought her husband hadn't noticed that he was being watched from across the street. He could see that the man was too busy watching his wife, or so he thought. It was amusing; but suddenly he got the distinct impression that he was receiving a warning from afar, that he had competition.

"Is something wrong?" she asked, Matt had become abruptly quiet.

He didn't want her to know that her husband was standing across the street. She deserved this night out and he would make sure she had a good time and maybe help her out in the process. To make Morgan's husband aware of what he was missing, he asked her if she wanted to go back inside. Matt made it his business to show her husband that they shared a bond between them, a bond that didn't really exist. He put his arm around her, kissed her forehead and told her that he was glad she was giving him the opportunity to become her friend and that he expected nothing more than friendship. Matt hoped he gave the guy the nudge he needed but it could easily go the other way. If it did, he would have to tell Morgan what he'd done and why. During their earlier conversations, Morgan revealed how she had initiated the separation and that her husband was one of the good guys. She further stated she had made a mistake and regretted her decision deeply.

Gage couldn't believe his eyes. Adam had told him that Morgan was going to this shindig tonight, alone. Yet, there she was on the arm of some Adonis like creature. He had to admit the guy was good-looking and he looked vaguely familiar for some reason. *Have I seen him before?* She seemed comfortable and rather happy with the stranger, maybe he was the reason she hadn't returned any of his phone calls lately or responded to his letter? Perhaps; his wife wasn't as unhappy as some of the McCleary brothers had led him to believe. It made him sick to his stomach knowing that his wife was with someone else. He watched them both walk back into the building. He just stood there staring at the blank space they had just left behind. *What should I do now?* He decided to go to the one place he found comfort when he was feeling down and alone, the McCleary's Bar and Restaurant. He hoped that Logan had taken the night off because he didn't feel like getting into another argument with him about Morgan. She had left him, and that was one piece of information that the McCleary brothers didn't seem to want to believe.

After a night of dancing and conversation, Morgan had to admit to Barbara and Matt that she'd had a great time. She thanked them for the wonderful night but insisted on taking a cab home. Morgan glanced down at her watch and hoped she would still have time to get to see Joe. She hopped in the first available cab and conveyed her address to the driver, opening her purse to pull out enough money to pay the fare ahead of time, adding a tip before setting aside the correct amount. As they approached her apartment building she glanced up at Joe's and noticed his light was still on. She rushed out of the cab and ran to the elevator, pushing the button as quickly as she could so she could get there as fast as possible. Morgan prayed that everything had gone well for Joe.

After a brief knock on the door, Joe greeted her. From the look on his face, Morgan could see that the day hadn't gone as well for him as she had hoped. Joe's first thought after seeing Morgan was to ask her how her night went, putting off any conversation about his day. *Just like him, to put my needs ahead of his own. Or is he changing the subject so he won't have to deal with his own issues?*

"My night was fine but I'm more concerned about you. It's obvious your hurting, Joe. Is there anything you want to talk about?" It was apparent that the man of steel had been crying. Obviously, he hadn't told Neil anything. If Neil knew anything he'd be here, she knew that for sure.

"My father passed away tonight," he said quietly before adding that the funeral was all arranged for the day after tomorrow. He had taken care of all the arrangements earlier. He didn't want his mother to have to do it when she was feeling so vulnerable. Joe told her that after his father had passed away he went back to his parents' place with his mom and picked out a suit for his father's burial. "I watched my mother as she fell apart before my eyes but at least I could be there for her."

He told Morgan that at least he and his father had made peace before he died. His father told him how guilty he felt about not having his only son in his life all this time. He went on to tell her that his father made him promise that things would be different for his mother. He wanted Joe to make sure that he kept in touch with his mother and he wanted his son to introduce Neil to her. Joe told her, with tears in his eyes, that his father regretted that he hadn't met the man who softened his son's heart. Joe added that he held his father's hand in his, the once powerful callous hands that were now frail from sickness, as his mother held the other and they were a family for the last time as his father slipped away peacefully.

"I'm glad my dad was able to find peace in the end and that my mother witnessed the exchange between us. She seemed to cry happy tears knowing that we had made peace. She knew that in the end he had accepted me for who I am and not who he wanted me to be. I knew all along that my mother followed him blindly because she loved him even though she knew that by doing so it would cost her our relationship. She personally didn't give a damn what my sexual orientation was but she didn't dare go against my father's wishes. It was their way, she said to me. Women of her generation didn't go against their husbands. It was a decision I think she regretted. "It will be interesting when Neil comes home from the medical conference tomorrow. I can finally tell him that I want to bring him home to meet Mom and by the way, *I need you to attend my dad's funeral with me.* I've been avoiding his calls all night. I'm sure by tomorrow he'll be chomping at the bit to give me a piece of his mind," he added, smiling at Morgan.

Joe walked toward the window and turned back to Morgan. "It's going to be a little weird for me and Neil, to be around my parent's friends and extended family after going so long without having any contact with any of them. I don't know what my father said to his friends and co-workers about my not being in his life." Morgan stood next to him and held Joe's hand in hers, offering her condolences and promising to be by his side if he needed her. She volunteered to call Neil tonight and give him the heads-up about what had happened since he's been gone so he wouldn't have to worry needlessly.

"If you'd like, I could call Neil so he doesn't worry about you. He should be told so he can fly back in the morning to be with you. I'll spend the night so you won't have to be alone." Morgan knew Joe wasn't up to making a call like that just yet so she made a mental note to call Neil for him. She picked up her coat and purse and told Joe that she was going next door to change into comfortable clothes, grab some things and come right back. She would also take the opportunity to put a call through to Neil's cell and grab some homemade soup her mother had sent over earlier that morning with Alex. Morgan was sure Joe hadn't eaten all day. The day had turned out to be such an emotional roller coaster that food would have been the last thing on his mind.

Morgan entered her apartment, hearing her phone ringing. She wanted to ignore whoever it was at first and then decided against it. She was quite pleased to hear Neil's voice when she picked up the phone.

He was worried and a bit frantic since Joe hadn't answered his cell phone all day. When Morgan informed him of Joe's father's death, he said he would cancel his morning seminars and fly home as soon as he could get a flight. Morgan told him not to do that. She knew he was due to fly out late tomorrow afternoon. The funeral was the day after tomorrow and since she would be there for Joe until he arrived there was no need for him to rush. She let Neil know that there was nothing he could do and she knew Joe didn't want him to cancel his plans. It took a lot of convincing on her part but she finally got Neil to relax and stick to his original schedule. Although money was not an issue for either Joe or Neil, acquiring a flight at the last minute would be costly and quite unnecessary.

"Joe knows you would be here if you could, Neil. He knew you would drop everything and he didn't want you to do that. Give me fifteen minutes to change and get back to the apartment; then you can call him and I'll make sure he answers the call. Neil, you know he loves you, right?"

"Yes I do. But this is the first time that Joe has ever needed someone and I feel bad that I'm not there for him when he needs me the most," he added with regret. "No matter how much he would want to push me away, I'm here for him." On that note, they ended their conversation and she went to change into more comfortable clothes.

While she was getting ready, she thought about her own mother. Morgan had heard many stereotypical things about gay men and women from ignorant people. Thanks to her mother, she had taken time to instill certain values within her own family. She knew that someone's sexual orientation, religion and color did not make a person any less worthy of one's respect. Ellie McCleary had always believed that he who is without sin should cast the first stone. She made sure her children believed and lived by that rule as well. She taught them that they were no better than the next person, and they should treat everyone as they would like to be treated. *I'm so glad my family accepts Joe for who he is.*

With soup in one hand and an overnight bag in the other, Morgan entered Joe's apartment to find him at the window staring out at nothing. *Looking at Joe like this, it breaks my heart. I know he must be thinking about all the time he lost with his mom and dad; I know he's thinking about what happened today and what lies ahead in his future.* He turned when he heard her approach, Morgan simply smiled. He knew she would do whatever he wanted, even if that meant sitting there in silence.

"You're a good friend, Morgan. I don't quite know what to say. This past year has meant a lot to me. You've been more like my family than my own. I never once mentioned my family to you. You must think we're a bunch of dysfunctional fools in comparison to your family." He reached over the countertop and handed a photo album to Morgan. It was loaded with pictures of a younger version of himself with doting parents at his side. There was some of him playing all kinds of sports. His parents were with him in every photo. The photos ranged from his younger years through college. The outside world obviously thought Joe had been a typical jock; not one person would have been aware of the conflicts he held within himself.

"You're lucky to have the bond you have with your family. I've always thought I had that with my parents. It hurt when I found out differently. My parents were proud and devoted in the beginning, right up until my college graduation. I thought they were proud of me and who I was until I introduced them to my first love, Patrick. I never thought that my parents wouldn't be accepting of him until that day. My father gave me a hateful look, one that I will never forget. After a few choice words in private, he handed me a one way ticket out of his life and my mother's as well. I thought it would get better, that it was just the initial shock of the news. But the phone call inviting me back into their lives never came. Other than me sending them gifts during the holidays, birthdays and the occasional letter to update them on my life, they never spoke to me directly. It was a one way relationship, just as though I had ceased to exist. I don't even know if they ever bothered to read any of my cards or letters!"

Morgan said nothing, she knew he had to vent. Joe was finally letting out the feelings he had kept hidden for so long. "After I met Neil and things started to get serious, I had a change of heart and wrote them a letter to let them know that I had found the partner I wanted to spend my life with. I even told them I was going to ask him to marry me. I don't know why I expected a response from them; perhaps I thought after hearing that I was happy…? I was hoping it would somehow make things different after they received my letter. Once again, no reply, what was I thinking, as if I had a magic wand. I thought they'd be happy for me, and that perhaps we could end the silence between us, but that didn't happen. I never asked Neil to marry me. I've never told another soul that story until today. Neil never knew about my plans to ask him to marry me. I'm sure some shrink would have had a field day with me, telling me that my decision not to marry Neil had to do with my parents and their disappointment in me. Thinking about it now, the therapist would have hit the nail on the proverbial head." Joe was getting a lot off his chest and what came next surprised even Morgan.

"I never knew this; apparently, my father had been keeping tabs on me all these years. He knew I was wealthy and doing well in my career. About six months ago, he started receiving pictures from the private eye he'd hired to keep tabs on me, including some with a beautiful Irish woman and myself in them. At first he didn't think anything of it. Then he noticed that the same woman was seen leaving the building every morning, often shopping and having lunch or eating dinner with me. He saw how happy I was around this woman so he made an assumption about what he hoped was the truth. My father believed that you and I were living together, that I was so bitter by the way he had treated me that I didn't tell them I had you in my life. For one brief second, while in the hospital, I thought about letting him die believing that I was the son he always hoped for, but I couldn't do it. I couldn't bring myself to degrade what I have with Neil by lying about us. I told him the truth, about who you were to me and about Neil. In the end, you know what he said?" *Joe seems so sad when he speaks of his father.*

"He actually asked for my forgiveness, for all the time we wasted. He wanted me to forgive him for hoping that I wasn't who I was. He cried, Morgan. He asked me to promise him that I would introduce Neil to my mother and to beg Neil's forgiveness, on his behalf. He knew there wouldn't be time for him to ask Neil himself. He told me that he didn't want me to repeat his mistakes. 'If you love Neil, then you should be with him. Don't waste another minute of your life second-guessing who you are.' He told me how much he regretted the choices he made, allowing me to walk away that day, never writing or calling me. I couldn't believe what he said next, that if he could go back in time, he would run after me and try to work things out. I can't help but wonder if he just felt guilty because of what he believed would happen to him in the afterlife. I'm not really sure, but for the first time in years, my father glanced up at me and seemed proud to call me his son. I looked into his eyes and I saw his love for me," he said as he wept like a baby.

Morgan hugged him as he cried on her shoulder, letting out the feelings he had bottled up for years. It was difficult to see a man like Joe cry. Joe was over six feet tall, well-built and had the body of a twenty year old. She had never seen him have a weak moment. It broke her heart to see him hurting like this, but it was a long time coming. The McCleary men were all so manly but they did cry on those rare occasions. When they did break down and cry, it broke her heart too.

Morgan stayed with Joe that night, hoping the sleeping pill his mother's doctor had prescribed that afternoon would allow him to relax and get some sleep. Morgan slept on his couch all night long; afraid that she wouldn't hear him if she slept somewhere else. She worried for naught; he never woke during the night. She shifted on the couch when she became aware of the smell of coffee brewing. While in a foggy state of mind, she thought she heard the sound of water running in the shower. She knew Joe was awake so she forced herself up into a sitting position and pulled her hair up into a ponytail. After straightening up a little, she sat back down and waited. Just as she heard the water stop flowing, the front door opened slowly. Neil walked in looking disheveled, as if he'd been flying all night. He was wearing jeans and a black V-neck sweater. He tossed his bag on the floor and spotted her sitting on the couch at the same time.

"How is he doing?" He asked, glancing down the hall for any sign of Joe.

"I think he's going to be okay. He's had a lot to process in one day but he's got his mother and other family members back in his life. I think that has made the situation easier on him. Since you're here, I'm going to go back to my apartment and take a shower," she said, motioning toward the door. "I think he needs you right now. If either of you need anything, just call." She picked up the clothes she had brought over the night before. "Tell him I love him and you too," she added before giving Neil a kiss and leaving.

Morgan took a long hot shower and fixed herself a light breakfast. Joe was never far from her thoughts this morning but she couldn't help thinking about her own situation when she thought about what his father had said on his death bed. *Maybe I'm a lot like Joe's father? Didn't I let Gage, the only*

man I ever loved, walk out of my life without a fight? Didn't I sabotage my marriage by leading him to believe that I didn't care about him or that I didn't want to save our marriage? As she sat in silence, she couldn't stop thinking about Gage and the woman she saw him with yesterday. *Is it too late for me? Did Gage move on with his life without me?* The phone rang; as she answered it, she was pleased for the first time in months to hear the voice of one of her siblings.

"Alex, how are you? It's so good to hear a friendly voice!" After the night she'd just had, she knew she needed to remind her family that she loved them. *Why does it always take a death for people to realize how short life is and how important it is to let the people in your life know you love them?*

"Why do you sound funny? Is everything alright? Did that actor do anything to you, Morgan? I'll kill him if he did," he rattled loudly into the phone.

It took Morgan a few seconds to decipher what he meant and a few more to assure him that her mood had nothing to do with Matt Hastings. She informed him that it had to do with Joe Kirby. Alex was saddened to hear that Joe had lost his dad as he took down all the funeral information so that he and the other members of the McCleary family could attend the wake to show their respects. The entire family would be there for Joe and Neil, extending a helping hand, because both had become part of the McCleary's extended family. She had been so focused on Joe and his father's funeral that finding out the reason for Alex's call had slipped her mind.

Within seconds, the phone rang again. Her mom wanted to cook something for Joe and his family and deliver the food to their home so that they would have one less thing to think about after the service. She offered whatever help she could without passing judgment on Joe's mom. She had Morgan promise to get the information so she could have the food delivered and make sure flowers were sent to the funeral home. During the course of their conversation, Morgan's mom, Ellie McCleary mentioned that her dad had heard from Jake's commanding officer earlier that morning and that Jake hadn't reported back to the unit for almost five weeks. Currently his status was not MIA, (missing in action). The officer told her father not to worry because it was not unusual for the men in this unit to remain silent for long periods of time. He added that he would be in touch if there was any further news. Her Mom also let Morgan know that her dad had called Gage to see if he could do some digging for them.

Ellie McCleary tried to change the subject by mentioning that Alex had called repeatedly inquiring if she knew anything about a certain actor Morgan was dating. Morgan let her know that Alex had too much time on his hands. She told her mother that Matt was the actor who played the lead on the movie adaptation of her book. She assured her mother that she and Matt were friends and that she had no romantic inclinations towards him at all. Morgan made a mental note to call Alex and find out what she could about Jake. If there was anyone who could get the family information on Jake's whereabouts it would be Gage.

Morgan didn't known how Joe would feel about the McCleary family's intrusion into his affairs; she hoped he wouldn't get annoyed by their pushy overwhelming nature. She knew her mom needed a distraction; she would definitely be cooking all afternoon. Morgan searched in her closet looking for a dark dress and low heels. After dressing she couldn't help but feel a little anxious about attending the funeral.

Funerals had always made Morgan nervous but this time was especially difficult for her. As she approached the Humble & Sons Funeral Home all her old fears came rushing back. It had been a long time since she had attended a wake. She knew she had to pay her respects but she hadn't done it alone in years. This was her first since Michael's death and she knew it would conjure up all the memories from that time. Before she always had someone to lean on, usually Gage, but this time it was different. Morgan loved Joe and Neil and so she would take a deep breath and be there for them no matter how distressed she felt.

She locked her car and headed toward the building when she heard someone call her name. It was Gage; he was dressed elegantly in a dark grey pinstriped suit, a white shirt and a grey and blue tie. He looked better than attractive, as though he had just stepped off the cover of GQ magazine. *That man personifies sex.*

Cars were pulling in every which way but still they seemed focused on each other intently. Morgan thought she was prepared for their first encounter but she found herself lacking the courage to speak to him. Gage lifted the tendril of hair that had fallen into her eyes and smiled at her. "I had to come. As soon as Alex told me the news I knew you would put up a brave face and come alone even though it would be hard for you. I hope you don't mind my being here? I couldn't let you go through this alone and I figured your friend would be too busy with his own family right now." She knew he meant Joe.

No explanation was needed. Gage knew how she felt about death and funerals; he knew it scared her more than she would care to admit to anyone else. With Gage close by, she knew she would be able to cloak the fear lying just beneath the surface. Before they went inside she had to ask him about Jake.

"Gage is there any news about Jake?" She could see by the look on his face that he was very concerned. He told her that Jake was good at his job and that he would make contact if he could. He told her that he put in some calls to find out what he could. As soon as he heard something he would let everyone in the family know.

Gage took her hand and led her into the funeral home. Neil was the first to greet the couple and seemed shocked as Gage introduced himself as her husband. He knew part of the story and was under the impression that Gage had moved on with his life, but the man standing before him acted anything but aloof. This was certainly a pleasant change of events since it was obvious that Morgan was still in love with her husband. Neil greeted them and thanked them for coming. He assured Morgan privately that Joe was doing well under the circumstances and that Joe's mother didn't know whether to cry at the loss of her husband or jump for joy to have her son back in her life. He was pleased to tell Morgan that Mrs. Kirby had accepted them both with open arms. Neil smiled as he told her that he was being introduced to all relatives and friends as her son-in-law, the surgeon.

"I'm glad for you both. I wish the reconciliation had happened under better circumstances but I'm happy that Joe reconnected with his father before he passed away. If you'll excuse us, Neil, I'm going inside to find Joe," she said, but before taking a step Neil mentioned that Joe had introduced her parents to his mother already.

"Your mom and dad were here earlier and introduced to Mrs. Kirby. I have the feeling your moms are both going to become friends. You just missed your brother, John. He left about twenty minutes ago. I've been introduced to so many people today that I don't think I'll remember any of them." Neil offered his apologies and excused himself before being addressed by a stranger who was vying for his attention. Morgan and Gage weren't at all surprised to hear that her mother had already been to the funeral home. If there was one woman who held the key to heaven it would be Ellie McCleary. She saw only the good in people and in turn she had them believing the same about themselves. Ellie McCleary inspired you to dig deep and be the best person you could be. Gage could only imagine the deep-seated fear in her heart as she worried about her son. He was sure that she would try to hide what she was feeling; not wanting to worry anyone else. He knew Ellie and she would be a nervous wreck deep inside where no one else would notice. *I wish that I could be in Syria right now so I could have a better perspective about what was going on. If I was there, perhaps I could report that Jake is safe.*

Gage asked Morgan if she was ready to pay her respects, letting her know that she had nothing to fear, that he was right beside her. He tried to lighten her mood, knowing how depressed she'd be as soon as she saw the casket. It was enough that she was worried about Jake; the last thing she needed was to see was a casket that would bring her back to a darker time in their lives.

"Do you know this will be the first time I meet the infamous Joe Kirby? I've been wondering about this guy, the man who's had the pleasure of spending so much time with my wife."

It seemed like a long way down the aisle and her anxiety didn't help the situation. It did make things easier knowing that Gage was standing right next to her. She knew she needed to cloak the anxiety she was feeling because Joe didn't need the added burden of worrying about her. Joe spotted her, greeting her with a giant bear hug. After meeting Gage, he introduced them to his mother. He was glad to see Morgan even though he knew she would be there. He was pleasantly dumbfounded to see her husband standing at her side. *Maybe this means something but I have my doubts.* He remembered that she was out last evening with Matt Hastings.

Joe had to admit that Gage Delaney was even hotter in person than his photographs alluded. *How did Morgan let something this hot, this ravishing out of her sight?* After embracing Morgan and thanking her for all she and her family had done, he turned his attention to Gage. Both men looked at each other, trying to intimidate the other. It seemed a little ridiculous considering their separate relationships with Morgan.

"So we finally meet. I was always curious about the man who let my girl walk out of his life. It never would have happened if she was my wife," Joe said, meeting the other man's glare. Joe could see his words hit a nerve but to his credit Gage didn't react. This was not the place to respond to the bait being taunted in his direction. Joe could see that Gage hadn't moved on with his life at all as Morgan had led him to believe. *If he was dating other women, they certainly didn't mean more to him than the woman decorating his arm at the moment. There is an interesting story here and I can't wait to hear it.*

Gage and Morgan stayed there for a couple of hours. She needed to be there for Joe and Neil. Joe announced that he and Neil had arranged for a late lunch and all were invited. He told Morgan he needed to get some food into his mom before she collapsed.

Joe and Neil invited Morgan and Gage personally. They would be meeting at a restaurant two blocks over. Neil had secured reservations for a private room in the back so that the family could eat something light before returning to the funeral home for the second viewing. Morgan offered her condolences to Joe, Neil and Mrs. Kirby before leaving. She told them she wouldn't be joining his family for lunch but promised she would return later that evening with the remaining McCleary family. Joe's mom had given her mom a key to her home so that she could let herself in to arrange the food she had cooked to be eaten after the viewing tonight.

"You've done enough already, Morgan. I don't expect you to sit here with me all day and night. I appreciate everything you've done and I'm going to be alright. I promise. Go home and relax and I'll see you later tonight at Mom's," Joe said, taking her in his arms and hugging her tightly. He turned to her husband and thanked him too for taking time out of his busy schedule to come to his father's wake. Joe knew that Gage had come for Morgan's sake, but still, he appreciated it. *I'm impressed with Gage; he was at Morgan's side when she needed him and without being asked.* Morgan didn't make the first call to her husband, Joe was sure of that.

Although Joe was well aware of Morgan's fear of funerals, he couldn't shake the feeling that Morgan seemed distracted by something else.

Chapter Seven

Morgan stood in the parking lot with Gage for a while, not knowing what to say to him. *Is this how our marriage is going to end? Have we become so incompatible that we have forgotten how to speak to each other?* Gage finally broke the silence and told her that she needn't worry about Jake. "I know you and I know you're worried. Jake is a smart man. If he's in any danger, he'll know what to do to stay alive. He was trained by the best." He hugged her for what seemed an eternity and casually asked about Matt Hastings, as if he had the right to. He said he had heard through the grapevine that she was dating again, that Matt Hastings was her new love interest. Morgan didn't miss that he'd said Matt's name with a note of disappointment in his voice. She realized, as he pulled away from her, that he really didn't want to hear her response.

"Matt Hastings is a friend; I met him in California on the set. What about you? I see you're out and about with a lot of different women, if the tabloids have even an ounce of truth to them. You may be able to hide from people who don't know you but I've always recognized you, even though you tried to dodge the camera," she stated with a smirk in retaliation.

Gage's smile was remote he didn't bother to comment at first. He didn't want to dignify pictures from gossip magazines.

Morgan should have known better than to embark on this subject with him. He thought she knew him better than that. He wondered if she was emphasizing the tabloids and the lies they wrote to take the focus off Matt

Hastings and her. She had to know what was written in the tabloids was rarely true. It was mostly leaked by the women he was with to insinuate something that didn't exist, so they could have their fifteen minutes of fame. He didn't like having his picture taken and she knew that. He had taken steps early on to have Alex's name put on all company documents. Alex agreed to do this for him and he understood the reasons behind the request. Alex also knew that it meant Gage trusted him explicitly because the entire company belonged to Alex on paper.

Gage took all the necessary steps to assure the safety of the people he needed to protect. There were no clear photos of him anywhere. That was a good thing because if what he was hearing about Jake was true, he might have to intervene. He had already started to grow facial hair but he knew there would be a target on his chest if he went back to Syria. Getting in and out of the country in one piece was going to be tricky. There was a very good chance he wouldn't be returning, but he was beginning to think he would have no choice but to go to Syria.

It was a shame that she had already left him when the business took off, otherwise she would be with him riding the same wave of excitement that he had experienced this past year. After all, it was for her that he had built this empire.

"I want you to know that if you need me, no matter what time it is, I'm here. You know that, don't you?" he asked as he lifted her chin so their eyes would meet. It was funny, but as he looked into the emerald eyes that he loved so much, he only saw distress and fear. Gage wished there was some way he could relieve her of this anguish she was feeling. If there was a way to take Jake's place in the desert, he would do it. He hated seeing her in such turmoil. He wanted to see her smile again.

Is she wondering why I wouldn't give her a divorce when she asked me? The McCleary's were an old-fashioned bunch and they didn't believe in divorce but she had to know that he would never hold her back from being happy. If Matt Hastings made her happy, he would give her the freedom she needed. It would kill him, but he would make the sacrifice for her. He would forever hold her in his heart, along with the memories of their time together. He knew that no future love interest would ever compare to his feelings for Morgan.

"I appreciate your coming with me today, Gage, but you don't have to accompany me tonight. I'll come back with Logan and Alex. They're both coming tonight, so I'll hitch a ride with one of them. It was truly nice of you to take time out of your busy schedule for me. Alex told me how busy you have been lately. I'm glad to hear the business is such a success. Gage, I never regretted one minute of it," she added, meaning their marriage. If their marriage was to end, she wanted him to know she enjoyed the ride and had no regrets.

Gage took her in his arms and hugged her tightly as he took in the scent of her. He didn't want to let go because he was afraid that this would be the last time he would hold his wife in his arms. She didn't seem to need him anymore and it bothered him more than he cared to admit. As he loosened his grip ever so slightly, while still holding her close, he looked into green eyes that had haunted him for a year. He couldn't help himself as he looked at those warm rose-colored lips quivering ever so slightly. The look she gave him said she wanted him to kiss her. He lowered his head and kissed her, perhaps for old time's sake or maybe desperate need. He meant it to be a light brush of a kiss just to say good-bye but it turned into something very different for both of them.

Gage kissed her softly, at first, and then intensified the kiss, as if his life depended on it. Within moments he decided he would let the kiss take them where it would and he would not regret the temptation. After all, she was still his wife and he wanted to make her feel his desire. He wore his wedding ring around his neck but it meant the same to him as the day she put it on his finger. Morgan had always been the light in his darkness, his special ray of sunlight. He knew he could reach her, sexually and spiritually they were connected as if they had shared the same space. If he was wrong to use her weakness of him to try to keep her in his life, so be it; to him, it was worth the risk. He wanted to hold her in his arms like this forever. What he saw in her eyes when he kissed her, he savored. Nothing had changed. She wanted him just as much as he wanted her. She kissed him back like there was nothing in the world but them. *How was she able to walk away from me and what we shared?* It made no sense. Gage knew that kissing his wife like this in the middle of the parking lot was not going to win him any points with her family. If any one of the McCleary brothers saw them, he was sure they'd kill him. But right now he felt like he was drowning and he needed her to rescue him. He couldn't let go of her; he held on to her for dear life.

Morgan knew she should get a grip and put an end to this madness. But she was having trouble concentrating on anything other than the fact that Gage was kissing her and helping her to forget everything happening around them. It wasn't just any kiss either; he was going in for the kill. *This was the way he kissed her when he wanted to make love to her,* and not just soft gentle lovemaking. This was the Gage who would tear the clothes from her body in desperation, the make love in the backseat of the car Gage. That was the impulsive lovemaking they had often shared. *I'm at a wake and in a parking lot, dear heaven; I have to try to gain my composure before someone comes outside and witnesses our animal behavior.* They were acting like two cats in heat. *Please,* she prayed to all that was holy, *allow me to gain my sanity.*

"Gage, I can't, not here," she whispered in his ear, as he kissed the exposed skin of her neck and her breasts. She was breathing short little breaths, almost panting, as he lifted his head. He led her over to her car and asked if he could follow her to her apartment. Morgan could barely breathe, let alone deny him what her own body, *craved.* She shook her head and hoped that neither one of them would come to their senses before they got to her apartment. She needed this as much as he did, maybe more. As she drove home all she thought about was Gage's hands touching her body the way he once had. As she drove down the highway she was lost in her memories, remembering the way he touched and worshiped her body, before the separation. *It has to mean something; maybe we have one last chance to make this work.*

They both pulled in directly across from her building. Fate must have intervened because there were rarely spots available at this time of day and never two at the same time. Gage jumped out of his car as fast as he could to be at her side. He was not going to let her change her mind, not if he could help it. If there was one place he knew her better than any other man, it was in the bedroom and he wasn't about to give up his only advantage. He couldn't walk away from her, not now, not if he had a fighting chance at winning her back. Gage took her key from her shaking hand, put it into the lock, opened the door and pulled her into his arms. After kissing her deeply, he trapped her body against the wall behind her. There were only two apartments on the floor she lived on and he was sure the other belonged to Joe Kirby. That meant they were alone, he could seduce his wife without interruption.

Gage lifted her dress, kneading her buttocks with his hands as he pressed himself against her. Morgan could feel how much he needed her. He tore her thong from her body, shoving the skimpy scrap of material into his suit pocket while his mouth was focused on playing havoc with her senses. She was breathing deeply and he knew there was no turning back for either of them. He would make sure she remembered this day forever. Gage turned her body away from his so that her back cradled against him. His hands roamed her body as he continued to worship the side of her neck with his kisses and his gentle nips. He held her loosely against him as her body convulsed with multiple orgasms. He undid his pants, turned her body and lifted her leg, wrapping it around his waist as he entered her. They rode each other with such force and intensity. When they climaxed he felt complete.

Gage locked the door and followed behind her. Neither of them knew what to say to each other. She asked him if he would like anything to drink or eat and all he did was smile. "Don't be so vulgar," she said as she tried to walk past him.

"I'm not being vulgar. You asked, I answered," he teased. "Don't cheapen what we have together, Morgan. I want you forever. I have always wanted you," he said as he held her arm and pulled her into his embrace again. Once again, he stared into her eyes as he undid the single knot that kept her dress in place and let the two sides fall open. Her dress was hanging off her shoulders and he helped move it along by slowly letting the silk graze her shoulders before falling to the floor. Morgan stood there wearing a skimpy bra. He kept his eyes locked on hers as he undid the clasp, all the while aware of how her breathing was becoming more rapid and labored. Gage lifted the love of his life into his arms and carried her down the hall to her bedroom while kissing her as deeply and mind-blowing as was physically possible. It was driving him insane having her naked body wrapped around his clothed one, something he would take care of immediately.

Morgan unfastened his tie, tossed it to the floor and began unbuttoning his shirt as they continued down the hall. She needed him naked as quickly as possible, there was no sense denying that she wanted him again. As he continued to kiss her, she thought she would die with pure lust for him. She yanked his jacket over his broad shoulders and let it fall to the floor. Morgan had already started unbuttoning his shirt; some buttons went flying when she pulled his shirt apart. There were clothes strewn everywhere; Gage kicked off his shoes impetuously, never letting go of her. When they reached the bedroom, he placed her on the bed and joined her. After today he would make sure she remembered what they'd once had together. If by some chance she could still walk away from their marriage, he would make sure she thought of him every night she laid her body down on this bed.

Gage held her in his arms, saying a silent prayer and hoping she would ask him to stay. She had fallen asleep in his arms after they had made love. He loved watching her sleep; the look on her face as she drifted off to sleep was always one of pleasure and contentment. He remembered the first time he made love and spent the night with her. Gage rested his head on his elbow and watched her as she slept, glorying in her beauty and the sexual satisfaction he saw on her face, basking in the expression of fulfillment he knew he put there. He would never get enough of her, she meant that much to him. Somehow, he would win her back.

His cell phone rang, it was his office calling, there was a problem with some blueprints. He had to take care of it immediately since the job's deadline was fast approaching. He thought about calling Alex but he was already sitting on a full plate. He would leave Morgan a note explaining why he had to leave. In the note, he asked her to call him later; signing it, he dressed quickly and left the apartment as quietly as possible. Luckily, he always kept an extra shirt in the car.

Morgan woke feeling wondrously fulfilled for the first time in a very long time. She expected to find Gage sleeping next to her but there was no sign of him anywhere. The thought of Gage and what they had just shared aroused Morgan's body. She'd hoped he hadn't left because she wanted him to stay. She arose from the bed and with only a sheet covering her body she went in search of her husband. She smiled mischievously as she searched for him. He always incited this erotic behavior in her. She didn't find Gage in any of the other rooms but she did find a note he'd left propped up against a vase on the kitchen table. She felt let down but she knew he had a good reason for leaving.

> *Dear Morgan, (My ray of sunshine.)*
> *There was a problem with a job and it needed my immediate attention. I had to take care of the problem personally. Have I ever told you that I love watching you sleep and by the way princess; you still snore. I hope to hear from you later on tonight.*
> *Forever and always,*
> *Gage*

Morgan took the letter and pressed it against her breasts. She hoped it meant something and that perhaps they were turning a corner in their relationship. Gage had always said that she was his forever and always and she responded with 'always and forever'. She glanced at the clock and realized if she didn't jump into a shower soon her brothers would be going to the wake without her. After a quick shower, she brushed her hair and put it up. She picked up the phone and called Logan asking if he could give her a ride. She didn't want to have to go alone and of course he readily agreed. With her ride assured and the time confirmed, Morgan went to her closet to pick out another outfit for the evening service. She hoped Joe and Neil would have too much on their minds to notice her wearing a different outfit. She would have to explain that while Joe was feeling emotionally distraught she was getting it on with her husband and not just once or twice but multiple times.

Logan called her from his cell phone a short while later to let her know he was outside. After a little last minute primping, she grabbed her purse, cell phone and locked the door. Logan was looking very masculine and handsome in his suit. He was the only brother who rarely wore a suit. His job never required more than a tee shirt and jeans so he did whatever he could to avoid wearing a suit. Weddings and funerals were the rare times anyone would see Logan dressed to the nines. But she had to admit that when he did clean up, he was as attractive as or more so than her other brothers.

She was surprised that each of her brothers had remained single. All of the McCleary men were a great catch, in her biased opinion and each one was a success. They didn't seem interested in rushing to the altar. They loved women for sure. *They each played the field a little too well.* But she had confidence knowing that a woman was going to come along for each of them. She couldn't wait to sit back and watch as they squirmed and fought against the idea of falling in love.

Logan reached over and kissed his sister on the cheek before asking how everything was going since she had returned home. "I haven't talked to you since you came back. Did you get everything packed up all right? I didn't even know you got back early until Alex stopped by the bar last night. Oh, by the way, is it true that you're dating the lead actor from the movie?"

"Yes, everything went fine with the packing and thanks for offering to fly out and help. As for Alex telling tales, that's all they are, rumors. He read more into a relationship I had with a friend than actually existed. Come on, Logan, you know me, if I was dating anyone I would have told you. You and I talk almost every day. Not that I'm changing the subject, but what do you think about Jake?" she asked with concern. "Logan, I'm really nervous. I have a bad feeling. Aren't you worried?" she added with a heightened sense of fear.

"I'm concerned but I have to believe that Jake is going to be fine. He learned from the best. You know, that guy you're still married to," he said vehemently, reminding her that she still had a husband and hinted without saying that dating the actor would have been in poor judgment on her part.

"Not that I *am dating, but if I recall correctly, the tabloids had pictures of Gage doing his fair share of dating while, still being married to me,*" she said sarcastically. Why she chose to have this discussion with Logan after the afternoon she shared with Gage she didn't know. Perhaps, she was fishing for information, thinking Logan could offer some insight into Gage's personal life. She was disappointed in herself for how trivial and immature she had sounded at the moment but Gage was the only man alive who could incite her to feel so intensely.

"Don't believe everything you see in those rags. Gage has always been around, just waiting for your call. If you wanted him back all you had to do was pick up the phone. Remember, you were the one who ended it," he said raising his brow. Logan was the only one who knew that Morgan had walked away, that it wasn't the other way around. Morgan abruptly changed the subject. The last thing she wanted to do was have her family speculating about their relationship by admitting what happened this afternoon to Logan. She decided to keep it to herself until they sat down together and decided what to do next.

Morgan and Logan discussed Jake and his situation while en-route. It was no surprise to Morgan when Logan told her he had offered to host a luncheon at his restaurant after the burial. Joe had accepted the offer but insisted on paying any expense it would cost Logan, Morgan knew that Logan would never accept money from Joe or his family, considering it an insult.

When the conversation meandered back to Jake, Logan told her that Gage had heard from a member of his old unit, confirming what they already knew, that no one had heard a word from Jake in over five weeks. He had gone into enemy territory searching for a British journalist who had gone missing. Everyone in the unit had returned with the exception of Jake. Gage had told Logan that if he heard any other news he would call him as soon as he could. It was much easier for them having been forewarned by Gage. Morgan found herself wondering if Gage had shared her bed to take her mind off thinking about Jake and the plight he was in. *I know my husband and he always felt responsible for the men in his old unit. Even though they are Jake's men now, I wonder if Gage feels responsible for Jake's disappearance.*

She began to think about Gage again and started to feel unsure. She knew Logan suspected that the pictures were all fabrications. *Perhaps there is something to what Logan just told me.* It would make what happened between them this afternoon feel more real, that maybe their relationship was on solid ground after all. She knew that they would have to talk about what happened and she hoped that when they did there were no regrets, because she had none.

"Logan, I can't believe that you were told Jake was missing over a week ago and didn't say anything to me. Why didn't you tell me?"

"You were out of town and as soon I heard something, I told John right after Gage told Alex at the office. Alex told me and asked me to keep it to myself until they were sure. The only one who didn't know anything besides you was Patti and you know how she is. It's hard enough for her to deal with her three kids, let alone handle news like this. As it turns out, we did the right thing not telling her, she fell apart this morning when dad and mom gave her the news. I was going to tell you when I flew out to California but you didn't need me. You're a lot stronger than you give yourself credit for, Morgan." Logan reached over and covered her hand with his, gently squeezing it. "Jake is going to be fine, you'll see. You need to take care of yourself, Morgan. Michael wouldn't want you to live your life alone and you know that. He would want you to get on with your life and be happy."

"I hope you're right about Jake. I have to say Mom is handling this better than I would have expected her to," she said as she told Logan about the conversation she had with their mother.

Logan smiled as he pulled into the parking lot. "Contrary to what some people think, I happen to know that Mom is a very strong lady. It's Dad who scares me a little. He's been pacing the floors, worrying about Jake. I just hope Gage finds out something soon. The old man's ticker is not going to be able to handle it if the news is bad," he added regretfully, after seeing the look on Morgan's face. "I didn't mean to upset you. I'm sure when we get the news it's going to be good news."

Logan parked the car in the first spot he found and turned off the engine. He and Morgan were joined immediately by Alex, John, Patti and her husband, Bill. After greeting each other, the siblings went inside to offer their condolences together. Joe was glad to see all the familiar faces and even happier to introduce them to his mother. Mrs. Kirby openly admitted that she was glad to know that her son had had such wonderful people in his life all this time.

After extending their respects, the McCleary's moved toward the back of the room where they sat and discussed the latest news about Jake's disappearance. Each one of them had their own opinion about what they thought should happen next. John, the F.B.I. agent, tried to lighten the mood and said not to worry about Jake knowing the enemy would never want to keep him. "Can you just imagine what he's doing to them now?" he added. "Let's face it; Jake is your typical macho soldier who we all know learned from the super soldier himself. He's a trained killer. He knows what he needs to do," he said as he looked at Morgan, implying that Gage had a lot to do with the man Jake had become in the military. "If there's a way out the mess he's in, he'll find it," he added confidently.

Alex let his brothers know that Gage was doing everything in his power to gain whatever Intel he could about Jake through his sources and that the family needed to ease up on Gage. He told them that, although Gage hadn't said so himself, he knew Gage was blaming himself for Jake's disappearance. Alex also told them he overheard Gage telling Jake's commanding officer that if anything happened to Jake he'd blame himself. After all, it was his idea that Jake train for the elite forces. Alex said that Gage hadn't been aware that he was standing outside his office while he was having a face to face computer conversation with Jake's commanding officer, an old friend. Alex admitted he heard Gage volunteer to fly to Syria, but Jake's C.O. told Gage that that was out of the question. Jake was a trained Seal; he would find a way to get back to the unit. If he didn't then the men is his unit would find him; and if by some chance he didn't make it back, Jake already knew the risk he would be facing and that Gage needed to be able to deal with it.

Alex waited until Morgan was out of the conversation before proceeding with a conversation he overheard that frightened him.

"Gage also contacted his C.I.A. connections and, from what I could understand, Gage has reactivated himself. He did that for Jake. We need to show him a little appreciation for what he's doing. I got the impression that no one else but us and whoever it was he was talking to knows what he did. I'm sure Morgan was kept in the dark too but I'm not sure that's a good idea. She deserves to know what Gage did for Jake," Alex reiterated. The brothers were shocked and they all knew the risk. They had to make this right with Gage.

"I didn't know Gage was feeling that bad. I knew he was concerned but he must be really worried if he reactivated Alex Summer," Logan said with concern as he glanced over at Alex and shook his head.

"Maybe we should give Gage a call and take him out to McCleary's tonight so we can talk to him. We don't have to let on that we know anything," John added, looking at his siblings for confirmation. "We could all use a guy's night out and then we'll just crash upstairs at Logan's. You don't mind do you, Logan? Maybe we can talk Gage out of this."

Logan wholeheartedly agreed. Right about now, a night out was just what they needed to numb themselves for a little while. He teased his brothers by saying he only hoped that there was enough liquor handy to take them all on. Morgan and Patti returned to the group and felt left out. When they were told about the boys night out they were a little confused but understood the male bonding that was taking place. The McCleary men hated to show emotion and somehow thought that if they got drunk together it would numb the pain they were going through. Logan offered to be the one to drop by their parent's house and kidnap their dad. If there was one person who needed a diversion it was him.

Morgan excused herself when she realized Joe was among the missing. When she found him, he was outside leaning against a car parked on the street side of the funeral home. He smiled at her when she approached him; he explained that he had needed to get some air. "I felt like I was suffocating in there. I think it's finally dawning on me that after tonight they're going to close that coffin and I'm never going to see the old man again. I didn't think I'd feel this way but I actually feel physically ill. I need to pull myself together before I go back inside. I don't want my mother to see me like this. She says I'm her pillar, that's a laugh," he added, before Morgan came over and embraced him.

"I don't think anyone expects you to remain in control every second. He was your father and despite what kept you both apart all these years, you still loved each other. It's never easy to say good bye to someone you love. You need to allow yourself to feel the pain or you won't be able to ever let it go." *Who am I to be giving this advice?* It took her this long to understand just what she was saying. Grieving is a process and each stage has its own validity. Morgan hugged him as tears fell from his eyes. The few pedestrians that passed by were obviously touched by his sadness.

As Joe pulled himself together, he told Morgan how much he appreciated her and her family and all they had done for him. Joe told her that Neil's family had stopped by earlier to show their respects. It was like one big family get-together as they all promised to stay in touch with each other and that included his mother. It was amazing, he relayed to her, that his father's death had brought him the family he craved. "I now have my mother in my life as well as Neil's family and believe me their quite a crew, too. They remind me a lot of the McCleary's. I didn't think it was possible to meet another family who would remind me of yours but Neil's family certainly does," Joe added.

"Listen, Neil has rounds tonight at the hospital and he has an early morning surgery that couldn't be postponed so he's staying at the hospital. He'll be back early tomorrow so he can attend the service, but I was wondering if you feel like staying at my place tonight? I could use a friend," Joe asked hopefully.

Morgan readily agreed since she knew she had no plans and the boys would be including Gage in their night out so she wasn't expecting to be hearing from him. Besides, Joe was her friend, he needed her and she wanted to be there for him.

Joe Kirby never admitted that he needed anyone and Morgan couldn't help but think that this could be a turning point for him. Joe was finally getting in touch with his feelings again and when all the dust settled she couldn't help but wonder how much his life would change. He had his mother now and perhaps he would open up more to Neil now that the past had found a resting place. She was convinced that the events of the past few days would allow Joe to move forward.

Chapter Eight

"Joe, are you sure you should be drinking like this?" Morgan asked as she watched Joe go to his bar and pour himself another glass of scotch. "You have to be there for your mom in the morning and you don't want to be hung over."

Joe tried without success to numb the pain with alcohol but he knew Morgan was right. No one expected him to be strong the entire time. "Hey did you hear the latest trend, drunk while emailing?" he asked, trying to lighten the conversation.

"What the heck is that about?"

"I heard about it before my dad's death and I was going to mention it to you, then it slipped my mind. There are so many people who email while drinking that a program was developed to protect people from themselves. You load this program into your computer and if you decide to turn it on after a night of drinking, like some of us have done, it has a safety mechanism that's set so that you have to answer a few questions before the computer will allow you to send an email out. I'll download the program into your computer if you want," he said slurring his words.

"Maybe I'll take you up on that. In the meantime, how come you haven't asked me about my night with Matt Hastings?" She continued to enlighten him about the gala that Barbara had invited her to and where she had met up with Matt. She went on and on with her conversation, unaware he wasn't listening as she was telling him how the night went, all the while speaking from his kitchen as she was trying to prepare him some food to help him evade a morning hangover.

"I'm glad to hear that you and Neil are finally moving into the penthouse together. It's about time your beautiful place was lived in. It was a pleasure to meet your mom, by the way. She's a classy lady and I could tell how much she has missed you. Joe, I'm sure if he were able to, your father would have called sooner. Keep the memory of him alive in your heart and remember that in the end he made sure you knew that he loved you." She should have known that she was talking to herself for some time now as she turned the corner with a cup of coffee and an omelet in hand. He hadn't participated in her conversation because he was sound asleep on the couch.

Morgan took off Joe's shoes and covered him with a blanket she found on the couch. She couldn't imagine what his emotional state might be like after all the highs and lows of the past two days. Three days ago, he was a loner with a boyfriend he couldn't really commit to and now he had the family he always craved and an extended family through Neil. Even Neil had admitted to her that their lives had taken an unexpected turn after Joe made peace with his father. Neil knew that Joe was finally able to make the ultimate commitment after he had freed himself of all the unwanted baggage he had carried around all these years.

Morgan went into the kitchen and cleaned up the mess she made, wondering about how things were going down at McCleary's. She couldn't stop thinking about what Alex had said earlier about Gage feeling guilty about Jake's disappearance. *Is that why he made love to me?* Did I help to ease the feeling of guilt for him? Perhaps he hoped by making love to me he could be forgiven for his unwarranted sins? In her naivety she had hoped that they were turning a corner and starting over, but at the present moment she found herself questioning his motives and not liking where her thoughts were taking her.

She reached for her cell phone and put a call through to her sister Patti to see if she had heard anything from her husband, Bill. She would try to find out what she could from Patti although Logan had admitted freely that they didn't share too much with Patti these days. She was an emotional mess; even Bill kept her in the dark about things that would have his wife worrying unnecessarily. The family had always contended that if you were to die, you would want Patti at your funeral. Morgan recalled an amusing moment when the family found her crying hysterically at a stranger's funeral. She'd had no idea that the funeral she was supposed to be attending wasn't due to take place until later that afternoon. Patti had given the family quite a lot to banter about with those antics.

It took only three rings for Patti to pick up her phone, a minor miracle since Patti always had some kind of crisis going on with one of the kids. There was only a three year difference between Patti and Morgan but it might as well have been a decade. Patti and Morgan were just so different. When they were growing up, Morgan always envisioned herself as a corporate leader or some other successful type. Patti, on the other hand, had always wanted to be a wife and mother, married to a doctor.

Patti's dream had come true but the doctor was a lawyer and the house with the picket fence and the three kids seemed to be more than she could handle. Bill had decided recently that Patti should have help so he hired a full-time housekeeper and a nanny. Patti was thrilled but still found her life to be complicated. Leave it to Patti to create chaos from nothing. Morgan blamed that on her father; he had always doted on Patti. He had insisted that she was fragile and needed a strong man to take care of her despite the harm Morgan vehemently declared he was causing. Patti would never be able to handle her own problems, she often told him, if he was always going to give into her tantrums and tears, fixing her problems for her. Her father knew what Morgan was saying had merit but he still felt it his duty to protect her. She was the eldest daughter and she always held a special place in his heart. He was still doing it today. If Bill didn't fix an issue at hand, her dad would step in and do the job. Life had turned out just the way they thought it would for Patti and now, instead of their father handling everything for her, she had Bill Forrester, an attorney and loyal husband who adored her and took care of her.

"Hi Morgan, I wasn't expecting a call from you, is anything wrong?" Patti asked, as she fought with one of her children in the background. "I thought it might be Bill again. When he called me, it sounded as if they were all in quite a drunken stupor down at McCleary's. I don't think any of the guys will be home tonight. What did you think about Gage leaving for Turkey this evening?" Patti hadn't given any thought about how her sister might feel after hearing those words until after she said them. "I'm sorry, Morgan, I didn't think. I was surprised when Bill told me. I thought you knew. He said the guys saw him briefly before he left. Apparently, John knew Gage had been in contact with his handlers from the C.I.A. and making plans to enter Syria through Turkey. Apparently he had been thinking about it since last week when he heard the dire news and was trying to make arrangements so he could hook up with some of his old connections in the region in order to find out what he could about Jake's disappearance." The phone was silent for such a long time that Patti was convinced Morgan had hung up on her until she heard a much softer subdued voice from her sister.

"Are the guys still at McCleary's?"

"Yes, were you listening to me? I told you I don't expect any of them to be home tonight. Alex took dad home a little while ago. From what Bill told me dad was feeling no pain. Bill said that dad felt a little better though knowing that Gage was on his way to Turkey, if for no other reason than to get information."

Morgan couldn't believe what she was hearing. Gage was actually going to Turkey and then entering Syria without discussing his plans with her. She needed to talk to John and Logan at once. *What were they thinking, allowing him to go?* It was bad enough that Jake was missing but now she had to worry about perhaps never seeing her husband again. *What does Gage think he can do that the military and the C.I.A. aren't already doing?* Morgan ended her conversation with Patti abruptly and walked out of Joe's kitchen and into his living room. She touched Joe's face with her hand and apologized for what she was about to do. She had promised him that she would spend the night but she needed answers and she needed them now.

As Morgan sat down to scribble a note to Joe, she heard the door open and Neil walked in. Apparently his morning surgery had been cancelled and he wanted to check on Joe. His sudden presence was a gift and Morgan was thrilled. She didn't like breaking her promise but she was worried about Gage. After Morgan's brief synopsis of the events that led to Gage leaving for Turkey, Neil told Morgan to try not to worry.

"Morgan, go and do whatever you need to. If there's anything that I or

Joe can do for you, let us know. You've done plenty for us," he added throwing down his jacket.

"I didn't want to leave Joe after promising to stay. He had a pretty rough night. Tell Joe that everything is alright and that I'll see him in the morning. Don't forget, after the cemetery tomorrow Logan has a lunch set up back at McCleary's," she added before picking up her bag and heading for the door.

Morgan hoped that her uber driver would arrive on time. The faster she arrived at McCleary's, the sooner she would get answers from John. As Morgan glanced down the street she noticed a car making its way over to her. If there was one person who could talk Gage out of this craziness, maybe she could. After all, they had made love numerous times and not once did they use protection. *For all I know we might have created a child together and now that child might never know his or her father because Gage felt the need to rush in and be a hero.*

She was shocked when the driver announced that they had already arrived at her destination. The bar seemed to be hopping but that rarely surprised her. McCleary's was always busy. The weekly crowd was usually made up of business clientele looking to unwind while the weekends were reserved for party crowds, on those nights there was barely room to breathe in the place. For a Tuesday night, this crowd was unusual. She wondered if Logan had some kind of promotion going on. The bouncer recognized Morgan, welcomed her immediately and asked if she was looking for her brothers. He informed her that they were in the back at a table in the corner and raising hell.

Morgan made her way through the crowd and finally arrived at the designated table, Logan noticed her first. He knew, by the look on her face, that she had found out about Gage. John turned to see who Logan had spotted; when he saw it was Morgan he made his way over to her and asked if they could go back to Logan's office, so they could talk. She browsed from one brother to the other, with a glance she promised that they would be hearing from her after her conversation with John.

John didn't know where to start as he ushered Morgan into the backroom. He knew he had a lot of explaining to do and he wasn't quite sure where to begin. He had to tell her the latest news; that might help her understand why they had unanimously come to the decision to support Gage's position and the choice he made. John held out a chair for Morgan and before she was able to get comfortable he began the story which led Gage to make the extreme decision he had made.

"Morgan, not everyone knows the entire story, but I'm going to confide in you because I believe you need to know the full truth. I owe Gage that, at least. Jake went under deep cover to search for a missing British journalist who had been taken prisoner by Isis. It didn't look good for the reporter since she had angered the men who took her by revealing, on national television, where their latest stronghold was located. The Americans and Brits bombed the stronghold shortly thereafter, killing many of their senior leaders. As soon as they reorganized and found another place to hide, they sent a small group back to find her and kidnap her; she hasn't been seen since. Her camera crew was found dead in a ditch on the side of the road, near their last reported location. It's believed that the group had different plans for the journalist, a more public death, if you will.

Jake learned where the camp was located, with the help of informants in a direct satellite feed. He also learned that the men who had her were actually men that Gage and his unit had travelled with on earlier missions. They were not Isis but they were taking her to them. Jake thought he might be able to gain her release from these men before she was turned over to Isis militants without anyone else getting hurt. He and his unit disguised themselves and made contact with a nearby tribal leader. His plan almost worked but the insurgents were warned ahead of time and demanded that the group who held the woman turn her over to them at once. Apparently, they didn't trust anyone. Gage thought that if he returned immediately he could convince the tribal leader to let him take Jake and the woman with him instead. The tribal leader was his friend at one time and Gage wanted to negotiate a peaceful resolution. He knew the man he had gotten to know didn't want to turn the woman over to Isis either but he felt he had little choice. Isis was getting stronger; the tribe knew they were no match for them. Gage knew it would be dangerous for him to go back to Syria but he had no choice. Alex Summer needed to be there to negotiate for the lives of Jake and the reporter. If he thought there was any other way, other than to resurrect Alex Summer he would do it.

"Morgan, this is exactly what Gage said to me just before he left, he said, "I am going, John. There's nothing you can do or say to stop me. Jake will be dead within a week if I don't go, judging by my Intel. I have one favor to ask in return." John hesitated, not really wanting to continue. John had rehashed the last conversation with Gage over and over. He had promised Gage that he wouldn't tell anyone about it until he had to.

John didn't know how to soften the blow for Morgan because, either way, his sister was going to get hurt. One or both of the men she loved might get seriously hurt and there was no way of making it sound any less dangerous for either one of them. He sat directly across from her, held her hands and continued his story. "No one knows for sure if Jake was captured or if he is living among the tribe. His men doubled back after being questioned but they didn't know why Jake had remained behind. Gage is the only one with ties to the tribal leaders and he's the only one who can get the answers he needs. If Jake was taken hostage, I'm sure his response would be in line with his training, but in the end remember, it was Jake who ordered his men to return to the camp. Our brothers and I believe that if Gage hadn't agreed to go back to Syria it would have only been a matter of time before Jake would have been discovered by Isis and killed in some public horrific way."

Morgan couldn't believe what she was hearing. If anything happened to Gage, a large part of who she was would die. She prayed for the safety of Jake and Gage and that Gage knew what he was doing. She hoped that Gage would bring them both home safely. She only hoped that this woman reporter appreciated what the two men she loved with all her heart were doing for her. Morgan understood the risk they were taking but it didn't make it any easier. She had always believed that, in their life, there was no room for mistakes. Everything that is meant to happen does happen for whatever reason. She knew that the reasons weren't made clear until much later in life or perhaps not until after death; but she believed with all her heart that this was true. She couldn't fathom any alternatives for her if either her brother or Gage did not survive this mission. This whole situation was inconceivable to her. Having to handle another death after all she had been through within the last year was unimaginable.

"John, no matter what you say to try to convince me otherwise, this whole scenario feels wrong. Gage is no longer in the military. He doesn't belong in that part of the world; this is not his war to fight. There's a bounty on his head in the Middle East, you, the rest of the F.B.I. and the C.I.A. know that. It's too dangerous for Gage; so many factions want him dead in that part of the world. I can't believe you of all people didn't try to talk him out of it! You know what he's getting himself into by going over there. I know Jake is in trouble and I want him home safely, just as much as any of you, but what about Gage? Did any of you stop to think about what could happen to him? You know John...there's a good chance that Gage will not be coming home." Morgan said the words as clearly as she could through her tears but she knew John didn't have any answers. He knew that Gage might be Jake's only hope to make it home. There was a chance that she would lose her husband, her brother or both and he didn't know what to say to sugar coat that reality.

She sniffled, grabbing a tissue from the desk before adding, "Gage is on his way to a part of the world filled with terrorists who want to see him dead. I may never see him again, John, and I never had the opportunity to tell him that I had never stopped loving him," she added in a low-keyed whisper as she beat on John's chest, as he came around the desk to hold her.

John took his baby sister in his arms and hugged her as tightly as he could as he tried to console her for the pain she was feeling. He felt guilty for causing it. His chest ached with knowledge that no one knew other than himself. Gage had made John promise him that he would not tell Morgan *everything he knew*. John knew that Morgan was aware of the Ghost; but what she didn't know was that the Ghost's identity was rumored to have been leaked and now the Ghost had a name, Alex Summer. There was a very good chance that those who wanted the C.I.A. agent dead would know the minute he entered their country. Alex Summer had a passport and even if he didn't use it this time, his picture was in a system somewhere; they had scouts at all the airports. John knew facial recognition software was used at all the airports for security reasons. So even if Gage was traveling with forged documents, his face would still be on a passport for all to see. It didn't matter how careful the C.I.A. was trying to sneak Gage into Syria. Isis and all the other militant groups that wanted him dead had their spies scattered covertly. Gage wanted Morgan and the rest of the family kept in the dark about most of the details. He wanted them to have confidence believing that he was relatively safe. Gage had asked John to take care of Morgan if anything happened to him. After spending the afternoon with her, he felt as though he was abandoning her. He had his doubts about returning safely from his self-inflicted assignment and it worried him. He didn't want to be distracted, not now. He had told John about the afternoon and emphasized how happy he was that the love of his life was back in his life. Gage had needed someone in the family to know how much Morgan meant to him, before he left. But it was one secret he needed John to keep.

Gage needed John's reassurance that he would take care of his wife in the event he didn't make it back. John had a sealed letter addressed to Morgan in his breast pocket. He had promised Gage that he would only give the letter to Morgan, if he didn't return. Gage knew she would be sad when she read it but he wanted to help her move on with her life without regret. The only way he could be sure of that was to convince her that his decision to go to Syria, although it hadn't been an easy one to make, was the only solution and that he had always loved her.

John held his sister in his arms as she sobbed knowing how Gage really felt about her and unable to tell her. It was Gage's choice to let her believe that he was doing this because he wanted to help Jake and because he missed the danger and excitement the job had offered him. Morgan knew Gage thought she would worry less and be able to disconnect a little if she believed that he had walked away from her to be a part of the action he craved.

Gage had shared his fears of the operation with John, telling him that he hoped his instincts were still as sharp as they once were because his and Jake's lives depended on it. John appreciated just how much danger Gage was putting himself in for their brother. The C.I.A. would help him as much as they could but if the operation went south Gage would be on his own, just as he had so many times in the past. The U.S. government couldn't sanction some of the things he was called upon to do. It was part of the job; Gage learned early on that it was not a job for the meek. John didn't want to think about the outcome if the extraction went sour. Will having her husband's star on the wall at C.I.A. headquarters be enough for Morgan to forgive the family for this decision? No one will ever know the sacrifice Gage Delaney made to save one of the military's best. Gage mentioned something else to John before leaving. He hadn't given it much thought at the time. Gage said he'd been in touch with someone who was going to help him with the operation. John had been so busy trying to deal with the situation at hand that he hadn't questioned Gage any further about the mystery man.

Morgan pulled herself together and begged John not to tell anyone how upset she was. She convinced him that it was better if everyone believed she was over Gage Delaney. She asked John how soon he expected to hear anything about Gage's arrival in Syria. John assured her that this Special Forces Op was highly sensitive and it would take time for Gage to put everything in place once he arrived. The tribe holding the reporter was supposed to hand her over to the militia soon. The militia would hand her over to Isis right away. Getting intelligence on any of these groups was difficult without direct contact. In the past, Gage had had time to build up trust with the local tribal leaders but Gage didn't know what to expect since he'd been hearing reports second hand. His Intel had informed him that Jake was a hostage and he knew that the reporter had not been turned over to the militia or Isis.

John had heard enough chatter through the Bureau to know how much trouble Gage would be in upon his arrival to Syria. Gage didn't believe the C.I.A. or the Bureau was operating with all the facts. First of all, he told John he didn't believe that Jake was in any danger for now. If the tribal leader believed for one moment that Jake was not who he said he was, Gage believed he would have been turned over to the militia and killed instantly, along with his men, and that hadn't happened. His men had left the compound without resistance. Knowing that Jake stayed behind told him that he didn't feel his life was in danger and that he had a plan of some kind. There was something else they were missing; it was the reason Gage felt the need to intervene. It was the only way he could be sure that Jake returned alive.

Morgan and John joined the others making multiple toasts to Jake and Gage. Logan and Alex smiled as Morgan approached the table. Logan stood up but Morgan insisted he stay seated while she greeted her brothers and her brother-in-law as she turned to John and told him she was going to call a cab and go home. John insisted that Kevin, one of Logan's bartenders, give her a ride home. "He's on the clock, I'm sure he won't mind. I'll throw him some extra money to make up for any tips he might lose," he said, before turning to Logan who readily agreed and shouted to Kevin to bring his truck around and take Morgan home. Kevin loved driving Logan's Escalade so it didn't seem to be a problem getting him to agree to take Morgan home.

Kevin and Morgan shared some small talk on the way home and although it was a nice diversion she found it difficult to keep her mind on their conversation. Kevin had to repeat what he said on a few occasions. Morgan was convinced that Kevin couldn't wait to drop her off. It was tedious, trying to keep their conversation flowing, and he was doing everything in his power not to make her feel uncomfortable. He smiled when they reached her apartment as he asked if she wanted him to park the truck and walk up to her apartment but she refused. He had already done enough for her.

"Thank you, Kevin. It was really sweet of you. Go back to the bar and make sure my brothers don't overdo it," she added, after thanking him again.

Morgan entered the building feeling worse than she had when she'd left. Going to McCleary's didn't get her the answers she was hoping for. She felt sick to her stomach, *why didn't Gage come and see me before he left.* Once again, she questioned whether the afternoon they had spent together was anything other than a onetime event. She believed in her heart that they had turned a corner and she didn't want to think about the events of the afternoon with doubts in mind. She opened her door, flung her keys into the bowl on a table and stood for a moment, trying to figure out what to do next. She felt alone and isolated. She wouldn't be able to share her thoughts with Joe. He had made it clear that he and Neil would be moving into the penthouse and she didn't dare worry him with her problems. She still believed that Gage was her future but in one afternoon he had appeared and disappeared from her life. She was afraid for him and Jake. For the first time, she questioned whether Gage was still equipped to handle the mission. It had been a long time since he was an active agent and that edge he was always talking about had to be rusty at best.

She took off her coat, hung it in the entryway closet and kicked off her shoes before heading to the kitchen to pour herself a glass of iced tea. She knew she would have to do a lot of soul-searching in the near future. She might have to make decisions about her future that she didn't want to make. She might be pregnant; that was a real possibility. If so, they would have to talk when he came back, if he made it back at all. *What were we thinking?* We didn't use protection in our haste but it never occurred to me that Gage wouldn't be by my side if anything happened. She knew she would be spending many sleepless nights worrying about Gage and Jake. *Will Gage bring Jake home safely?* If she was pregnant, it saddened her to think that Gage might not be there to celebrate the family he had helped to create. Financially she was set and raising a baby alone would be difficult but she knew she was never really alone. The McCleary family would always be there for her and she had a great group of friends. Joe and Neil were more like family and they would always be there if she needed them.

She glanced over at the clock, it was getting late and she needed to get some sleep if she was going to be there for Joe and Neil in the morning. The closing of the casket would be the saddest moment for the family. Morgan remembered the day they closed the casket over Michael's beautiful, peaceful face. It had been so hard for her. She had wanted to lie next to him and take him in her arms so he wouldn't be afraid. She remembered feeling as though she were abandoning him, leaving him all alone in the funeral home and then at the cemetery. The whole service had been devastating. Morgan knew that Joe, having been estranged from his father for so long, was going to make it difficult for him to say his last good-bye. It was uncanny how, in the space of one week, she and Joe's lives had been turned upside down and inside out. They were both suffering a loss that could change their futures forever.

The church was crowded with family and friends, personal and professional, and she could see that Joe appreciated the turn out. Morgan knew her parents were watching her, she had the feeling that her parents were never quite fooled by her assertions that she had moved beyond Michael's death or that she was moving on with her life, without Gage. They were both aware that Gage had left for Syria and she knew they wanted to talk to her about it. Morgan was sure their decision not to speak about it had more to do with her readiness to talk, not theirs.

John sat on one side of her, Logan on the other as they waited for Morgan's reaction while the casket was being wheeled down the aisle. Both brothers knew she was strong but they thought that seeing death so soon after the news of Gage's decision was going to be too much for her. But, she seemed somewhat at ease. Either their sister was a lot stronger than they thought or she was masking what she truly felt so she didn't have to deal with it publicly. Logan looked at Alex as he mentioned that he was extremely busy at the firm. He had stepped up to replace Gage but didn't know how Gage had held it together with such ease. The brothers conversed and Alex mentioned going to Morgan for some help. Logan thought that asking her to help right now would be a good thing; working would help keep her mind off things.

Alex didn't want to let Gage down and he was doing everything he could to keep up with the work but he needed help badly. Gage had often told him he had faith in him, that he could do it. Alex wrestled with the idea of asking for Morgan's help since she and Gage had run things in the past. Perhaps, if he approached the subject during a normal conversation, he could feel out her willingness to help or not, without coming out directly and asking for it. Either way, a decision had to be made soon because he couldn't do all the work he and Gage had done while working together.

"Are you keeping it together?" John asked, taking Morgan's hand in his.

"I'm fine, John. I can handle it," she whispered softly. John had always meant well. Even though she had a closer relationship with Logan, it seemed she needed John's strength at the moment. He knew the secret she kept close to her heart. Morgan realized he shared her fears with her as she sat peacefully listening to the sermon, hoping she would find peace in what was offered. If Jake and Gage were called home, she had to prepare herself to be able to deal with that possibility. Besides, she had to be prepared at least for her parent's sake. They would find the loss of their son unbearable; she had to put on a brave face so they wouldn't have to worry about her as well. As Morgan listened to the words, she couldn't help thinking; *Will I be able to handle the loss of Gage in my life again and, this time forever?*

Joe and Neil couldn't thank Logan enough for all the work he'd done. The presentation was lovely and there was plenty of food and drink for all. Joe was surprised at the turnout; very few of his friends and colleagues had known anything about his family. Morgan was happy to see Joe talking to old friends and family members; he hadn't seen some of them in many years. She heard him laughing for the first time in days as they shared familiar stories about his dad. Joe was happy talking about his family and the life he'd led as a much younger man.

Morgan helped Logan as he brought out another tray of chicken, taking a moment to glance at Joe. Some of Joe's co-workers had stayed to eat something before returning to work, at Joe's request. *He definitely seems to be a changed man these days.* Next, Morgan took the time to speak to her mom and dad about Gage leaving for Syria. She knew he had left and headed first for Turkey; and later would be making his way into Syria through some rough terrain, to try to keep his whereabouts a secret. She answered her parent's questions curtly; then she dropped the subject completely. The last thing she wanted to talk about was Gage, it was too painful.

Chapter Nine

Barbara hated to bother Morgan with another phone call instead of meeting with her in person as they had so often, but Morgan had been avoiding her. Barbara knew Morgan had a lot on her plate but deadlines had to be met and she was getting pressured, it was her job to make sure those deadlines were met. It had been five months since Gage had left for Syria. Although Barbara understood her despair, she had to push Morgan to complete her latest manuscript. She knew Morgan spent a lot of time at the company, leaving very little time for writing but she had to remind Morgan that she needed to focus on her career. Barbara was being pressured by Darien Preston, her boss, to push their favorite authors so they could have their books out for the next holiday season. Barbara anticipated Darien's call long before he made it because of the influx of emails she received requesting to see a working copy of Morgan's latest novel. Morgan had established herself as one of their most sought-after authors and the requests were pouring in. Her fans were extremely loyal and demanding.

Morgan's readers wouldn't accept any publisher's suggested reading lists while they waited for her next book. Barbara had to try to push Morgan without pressuring her. She had to try to convince her that everything would turn out just fine, even though it had already been five months since Gage had left, whether Barbara believed it or not. Barbara knew firsthand what losing her son had done to Morgan. She feared for Gage and her friend's well-being.

Who does Gage Delaney think he was anyway, running off to Syria thinking he can take on a foreign power all by himself? Does he think he's the next James Bond? Didn't he realize that his rash decision to act the hero would have a ripple effect on his wife and her life after he left?

Barbara hesitated, wondering just how she would begin her conversation with Morgan. She rarely became emotionally involved with her clients but Morgan Delaney was different. She possessed such a warm personality; Barbara couldn't resist being drawn into her world. She dialed her number and waited, hoping Morgan would answer this time.

Morgan was just putting away the last of her laundry, getting ready to sit down and finish the last page of her manuscript when the phone rang. It was hard for her to ignore the phone when she desperately yearned to hear news of Gage and Jake.

Barbara was ecstatic when Morgan informed her that she was working on the last page of her manuscript. Barbara let her know how worried she had been about her since she had avoided most of her calls for the past five months. They spoke, briefly about the manuscript; Morgan kept the conversation short, avoiding anything that wasn't business related.

She looked down at her once flat stomach, now sporting a tiny pouch, telling her friend that there had been a lot of changes in her life since they had last spoken. She decided to lighten up a bit as she filled her in about how Joe had finally moved out of his apartment and into his penthouse with Neil. Morgan let Barbara know that Matt Hastings had kept in touch with her, that he would be arriving in New York in another month or two to begin filming his new picture. She and Matt had remained friends and Morgan had to admit she liked having him in her life. Whenever he was in town they would try to get together, even if it was for just a cup of coffee.

"I'm glad to hear it. But we seem to be avoiding the big elephant. What's going on with you and Gage?" It had been months since the two women had talked and the last thing Morgan wanted to do was to tell her friend that she feared Gage and Jake could be dead. She couldn't bring herself to say the words because by doing so it would bring the truth closer to home. They had been missing for months now. She explained what she could to Barbara. Her friend was shocked to hear what had transpired but helped to bring everything into focus. Morgan, she knew, had a lot to deal with these past few months. Barbara understood that she wanted to do it privately. She tried to reassure Morgan that both men would return home safely, but it was one hope she found a little difficult to believe herself. Before disconnecting, Barbara tried to offer some advice to Morgan, to use this experience and write about it. It could be therapeutic and financially beneficial for her. Her fans would love to read her personal story, she thought.

Morgan thought about the things she had shared with Barbara and wondered what Barbara would have thought about the one bit of news she had left out, smiling at her bulge as she looked down and cradled her unborn child. Morgan hadn't told anyone that she and Gage were having a baby. But that secret would be out soon because in another month she wouldn't be able to hide her pregnancy any longer. She was sure her mother had sensed something was different, but to her credit she had said nothing and Morgan couldn't be any happier because she wasn't ready to talk about it. For all her family knew, the baby's father could easily be *that actor guy's* child they all referred to Matt Hastings as.

Morgan glanced over at the clock realizing she had very little time to get herself ready to go to the office. Alex depended on her help and she was grateful for the distraction. She worked all day and wrote well into the night finalizing her manuscript, getting it ready for publication. She didn't have time to let her thoughts wander into any painful places. She reached for her black pencil skirt and stepped into it. She wasn't surprised when she had trouble with the zipper; it was time to buy some comfortable clothing. She threw the skirt to the side and reached for an A-line dress. She stood in front of the mirror, stepped into her heels and studied her reflection. Gage would have been thrilled with the idea of becoming a father again. It tore at her heart strings knowing he had no idea their child was growing inside her womb and that he might not be there for their child's birth.

The office was buzzing when she finally arrived; Morgan couldn't help but wonder what all the chatter was about. As she entered Alex's office, she noticed that John and Logan were also present. The first thing that entered her mind was the possibility of news about Gage and Jake. She watched as their facial expressions went from joyous glee to somber terror almost instantly. Morgan feared what might come next. It didn't take a rocket scientist to figure out that the bad news concerned Gage. She felt sick to her stomach, without waiting to hear any news; she went into Gage's office to prepare herself for what was to come. His office had become the place she had called home for the past five months.

John asked Logan and Alex to give him some private time with Morgan before joining them. He knew that Morgan suspected the news was bad and he was also aware that he was the only one who knew Morgan and Gage had reconciled. This was going to be a difficult conversation but still one they needed to have. John stood at the door and watched his sister staring out the window, knowing that she was looking at nothing in particular, being torn apart inside while tears flowed down her cheeks.

"Morgan, there was some good news about Jake and the journalist this morning. That's what all the commotion is about. Apparently, Gage secured their release last night and had them escorted directly to the nearest safe house until they could be picked up by U.S. military in the area. Jake didn't get to see Gage but he did get to speak to him via satellite connection. Jake and the reporter are being debriefed as we speak; they'll be allowed to return to friendly soil very soon. "I was able to speak to Jake for a few seconds, he's in good spirits and he told me he wasn't being held prisoner. His cover was never blown, which is what Gage believed to be true all along. He said when Gage arrived on the scene his cover was more convincing and highly plausible. The tribal leaders were convinced that Jake was a friend. Any doubts they had vanished when Gage arrived. It seems Gage has as many friends as he does enemies. Jake had convinced the locals that he had fallen in love with their prisoner and wanted to take her for his wife. He begged them to let him have her and not hand her over to the Isis militants. Until Gage arrived, he hadn't been able to convince them that the idea was sound. Gage convinced the men not to hand her over to the militia and asked the tribal leaders to help Jake and the journalist escape with his assistance. Jake told me that Gage had a good relationship with the leader but it was going to cost him if the tribal leader had to tell Isis the reporter escaped. I don't know much beyond that, other than Gage offered them something worth more, something so valuable that he was able to secure her safety and eventually her freedom and Jake's. I'm sure Jake did whatever he could to make sure the reporter was protected while they were at the camp but until Gage got there he couldn't secure her freedom." John could see that Morgan was visibly happy for Jake.

"I'm just as happy as you are that Jake is coming home, John, but please get on with it. I know you have intelligence about Gage." Morgan took in an exasperated breath as she tried to prepare herself for the worst. Devastating news would mean she would be raising her child alone, without Gage, and her heart would be torn apart once again.

John had said he'd keep her in the loop with every new update but he didn't have much to go on when it came to Gage. There was very little he could tell her other than what Jake had shared when he was debriefed. He hoped that Gage had gotten out of Syria in one piece. Now that the reporter and Jake were safe, John was convinced Gage would be running from Isis. John also confirmed that the military would be ordering the bombing of all known Isis hideouts in the area and if Gage hadn't already left the area, he'd be right in the middle of another conflict, but this time he'd have no back-up plan. Gage would be alone with his life hanging by a thread.

"Jake said he wasn't with Gage when he secured the release of the journalist and since it was Jake's mission to get the journalist home safely that had to be his first priority. He asked to be allowed to take his unit back to go after Gage but he was ordered to stand down. The commander said Gage knew what he was getting into. He was told that the C.I.A. would take over and do what they could to extract him. Jake feels tormented by that decision but he doesn't know what else he can do. He was given orders, Morgan, and it's his job to follow them regardless of his personal feelings." John knew what he was asking of Morgan was difficult, but what choice did Jake have. "We have to believe that Gage found a way out of the country," he said, taking her into his embrace as she cried whatever tears were left.

Morgan didn't know what to do. It seemed as though time had stopped; she was left alone with her fears. She was terrified of the thoughts that were racing through her mind as she tried desperately to come to terms with the information John had just given her. She had a child coming into the world shortly and she had to find a way to pull herself together, to be strong for both of them. Morgan thought about sharing her good news with her family but she was glad she had decided against it. It was best that her secret remain just that, *her secret*. She was glad that the announcement that she and Gage were having a child would wait until Gage returned, or until she heard something about his fate. She hoped he would return soon, otherwise an announcement would be unnecessary; everyone would be able to see that she was with child. Morgan promised herself she would never give up hope that Gage would find his way back to her and their child.

"I have work I need to do, John. If you'll excuse me," she said as she glared at him, knowing John wanted to take her pain away. He didn't want to leave her like this but he understood her need to be alone after what they had just discussed. He watched as she shuffled some papers on her desk, trying to look busy as he left the room. This was going to be a rough time for them but somehow, as a family, they would get through this. He would leave her with her thoughts and gather the rest of the family to decide what to do next. John decided not to give Morgan the note from Gage. He still held out hope he was coming back.

Morgan worked tirelessly to keep her mind off Gage and it worked for a time. As day turned into night, she was diligent with her work and she kept her emotions at bay, but it was becoming difficult as she grew tired. She hadn't noticed until then that the office had cleared out. It was very late and she knew she should leave but she dreaded being alone in her empty apartment. If she had thought about it, she would have had dinner delivered to the office earlier but in her attempt to keep busy that was far from her mind. Morgan was suddenly jarred from her seat when she heard someone enter the main office. There was security in the building but they usually stayed in the halls or the lobby, unless there was trouble. Suddenly, staying so late didn't seem like such a good idea.

Alex had come back to the office to drop off some paperwork he needed for the morning and was surprised to see that someone was still there. He was doubly surprised to see his big sister working late into the night again. *What is Morgan doing in the office at this time of the night?* Alex made his way to Gage's office. He could see by the look on her face that she was startled and frightened by his arrival.

"What are you doing here so late? Do you have any idea what time it is?" he added, with a note of concern as he motioned toward the clock.

"I didn't realize the time had passed so quickly. I'm packing up now. What are you doing here?"

"I wanted to drop off this paperwork; I need it for a meeting tomorrow. Have you eaten anything?" he asked, knowing she hadn't left the office all day.

"I am hungry, and if you're offering?" she teased not wanting to admit that she needed to take care of herself for the baby's health, including her own.

Alex reached for Morgan's coat and helped her into it. "It's late but I think we can grab something to eat at the bar on the corner. Do you feel like having a hamburger? That's about the best we're going to get at this time of night, unless of course you feel like taking a ride to McCleary's?" he added with a smile. "I'm sure Logan would gladly fix you whatever you want."

Alex and Morgan jumped into his car as the valet pulled up to the curb. They decided to leave her car in the lot until morning and drove to McCleary's hoping it wouldn't be too crowded when they got there. Morgan wasn't up to dealing with crowds but she was hungry. *No matter what, I have to make some changes in my life, if not for me, then for the baby sake.*

Logan was surprised and happy to see Morgan and Alex as they walked through the door. He guessed they'd had a long night at the office and hooked them up with a private table in the corner so they could talk freely. Alex tried to lighten the mood by filling Morgan in on the family's latest news but that didn't stop a well-meaning waitress from congratulating them on Jake's homecoming. Morgan was quite surprised to hear that the journalist would be joining him when he arrived in two weeks. Morgan's mind began to wonder, she couldn't help thinking about Gage. She wanted to be happy for Jake and she was, but she feared for Gage because the longer the family went without news, the harder it was for her to believe that he would be coming home at all. She tried with all her might to stay focused on the immediate conversation.

Alex told Morgan he was convinced there was more to Jake's story than what they were being told. The fact that Jake was bringing this woman home was major and Jake had to have a reason for it. "Mom and Pop are thrilled that Jake is coming home but they're very concerned about the effect this woman will have on you. Morgan, everyone wants you to know that we haven't given up on Gage. We all believe that he's still alive and will be coming home. You do believe that, don't you? Everyone feels guilty, knowing that we're having a party to celebrate Jake's return."

"I hope you're right about Gage, but for now I don't want to talk about it. I don't mind everyone celebrating Jake's return. You should, it's the right thing to do," she said lifting the menu, trying to ignore the talk about Syria on the television in her line of vision. She watched as little news as she could and she read the newspapers even less. Not seeing or reading news about Syria made it less real. It hurt too much and she was frightened for Gage.

She was craving one of Logan's spicy pasta dishes; although it was late she was going to order it anyway. Normally, she would have ordered a light salad but today was special and she was going to order from her heart, not her head. When Alex asked if she wanted a drink, she politely refused and hoped Alex wouldn't insist. The waitress took their orders and rushed back to the kitchen to place them. She came back and told them Logan would be joining them momentarily. He had sent salads, bread and a bottle of wine to the table immediately. The waitress offered to pour the wine for them, Alex consented but Morgan asked for a glass of iced water instead.

Alex had been speculating for a couple of weeks; he noticed Morgan's mood often changed at the drop of a hat. He originally thought her mood swings had to do with everything that was going on in her life, but lately he had a gut feeling that it was something else entirely. They spent a lot of time together and he had noticed her growing abdomen. But he didn't want to mention anything to her. She was wound so tight and besides he didn't want to intrude on her life. He hoped she would tell him when she was ready. He wondered if the father knew about the baby's existence because he hadn't seen the actor around for a while.

Maybe Logan had picked up on it too; perhaps he'll talk to her. After all, she and Logan had a much closer relationship than he and Morgan did; they seemed to share a lot more about the intimate details of their lives with each other. Alex didn't know what to say to Morgan. They barely said a word to each other as they picked at their salads, until Logan approached five minutes later. *I think we might have said about ten words between us while we were both waiting for Logan. I'm glad he's finally here.*

Logan kissed Morgan on the cheek and asked how she was doing. He immediately noticed that she hadn't touched the wine and it was her favorite. They had a brief conversation about what was going on at the office, other than that Morgan had very little to say. As Morgan took her second bite of the dish she loved so much, she immediately felt nauseous from the smell of the fresh cheeses Logan had used. As fast as she could, she excused herself and ran to the ladies room. Logan took one look at Alex and another at his sister and demanded an answer with a silent stare. Alex motioned with a hand over his stomach; Logan squirmed in his seat with shock and disbelief.

"You have got to be kidding me. What about Gage? He's gone through a lot for this family. How do we explain this to him? This happened on our watch. He's not going to be happy when he comes home and finds out that Morgan is having a child with some actor she met on the set, damn," Logan added, whispering in a disappointed tone as he ran his fingers through his hair. It was obvious that Morgan wasn't feeling well and he didn't want to push her for answers, especially in her condition. For now, he would let his questions linger in his mind. But the fact remained that he was shocked and so would the rest of the family be when they heard the news. Before Morgan returned, he asked Alex to keep what he knew to himself for a little while, at least until he had a chance to talk to Morgan about her situation and what her plans were.

Logan stood up as Morgan returned and asked if he could get her anything else to eat. He hinted that maybe it was too late to be eating something spicy. He told her his stomach couldn't take spicy foods this time of night either. "Perhaps you'd like a bowl of fresh soup and some bread?" Morgan felt much better after eating the soup that Logan had brought her. The nausea seemed to pass and not a moment too soon judging by the looks she was getting from her brothers. She knew that Logan and Alex were suspicious. *Since I ate something perhaps they'll be thrown off guard.*

"Did Jake mention anything about what he thinks happened to Gage once he and the reporter were freed?" she asked, hoping she could sway their thoughts to a topic other than herself.

"When I spoke to Jake, he said Gage was last seen with a Shiite cleric who he had befriended years earlier. It was with the cleric's help that Gage negotiated the release of the British journalist. Jake had no idea what Gage promised to gain the release of the journalist when they were so close to handing her over to Isis but he had to have made it worth their while." Logan wondered if he had said too much. "Gage nearly choked when he was told what Jake said to convince the Shiite tribe to keep the woman at their camp longer than they had wanted to. Apparently, our brother said that he wanted the woman, as if had a right to do so. He was convinced it was the only way he would be able to leave the camp with her and bring her home safely. Gage played along with the plan but once Jake and the woman left the camp, Jake had no knowledge of Gage's whereabouts or his circumstances. Jake insisted he never felt that his life was in any danger while he lived among the Shiites. In fact, he believed the men thought he had gone insane, wanting to take a journalist as his wife." Logan was trying to make light of the situation and trying his best not to reveal too much. Jake had told him that he suspected Gage had to give up a lot in order to convince the men not to turn the reporter over to Isis. He could only speculate what Gage had offered the Shiite leaders in return. Jake was worried and he let Logan know just how worried he was. Logan decided to keep that bit of information under wraps to spare Morgan from any additional heartache.

Logan wanted to tell her that Gage was going to be on his way home soon and that everything was going to be alright but he wasn't so sure anymore. He hoped his deepest fear would not come true. He knew Gage and the man he was; more than likely he had offered up Alex Summer in return for Jake and the reporter. *It really was the only deal that made sense.* He could only wonder what the future would be like for them but he always remembered what his mom had said to her children over the years, **"There are no mistakes in life, everything happens the way it is supposed to and although you may not understand the reasoning, there is a master plan."** Well Mom, I guess your theory is being put to the test in a big way right now. I only wish that I had your faith to believe things would turn out okay.

Chapter Ten

Morgan was stirring in her sleep as the sound of a phone ringing disturbed her. She grappled to pull herself from a seldom peaceful slumber. While asleep, Gage had come to her safe and sound. Her dreams were so vivid; Morgan was convinced it was his way of letting her know that he was alive and well. The connection they shared was that uncanny. When she picked up the phone, her mother told her that they had finally received word that Jake and Reigh, the journalist, would be flying home in the next couple of days. Her mother was calling to ask Morgan to come to the celebration on Friday. They were having friends and family over in honor of Jake's homecoming. Ellie excitedly told Morgan that she and Logan had planned the whole thing out last night as soon as they got the news. She was making all the calls today, hoping everyone would be available. Her mother was thrilled that Jake was finally coming home and she wanted to celebrate. *Who could blame her?*

"Mom, don't worry, I'll be there. Just don't expect me to stay. I'm doing this for you. *Is there anything you want me to bring?*" she asked, trying to sound as enthusiastic as her mother.

"You have enough on your plate already, Morgan. Between keeping long hours at the company and your writing, I don't know how you do it. Having you there is more than enough. Besides, I was hoping I could talk you into putting aside some time today to stop by for a visit. It's been a long time since we've seen you. We haven't seen you since Joe's fathers' passing. I've been really worried about you." *Had that much time past since she'd seen her parents?*

It had been six months since Gage had gone missing and with Jake's homecoming postponed, everyone was growing anxious to hear any news about Gage. Ellie knew what Morgan was going through, more than anyone. She suspected that Morgan wasn't estranged from her husband, not as much as she tried to make everyone believe she was. Morgan and Gage were meant to be together; *I hope they find their way back to each other.*

"I'm going to be fine, Mom. You don't need to worry," she added again halfheartedly.

"I have to tell you, I was a little surprised to find you at home at this time of the morning. Alex tells me you practically live at the office. Morgan, you're not doing *him any good if you get yourself sick. You need to take care of yourself.*" Morgan knew who she was referring to, and it wasn't Alex.

"Mom, I appreciate the advice and I am trying, really. I took the morning off today, didn't I?" she said, knowing the only reason she took the morning off was to go to her monthly doctor's appointment. If there was one thing she was going to do, it was to take care of their child. She was a little over six months along now and she needed to share her news with her family before she gave birth. "Mom, I was thinking of calling Alex, and telling him I decided to play hooky today. Do you think we could go to lunch?" *No time like the present,* as she contemplated telling her mother the news right after her visit to the doctor.

"I miss you terribly, if having lunch at a restaurant, instead of allowing me to give you a home-cooked meal, is the only way I can get to finally see you, I accept your offer, with a smile, I might add. Where would you like to go?" Ellie was delighted that she would finally get the chance to see Morgan and make sure her daughter was doing as well as she let on.

Morgan smiled at her mother's abrupt way of telling her it had been a little long between visits. As mothers and daughters go, they were closer than most. She tried, once again, to reassure her mom that she was fine. She would pick her mother up directly after her appointment. They decided on a nice quaint restaurant that had just opened, one her mother had been curious about. Two women her mother knew had opened the restaurant after spending so much time volunteering during the aftermath of Super Storm Sandy. The two women enjoyed cooking so much that they realized they might be able to make a go of it in the café business. Morgan hoped they could talk privately there. She didn't need everyone in town talking about her pregnancy, not yet anyway.

Morgan got ready to leave for her pre-natal appointment after placing a call to Alex to inform him that she wouldn't be in today. He was actually happy to hear it. She grabbed her keys and drove to her appointment. It went well, no surprises. Dr. Cohen did another sonogram for her and took some pictures for Gage. When he came home, he'd be able to see every stage of their child's development. Dr. Cohen had been a retired reservist; he knew what Gage had given up to serve his country. Although he didn't have to do several sonograms, he would always do what he could to help a fellow soldier.

Morgan started the car, began to put the car in gear and changed her mind. She pulled the pictures out from her purse and glanced down at them. She sat in her car looking intently at her little boy, as she did; it made her think about Michael and all the happiness he had brought into their lives. She needed Gage; she didn't want to do this alone. The idea of raising a son without him saddened her. She ran her hand over her stomach and spoke softly to her unborn son.

"It could be just the two of us, little one," she whispered. "I know your daddy is trying his best to come home to us, but I'm not so sure he's going to be able to anymore. If that happens, I promise I'll take care of you and Daddy will take care of your big brother, Michael, for me. Did I ever tell you about your big brother? He was so courageous. He was a lot like your Dad. I'll show you pictures of him when you come into this world and I will tell you some great stories about them," she added, with tears in her eyes.

After pulling herself together Morgan headed toward her parents' home, it was a fifteen minute ride from the doctor's office. She arrived and noticed an unfamiliar car in the driveway. The last thing she wanted was to have to be pleasant to one of her mother's bridge club friends. She was tempted to wait until the person left but that could take all day. She was going to have to go into the house and face the situation respectfully and graciously.

Morgan entered through the side entrance; it allowed her access directly into the kitchen. She dropped her purse on the center island and went in search of her mother. As she approached the living room, she heard a familiar voice. It sounded like one of Logan's employees. Sure enough, it was Lizzy; she and her mom were busy planning Jake's homecoming menu. They both looked up and greeted her with a warm welcome. Lizzy let her know that they were just about finished. "Your Mom is very excited about the lunch date."

Her Mom looked up and smiled, "I'll be right with you honey, why don't you get yourself fresh lemonade while you wait. Did I tell you that Reigh is coming home with Jake? The journalists name is Reigh McGuire, by the way." Ellie was so preoccupied with her planning that she hadn't noticed that Morgan was looking a little puffier than usual. Her mother was going to notice at some point and she would have to explain her pregnancy.

While Morgan sat waiting, sipping her glass of lemonade, she reached over and nibbled on some nuts her mother always kept on the table. The strange look her mother gave her startled Morgan. *Why is my mother looking at me like that?* She realized, a moment later, that she had been eating nuts and she had never cared for nuts, at least not before today. When Lizzy left, Ellie McCleary turned to her daughter and asked her if there was *anything at all* she wanted to share with her.

"I was going to wait until we were at the restaurant but I might as well tell you, it would be more private to talk here. Mom, maybe it's better if I show you," she said, making her way past her mother and into the kitchen. She took the pictures from her purse and handed them to her mother. "I think this will explain everything."

Ellie McCleary stared at the pictures and didn't quite know what to say. This was Morgan and Gage's child, without a doubt. Everyone in the family would assume the actor was the child's father, but she knew her daughter better than anyone. Her daughter only had eyes for Gage Delaney. Her son-in-law was the father of this child, she'd bet her life on it. Though Ellie hesitated before speaking, she wondered when the reunion had taken place. Nearly everyone believed Gage and Morgan were heading for divorce. She reached over, hugged her daughter and congratulated her.

"Aren't you going to ask me who the father is?"

"It's Gage, of course, I don't need to ask. Am I wrong?" Ellie smiled at the pictures of her grandson. She had three granddaughters from Patti and Bill; Michael had been her only grandson, until now. Michael must have heard her prayers. She prayed every night that he would use his influence to watch over his parents. Ellie knew Michael must be smiling down from heaven, giggling at the lot of them, asking his Nan, *"How did I do, Nan? My brother will make them smile again. I had a little talk with him before he came to you. I don't know if he'll remember our conversation but I told him, Nan, we don't want Mommy and Daddy to be sad anymore."* It was as though she could envision him speaking these words to her. Sometimes, during quiet moments, Ellie could still hear her grandson speaking to her as if he were still with her. Once in a while she watched from her porch as children played in the surf. She remembered how she and Michael loved to sit on the porch and watch the locals surfing, an activity Michael had always hoped to be healthy enough to actually enjoy.

"I just thought you would think I'd had an affair with Matt Hastings." She was pleasantly surprised when her mother laughed and said she'd never doubted her feelings for Gage, not ever.

"Why didn't you say something to my brothers when they insinuated I had been unfaithful?" Ellie McCleary loved her sons but thought they deserved to stew in their own juices, perhaps eat a little crow thanks to their assumptions regarding their sister. Once again, they were interfering in her business, a place where they didn't belong.

"I had no doubt that eventually both of you would find your way home. It was always obvious to me, knowing how Gage felt about you, his love for you has never changed and he wears it like a shield of armor. All anyone would have to do is watch the way he looks at you. That kind of love is special, Morgan, it can never die. Whatever made you run from your commitment to him was never strong enough to keep you from each other forever. I wish he was here for you now. I'm sure Gage would be thrilled by this wonderful news and, more than anything, he'd be happy to have his wife back in his life," Ellie McCleary spoke with unquestionable confidence.

"Mom, I haven't told anyone about the baby yet. I'm not sure I want to until we hear about Gage, or, until I can't hide the pregnancy any longer," she added pointing to her once flat stomach.

"Morgan, this should be a joyous time for you, a time of celebration for the whole family. But, I agree with you, you're not going to be able to hide your pregnancy from anyone for too much longer." Ellie tried to make Morgan feel better but it wasn't working. So they agreed to go to lunch and talk about Jake's homecoming party instead.

The restaurant was a pleasant surprise. It was owned and operated by two widows, friends of her mother's; they had decided after hurricane Sandy that they wanted to do something meaningful with their free time. They had loved the revitalization in Rockaway and if the hipsters could do it, why couldn't the elderly, they often joked. The restaurant proved to be a great idea because the Walking Stick had been a hot place since its opening. There was a waiting list when they arrived but her friends had a table reserved for them. Morgan looked around; she couldn't believe all the Irish crystal and lace. The cafe was beautiful and she was thrilled to be the first member of the family to share this new experience with her mom. She would definitely suggest this place to the rest of the family and her friends if the food was as good as the ambiance. The two women had a small Irish gift shop to the right of the café's entrance, slightly removed from the dining area. Judging by the hustle and bustle, the little shop had been a clever addition. Morgan could see expansion in its future, thanks to the heavy beach crowd.

"It's so nice here, so warm and quaint. It feels like home. Your friends did a wonderful job. I can't wait to taste the food," Morgan said glancing down at the menu she had just been handed. "Do you have any suggestions?"

The waiter took one look at Morgan and said what he said to all the patrons. "I can't suggest anything on this menu is better than anything else. Everyone who comes in here raves about everything they're served. Bess and Nelly should have bought this place from the previous owner years ago. Before the storm, it was a nice mom and pop diner; what they did to it was unbelievable. I can't tell you how often they are approached with offers to buy the place and people pleading for them to cater large functions. But the women love this place. I think that they will add catering in the near future. I give them a year, maybe less, before they'll be searching for more space," he added with a smile.

After the waiter left, her mother took a few minutes to tell her a bit more about her friends. Now Morgan was a little more familiar with Nellie and Bess. She realized what they were doing had nothing to do with money at all. Both women were well-off and didn't need the restaurant to help them make money. This little bistro, as they liked to call it, was a place to gather and eat with friends and family. The two women loved making their friends and family feel whole again after the storm. Super storm Sandy had changed a lot of people and the way they lived. Morgan remembered the blank look on all her friends and family's faces after the storm. It seemed like none of them could believe what they had lived through. Some of the families, even now, had not been able to put their homes back together again. Life went on but nothing was the same. Many often said they didn't sweat the small stuff any longer.

After that storm had passed, the two women took the first step toward their future by volunteering to cook and take care of their neighbors. Before they knew it, they had found their calling. The restaurant was lovely and each day brought new customers who fast became new friends.

"Do you think there's any truth to what Alex believes, about Jake bringing this woman home?" Morgan asked her Mom, trying to keep the subject from drifting to Gage.

Ellie McCleary put her fork down and thought for a moment before speaking. "I have my suspicions just like everyone else but Jake will be home on Friday and I'm sure he'll enlighten us. There's no use going off on a tangent, trying to guess, when all we have to do is wait until he arrives to find out."

All in all, Morgan was relieved to have shared her baby news with someone else, especially her mom. Somehow, by saying the words out loud, her pregnancy was validated and it helped to authenticate her relationship with Gage. After lunch, she dropped her Mom at the house, promising not to let so much time pass between visits. For the first time in months she was looking forward to going back to her empty apartment. The afternoon spent with her mother, talking about the arrival of the baby and whether or not she was going to move back into the house she and Gage once shared, left Morgan with a lot to think about. Other than acknowledging the fact that she was pregnant she hadn't given much thought beyond that; it was time that she did. She knew Gage would want her to move back into their house. Besides, she had no idea how long Gage would be gone and he would want her to prepare for the arrival of their baby. Morgan decided she would have to be strong for all of them and begin to make the preparations for the birth of their child; this had to be her first priority.

Morgan looked through the catalogues she had picked up recently in the doctor's reception area, to order things she would need when their baby arrived. She ordered a bassinet, a dresser and a dressing table; that was only the beginning. She also purchased some clothing, diapers, additional baby items and some of the softest cuddly toys and arranged to have everything delivered to their home.

She didn't order a crib because she decided to use the crib Gage had built for Michael. It was the only thing Gage hadn't donated to the woman's shelter after she had moved out of the house they had shared. He had decided that he would get rid of anything that might remind her of Michael when she returned home. Gage had told her that he'd kept the crib and stored it in a corner of the attic. She would have John or Logan bring it down when she was ready for it.

Next, she called a moving company to price packing and moving her apartment furniture as soon as possible. The movers were going to send over a man in the morning to work up the price for her, Morgan was told, providing everything worked out, they could move her things to the house the following week. Without breaking her stride, she called the management company to let them know that she would be moving in another week. With that done, Morgan called the utility companies only to find out that Gage hadn't turned anything off. Gage probably thought he'd be away for a very short time, it was the only explanation. Finally, she was finished for the day as she sat back on the couch. For the first time in a long time, Morgan felt contented, knowing that what she was doing was what she was meant to do. *I actually accomplished a lot in one day.*

Morgan took a well-deserved break and then called Alex to ask him if Gage had left the key to the house with anyone. Alex told her that he thought Gage had given the key to Logan; that she should check with him.

Alex let her know that he had reservations about Morgan going over to the house alone and rehashing any memories that would make her feel worse than she was feeling already. *I can only imagine how guilty Morgan will feel when she enters the house she shared with Gage knowing she's carrying another man's child.*

"Do you really think that's wise? Won't it be a lot for you to handle?" After all, Alex knew Gage was still in love with his sister and had gone to Syria risking his own life to save their brother.

"Alex, I'm fine." She told him not to worry, that she had everything under control and this was something she needed to do.

Morgan got the keys from Logan, but not without having to listen to the same warning she had gotten from Alex. She knew what they were thinking. They were both under the assumption that she was going to the house to feel close to Gage and if truth be told, they were partially correct but she knew she had some major renovations to do and not much time to accomplish the task. She pulled up to the house they once shared and smiled, whispering to their unborn child that they were finally home. She also glanced at the Angel pin she kept on the visor of the car. Michael had given it to her for Mother's Day the year before he died. It was a silver representation of the arc Angel, Michael. She always thought of her son when she touched the angel's face. *"Well Michael, what do you think of the fine mess your parents have made of their lives? Put in a good word for me and keep Dad and your brother safe. With your help, I'll get through this,"* she whispered, touching the face of the Arc Angel Michael, her protector. Morgan pulled the car into the driveway and turned off the engine.

She hesitated before opening the door, afraid that if there were any remnants of another woman in the house they had shared, it would leave her feeling wounded. Turning the key and pushing the door open for the first time was just as nerve-wracking as it had been the first time she and Gage had done the same thing. She was excited and terrified at the same time. Morgan dropped the keys on the table in the foyer and made her way into the living room. As she looked around she realized that nothing had changed, it looked the same, as if she had never left. With the exception of some pictures, everything was as it had been. He hadn't changed a thing. Looking closer, she noticed that the pictures on the walls were mostly of her, Michael and Gage. He hadn't purged himself of her as he had led her to believe. This was certainly no bachelor pad, something she had created in her mind. The boxes he sent her were things they had stored years earlier. Had she taken the time to give it much thought, she would've figured that out for herself. They were all old memories; he had thrown in a few newer pictures and mementos to fool her. She could see empty spots on the wall where pictures once hung. *What was Gage thinking?*

Morgan made her way up the stairs entering the only room they had completely gutted and reconstructed, a beautiful master bedroom with walk-in his and hers closets, a bathroom suite with a sunken tub and a fireplace. The views of the Atlantic Ocean were beautiful, visible from any room in the house. The view from the spa tub was just spectacular. Gage was careful, keeping the beauty of this ocean front home and its entire splendor just as the original owner had intended, with modern additions added. It was built in the late 1920's by someone with a lot of old money. It was a nice size home, although it had fallen into disrepair, Morgan and Gage fell in love with it at first site. Gage had promised to make it a home they would live in forever and he hadn't let her down. Gage was great at anything he did and renovating this home was no exception.

Morgan looked at the oversized tub with floor to ceiling glass behind it, which allowed for a beautiful view of the ocean in the daytime and the stars in the sky at night. Gage insisted they needed this addition and as she eyeballed the tub she couldn't help going where her mind was taking her as she recalled the fonder memories of the times they had shared in that tub. Gage was an expert lover and she learned a lot about herself from him. She relived some of those special moments as she stared at the large tub. She knew this wasn't helping her situation so she decided to exile certain thoughts from her mind before her breathing became more labored.

She decided to investigate the other four bedrooms to see if Gage had done any other renovations since she'd left. Each of the rooms was meticulously decorated just as she had left them. The only room that seemed to have been touched was the bedroom directly opposite the master bedroom, the only room that left her feeling a little apprehensive.

She glanced around the room and was surprised. He had ripped down the wallpaper she had carefully chosen. All the furniture was gone; other than the hardwood floor, the room was bare. Not one remnant of Michael had been left behind. *Well, won't he be surprised when he returns home to find a very different kind of room, one that I will decorate for the arrival of our son.*

She checked the phone. Everything had been kept on so it was obvious that one of her brothers had been taking care of the bills, as well as seeing to it that the housekeeper was still on the payroll. Everything was meticulous and there wasn't a dust bunny to be found anywhere. Thanks to Katie and Belle, the best housekeepers on the planet. The two women had made Gage's life so much easier since their separation and Morgan was going to keep them on the payroll.

With everything in place and the movers arranged, Morgan was pleased with herself. Things were coming along smoothly and she was excited about the move. It was time to come home; it was time for both of them to come home. Her first thought was to attempt to decorate the baby's room on her own. Their baby was all she had of Gage and Michael; she was going to protect him at all costs. Doing work around the house just wasn't wise in her condition. She would be avoiding the family over the next few weeks but this time it was because she was busy making arrangements to move back into the house and preparing for the baby's arrival. At least on Friday she would see them all at McCleary's for Jake's homecoming party, and she would explain her plans to them.

Meeting with the decorator had been exciting and Morgan loved her design ideas for the baby's room. She gave the decorator the go ahead to start immediately. Morgan felt as though her life was finally moving in a positive direction.

Alex couldn't help noticing Morgan's change of mood at the office. He had thought that her trip to the house would surely upset her but it seemed to be having the opposite effect. He had to admit he was pleased, but it made him a little nervous. He had meetings earlier in the week and had just returned from business in London so he hadn't had a chance to talk to Morgan or to touch base with Logan yet. He wanted to ask Logan if Morgan had said anything to him about the baby and he would definitely make that call today. She had said she would be in the office most of the day today so she wouldn't suspect anything if he dropped in on Logan at McCleary's for lunch.

Morgan was at her desk when Alex managed to find a free minute to come in and see her. She motioned for him to come in even though she was on a call. He thought he overheard her going over plans for the baby's room even though she gave Gage's address to whomever she was speaking to. *What the heck is she doing?* She can't barge into the home she had once shared with Gage with another man's child. It just wouldn't be right.

"I've moved back into the house," she said to him as she ended the call. "I found this wonderful decorator and she has been busy working on my redecorating plans; as we speak she is implementing the last of them," she added, not before noticing the perplexed look on his face. He was probably deciding how he would break the news to her that she had lost her mind. *I know almost everyone still believes our baby is the result of a one night stand between Matt Hastings and me.*

"There's something I think you need to know, Alex. Please sit down, it would probably be easier to explain if you weren't hovering over me the way you are now." She was so proud of Alex and how he stepped up to the plate for Gage. It meant selfishly that she and Gage could take a break when he returned.

"I am pregnant, as I know you've suspected. This baby is Gage's child, Alex." She could see his expression change as she admitted the truth to him. It was not Matt Hastings child as he had suspected, she told him with assurance.

"How could you and the others actually think that I would betray Gage? I know we weren't living together this past year, Alex, but it was because I was a mess emotionally. My leaving had nothing to do with the way I felt about Gage. I was having issues dealing with Michael's death and every time I looked at Gage I saw Michael. Before long, I found myself avoiding him just so I didn't have to be reminded that my son wasn't coming back to me ever again. After Michael's death, I began to disappear, crawling into an empty shell. I was physically here but I had checked out emotionally. I allowed my life to end with Michael's death. As soon as I realized what I'd done and what I'd done to Gage, I knew I needed to get away, by myself. I had to find myself again. It was difficult, sometimes heartbreaking, but I think I turned a corner. I still miss Michael with all my heart but I know he would want me to go on."

Alex couldn't believe it. Morgan is pregnant and with Gage's child, imagine that. Other than admitting that the child was Gage's, everything he heard her say after that was nothing but a bunch of static. He realized he should have been listening more intently because he was certain it was important but having Gage back in her life changed everything. This was the greatest news she could have told him because he knew better than anyone what Morgan meant to Gage. Gage had found a way back into her heart just as he had promised he would. Alex gave a sigh of relief as she laughed out loud. She wasn't surprised to hear that he wasn't the only one who thought Matt Hastings was her child's father. She assured him that Gage was the father, that she had never been unfaithful to Gage Delaney. Alex had to admit *he was relieved to hear this news.* He knew how much Gage wanted Morgan back in his life. Gage had talked about nothing else at the start and the end of each and every day.

"Jake's coming home; and with this news, I'm sure you'll knock one out of the park. Now, if we could only get more information about Gage's whereabouts everything would be as it should. Will you need a ride to McCleary's?" Alex asked with excitement.

"I'm not sure what time I'm going to be able to get there. I have to go to the house; I'm meeting with the decorator. Other than that, I think I need some time alone to prepare myself before I see Jake and the reporter. I'm certainly happy he's home, but since Gage is still over there, I feel as though it's our fault he isn't home. I also have to find a way to let go of any feelings of blame I might be harboring before I meet this reporter. If Gage hadn't gone over there to help Jake, he would still be here with me. I know it's not really anyone's fault he went to Syria but I can't help but feel the reporter is part of the reason for his absence in my life."

Alex understood what she was going through but he also knew his sister. Somehow she would find the strength to forgive before Friday night. He had that much confidence in Morgan. He had faith; even though her pain was new and raw, she would make it through the night without incident at the family party. Alex knew Morgan was one classy lady.

Morgan had kept busy with the nursery after talking to Alex. Her thoughts of Gage were constant and her daydreams of him felt real. She looked forward to falling asleep that night so she would be with Gage and they could talk. She felt that the love between them was powerful, that even at this distance Gage had found a way to communicate with her through her dreams. Through her dreams, she and Gage could have active conversations in places she knew she'd never been. Gage would hold her in his arms and tell her there was nothing for her to worry about. He often told her that he had an angel who was looking out for him and that everything would be alright.

While standing in the nursery, Morgan let her mind wander; it was getting late. Her dreams of him kept her from going insane. She knew the danger he had put himself in and it was all for her and her family. She pictured Gage standing next to her. Morgan smiled at him and asked him what they would do without him. Gage lifted his head and whispered in her ear that she would have to find a way if it came to that. That last comment was enough to startle her back to reality.

Morgan was sweating, startled from her dream about Gage, as she got up from their bed and made her way to the kitchen. She needed to get a glass of water. She had to calm down; her nervous rapid breathing wasn't helping her or the baby. Why did Gage say that to her? He had always been positive before. Morgan remembered she'd had the same meandering thoughts just before she'd gone to bed.

Chapter Eleven

McCleary's was alive with thunderous applause as Lt. Col. Jake McCleary entered the room with the British journalist on his arm. The journalist, as everyone had referred to her up to this point, was being introduced to them as Reigh. Morgan had arrived minutes before Jake. It was the last thing she wanted to do but, like Logan had said to her earlier in the day, Gage wouldn't want her to have any ill feelings toward this woman or Jake. Gage had made the choice to go to Syria on his own and he wouldn't want her to judge someone else for the choice he'd made. *It's easier said than done, how can I put aside my feelings?* Somehow, for Gage and the well-being of their unborn son, she would have to try. It didn't do her or anyone any good to harp on what had happened.

"You know he's feeling a lot of guilt, don't you?" her father whispered in her ear as he placed his arm around Morgan. "You'll have to let him know you forgive him or his homecoming will be in vain. Jake will never be able to live with himself and get on with his life if he believes that you blame him for Gage being left behind." She knew that Gage and Jake believed and lived, *'leave no man behind'*. The order to leave him behind had to have been difficult for Jake.

Morgan looked into her father's adoring eyes and her demeanor softened. She was being given the chance to parent again and suddenly she understood what her father was asking her to do and just what it would cost her to do it. She had to find it in heart to convince Jake and Reigh that she held no ill feelings toward either of them. She knew in her heart that they weren't responsible for Gage's disappearance and no matter what the final outcome was, she couldn't blame either of them, otherwise it would become a burden for life and reflect on her son's quality of life. Gage would want Jake to be in his son's life and she had to admit, it was getting easier to let go of the anger she had been experiencing. In her dreams, Gage convinced her to let it go, if for no other reason than for their son's future. Morgan sighed and prayed for help so that she could be the person Gage would want her to be.

"Morgan, when your Mom told me about the baby, I was thrilled. It will be nice having another little man around to play ball with, rather than having to play the pretty, pretty princess game." They both laughed; Morgan recalled walking in on her macho father playing the board game, *pretty, pretty princess*, with his granddaughters. She remembered he had a crown on his head and a big blue necklace around his neck. Morgan remembered how silly he looked but he took it in stride. *Anything to put a smile on their faces*, he had said. "I'm really happy for you, Morgan, and no matter what happens when all is said and done you know your baby will have the support of everyone in this room," he said, looking around at all her brothers and her sister Patti. If anything happened to Gage, he knew this group of men would step up to be there for her and her son, along with his other daughter. "He'll never lack for a male figure in his life, but I haven't given up on Gage. My son-in-law is very capable of handling himself, as you know. I wouldn't count him out just yet," he added as an afterthought, giving her a hug.

She hugged her father, promising him that she had let go of the anger. She told him that she'd been busy preparing the house for the baby and didn't want to hang on to any ill will. At first, he was startled that she had moved back into the house she had shared with Gage. Making all the arrangements with the mover and the decorator without asking for any help, he knew, it was her way of distracting herself from her worries and anger. *It'll be nice to have my girl back in town and close by.*

Jake hadn't had the chance to make his announcement before he helped Reigh out of her coat. The entire room went silent as they stared at the pregnant woman standing before them. Reigh McGuire seemed a little nervous. The room fell silent but Morgan was sure the real shock was yet to come.

"Everyone, I'd like you all to meet my wife, Reigh McCleary. Reigh and I were married two days ago in Germany on the way home. Mom and Dad, Reigh is carrying your fourth granddaughter, I'm afraid. Maybe next time, Pop," Jake shouted to his father standing with Morgan toward the back of the bar. "I'm pleased to announce that my little girl will be arriving in about two months." Jake waited for some reaction, any reaction. Apparently, everyone was shocked. John was the first to take his new sister-in-law in his arms to hug her, welcoming her into the family. It didn't take long for the rest of the family to show Reigh they wholeheartedly approved. Ellie McCleary was delighted and overjoyed, knowing that she was going to be adding two more grandchildren to her family tree.

Morgan motioned to her parents and Alex not to make the announcement about her child yet. She decided that she didn't want this day to be about anyone other than Jake and Reigh. Besides, there would be plenty of time for her to tell everyone the news. She was happy for Jake and excited that her child would have a cousin to grow up with. Patti's kids were terrific, but they were older and by the time her child would be old enough to play, Patti's children would be practically grown. As Morgan made her way toward Jake and Reigh, it felt like the parting of the seas. It seemed that everyone was nervous, anticipating her reaction. Jake moved forward, as if to protect Reigh, should this meeting not go the way he hoped it would. He had enough guilt in his heart without Morgan making Reigh feel bad.

"Jake, I'm very happy for you," she said as she gave Jake a hug, offering her new sister-in-law a hand in introduction before welcoming her into the family with a firm hug. Jake couldn't have asked for more from Morgan and he wanted her to know how appreciative he was. *This has to be hard for her.* He would let her know when they were alone. Reigh sobbed like a baby as she hugged Morgan and thanked her for allowing Gage to come to Syria and not hating her for his decision to do so. Reigh let Morgan know how apprehensive she had been to meet her, under the circumstances.

"Gage really saved our lives," Reigh added with tears flowing.

"Reigh, you have nothing to feel guilty about. Gage made the choice to go to Syria on his own and I've come to terms with his decision. Gage wouldn't want you or Jake to feel any guilt. Congratulations on your marriage and the baby. I'm truly happy for you, really" she added, hugging them both. Morgan used this time to sneak away to the kitchen, knowing she could leave via the backdoor without anyone being the wiser.

Logan knew how hard that little speech had been for his sister but he was proud of her. It wasn't a surprise to any of them really because they knew how hard that speech had been for her. Morgan was a strong independent woman and she could certainly handle herself. Hadn't she handled all of the McCleary brothers for years? Alex reminisced, *that was one of the first things that attracted Gage to Morgan. He admired her strength, knowing that she could handle her brothers so well.* That meant she'd be able to handle him, and he knew it. Joe Kirby had been invited to the homecoming party as well and offered the couple his well wishes. He noticed Morgan was making her way toward the kitchen and rushed to intercept her. He had agreed to attend the party because the matriarch had asked him to join them. But he believed Morgan might have needed him there as well. Alex made his way over to Morgan at the same time. He hugged her and whispered something in her ear. Joe looked at her with a questionable glare. *Did I just hear what I think I did?* Logan glanced over at Joe. *Judging by Joe's expression, I think that Alex has just let the cat out of the bag.*

Logan wondered if Morgan had made any decisions about what she was going to do. Alex was correct, based on their recent conversation; she had already started moving back into the house. He would definitely be stopping by to talk to her and let her know that he knew about the baby and that Gage was the father. Logan had had visions of the brothers making a trip to L.A. to deal with Matt Hastings. *I'm so glad that Gage is the father and not Matt. I'm too old to pick fights or get involved with anything like that.*

Joe offered to get her coat, help her sneak out of the party and take her home. Morgan asked Joe to give her a second as she pulled her dad to the side and told him she was going to sneak out the back without offering individual good byes. She informed him that it was too much for her to celebrate Jake's homecoming knowing Gage was on the other side of the world and perhaps in a lot of trouble. He understood her emotional state and was thankful that she had put in an appearance.

Joe McCleary hugged his daughter and let her know that he was glad she had her friend Joe to keep her company. He let them know that if anyone noticed the two had disappeared, he would make their excuses for them. It seemed as though almost everyone was busy celebrating and hadn't notice they had taken off. There was one person who did notice but he didn't let on, nor did he try to stop her.

Jake knew his sister's heart was breaking and there was nothing he could do to help her right now. He empathized with her and understood her reasons for needing to get away. She had probably felt as if the walls of the restaurant were closing in on her. He had felt that way when he'd boarded the Black Hawk that would take him and Reigh to safety, far from enemy fire.

I hated leaving Gage stranded in Syria, it was the toughest thing I'd ever done in my life. He would never forget the feeling as the Black Hawk lifted off the ground; *it felt as though I couldn't breathe.* The sound of the engine and the blades as they spun were deafening; *it had never bothered me as much as that night.* He had felt as though he were letting his brother down. *It didn't matter that I was following orders.* He made a promise to himself that night that he would find a way to return. *Gage gave up more than his freedom to come to my aid* and how did they repay him, by leaving him behind in a hostile country with people who were hunting him down, trying to kill him. Jake knew better than anyone what Isis rebels would do to Gage first before killing him. Isis wanted Gage dead but they would make sure he suffered while they tortured him first. *How can I protect Morgan from that possibility?* He only hoped that Morgan could find it in her heart to forgive him. *But will I ever be able to forgive myself.*

Logan and his parents had gone through a lot of trouble to plan this party and Jake couldn't run out on them yet. But at some point he knew he would have to sit down with Morgan and have a truthful conversation about what had happened in Syria and where things stood at this moment. If he could change anything he would, but for now there was nothing he could do; his hands were tied. He had been given a short leave to come home and when it was time to report back he would find a way to convince his superiors to allow him and his team to go back and rescue Gage if he was still alive. Reigh would not be happy to hear what he intended to do but there were some things she was better off not knowing just now. He had promised her that he would consider leaving the military after this issue with Syria and Gage was resolved. It was something they talked about after being rescued. There would be no more danger for either of them, for the sake of their unborn little girl. Their little girl needed both of them in her life and he promised himself that after this last mission to find Gage, he would resign his commission and retire from military service.

"Jake, I'm so pleased to have you home and Reigh is wonderful. I think she's a perfect fit for this family. Don't you agree?" Joe McCleary asked his wife. He gestured towards Reigh, "She is obviously able to hold her own with your brothers; they seemed to take a liking to her. I am very impressed and pleased that you have finally found someone to quiet your untamed soul. I had my doubts that this day would ever come," he added joyfully offering his glass in salutation of the couple.

Jake embraced his dad in a bear-hug and offered up these words, "I love her, Dad. I didn't think I was ever going to find *the one who was right for me*. But, I love her with all my heart and you will too when you get to know her," he said, admiring Reigh from afar.

Ellie McCleary stood next to her son and smiled as she witnessed the love he felt for his new wife. *Someday my other rascals will fall in love as well.* Maybe they would eventually appreciate what a good woman could mean to them instead of the jezebels her other son's brought around to McCleary's. But not one of her sons had ever taken any of these women into her home. The bar scene was for the young and she and Joe looked forward to quiet nights at home in front of the television. She stayed out of her children's lives. She had done her job as a mother, now it was up to them. As a matter of fact, when she was in attendance, on that rare occasion at McCleary's restaurant, speaking to the young girls on her sons' arms was interesting, quite amusing and somewhat entertaining. Her sons were scoundrels for sure; she, more often than not, wanted to warn those young innocent ladies to run away from them, as far away and as fast as they could.

John tried to stay focused on the party, not on the news he had received prior to Jake's arrival. He had been notified this afternoon that body parts were discovered at a site near where Gage was last seen. Whoever it was, the poor soul had been savagely tortured and cut into pieces. The attack was so brutal that the young military coroner had vomited in a corner after seeing the pieces scattered about. It was obviously another statement from Isis. Apparently the person had been tortured slowly and methodically. No doubt the assailants had taken pleasure as they cut off his limbs one by one, while keeping the man alive while he suffered dismemberment. At least that was what they assumed. John hoped the preliminary report he had received was wrong and that it wasn't Gage. The coroner insisted he would try to identify the dismembered body as soon as possible. The only positive identification so far was that it was a white male, and probably an American.

John knew he would need to tell Jake what he had found out, but for now he would let it rest until after the party. Perhaps, he would take Jake aside in the morning and tell him in private, away from the family. They could decide then what, if anything, they would tell Morgan or the rest of the family.

Chapter Twelve

Joe was shocked that Morgan had so much news to share and hadn't told him sooner. Morgan told him she hadn't called him because she didn't want to bother him knowing he and Neil had just taken major steps forward in their lives. *This woman is truly amazing!* He was surprised when she asked him to drop her off at the house she had shared with Gage. What she told him next was a shocker. He couldn't believe she had moved out of the apartment and he was concerned by her decision to do so. As he followed her directions, he noticed that the house was located in a more exclusive part of the neighborhood. He was pleased as they approached her driveway; Gage Delaney certainly appreciated good architecture.

Joe admired this huge old beach house with wraparound porches facing the ocean. He noticed it was old but he could tell it had been completely renovated and restored. The house had been done with taste and class, at least what he had seen so far. *My mother would have been proud to see this place*, to see how Gage had restored it to its original luster, or what he thought it would've looked like in 1920. Joe's mother was a member of the historical society and she loved to see older homes being restored rather than torn down and replaced with mini mansions, something one would expect in this area. Joe knew this was one home that would have impressed even the worst critic.

Mr. McCleary had nudged him on the way out the restaurant and handed him a shopping bag which he was sure contained dinner for him and Morgan. Joe reached into his trunk, after they parked the car, and took out the great smelling bag before he followed Morgan up the walk to her fabulous beach house. The place was amazing Joe could see they had put in a lot of time into its decor. He made his way into their oversized country kitchen and dropped the bag of goodies on the counter. He thought about what it must have been like for Morgan and Gage during happier times, she and Gage preparing great meals together in this state of art kitchen while Michael played in the nearby family room. He was impressed with this very open concept.

"Your dad took care of us. He gave me our dinner just before we walked out the door…there's enough for the three of us," he teased before adding, "I still can't believe my girl is having a baby and a little boy to boot. If he needs any pointers when he gets a little older, Uncle Joe is available. If you ever need a babysitter Neil and I would be thrilled to help out. Who can do a better job watching your son than a kid at heart and a doctor on hand just in case I do anything foolish to put your child in danger?" Morgan smiled and told him she might have to take him up on his offer.

"Do you want me to show you around? I know you will definitely appreciate all the work and attention to detail Gage put into this place. It took him years but when it was finished it was quite impressive." She reached into the bag her father had sent over with Joe. She hadn't thought about dinner and she certainly wasn't up to preparing anything for the two of them. *My Dad is fantastic; he thinks of everything.*

"I'm sure you had something to do with this. Your design schemes are written all over the place." Joe said as he walked through the hall. "I want to see the rest of the place but it can wait until after dinner. I have strict orders to see that you eat enough for two."

"I guess you're right, we should eat before the food gets cold. Sit down at the table; I'll get the plates and utensils. It's been a while since we've had the chance to talk and I'm sure you're curious about a few things as I am of certain events in your life. Shall we start with you first, how are things with you and Neil?" she asked as she made her way back into the kitchen.

"We're good. Everything is great between us. We had no trouble settling into the penthouse and Neil loves being so close to the hospital. He's amazed that I chose to live in the other apartment after seeing the view from the rooftop terrace of the penthouse. I'd say everything between us is just about perfect. My mother is a frequent visitor these days and she and Neil get along like two peas in a pod. We see his family on occasion, not as much as we see my mom, but often enough. I really miss you though. It's been tough getting used to not seeing your face every day. We can't let so much time pass between visits," he added, waiting for her response.

"You're right, I promise to visit more often. You and Neil have been such a major part of my life this past year. Not seeing you or my family these past few months is inexcusable on my part. I take full responsibility and now that my secret is out I won't let that much time pass between visits." Morgan served the food but she had to admit she hadn't thought she was hungry; however, the smell of the food from McCleary's was hard to ignore. They each enjoyed the food commenting on how lucky Logan was to have hired a chef with such talent. All in all, McCleary's was not your typical bar and grill food. She didn't know how Logan did it but the food he served was always excellent. He had hired a new chef about a year ago, she was unbelievable.

Lizzy had been hired as a temporary cook while she put herself through law school. Morgan often asked Lizzy why she was wasting her talent cooking for Logan. Morgan suspected Lizzy had other reasons for staying at McCleary's. It seemed clear to Morgan that Lizzy felt something more for Logan than she let on. *My guess is that if Logan ever chose to ask Lizzy on a real date, he wouldn't be disappointed.* Morgan once hinted that to Lizzy and though she agreed she made Morgan promise never to speak about it again. *I wonder if that was such a wise promise to have made to Lizzy.* It would be good for Logan to have someone like Lizzy in his life.

After clearing the dishes, Morgan offered Joe that promised tour of their home. Joe was visibly more impressed with every room they entered. She decided to save the master suite for last because she knew he would be blown away. Joe smiled as he stepped into the baby's room. Two walls were light teal and the other two a deep ocean blue. The colors gave the theme away, nautical of course. One wall sported a beautiful seascape mural, the fish and other sea creatures under the water were amazingly colorful; to the naked eye they seemed animated. The furniture was exquisite and very tasteful which proved his original theory, that Morgan had more to do with the home's renovation than she was admitting.

Morgan told him that she had saved the best room for last, clasping his hand and dragging him along. By the look on his face, she was right to have waited. He was taken aback, imagining how much thought went into this project. Gage was definitely in the right field. He had a keen eye for architecture and it served him well. Joe would definitely be recommending him to all his family and friends in the future. He was seldom surprised but this was mind-blowing. He only wished he had the pleasure of seeing Gage's work before he had renovated the penthouse.

"This place is amazing. You must be proud of what you've both accomplished here."

"We were pretty pleased with ourselves when it was completed. I was afraid that after we split Gage would sell the place. We picked this place because of its location and the neighborhood. We knew we would eventually have children and we wanted them to have family close by," she said, getting a little melancholy.

Joe was happy for her, squeezing her when they both heard the door open. They weren't alarmed; their instincts served them well; it was her brother, Jake. He shouted her name. She yelled back to let him know they were upstairs. Jake was surprised as he reached the top of the stairs as he passed Michael's room. All of Michael's things were gone, replaced with nursery items. *This is a good sign, I hope.* Joe thought this would be a good time to leave, to let them talk. He told Morgan he'd be in touch later that night. Obviously Jake needed to talk to Morgan, alone. "I'll lock the door on my way out. Goodnight, Morgan, and Jake, I'm glad you're back," he added, patting Jake on the shoulder.

"I was hoping to talk to you before you left tonight. I wanted to apologize to you. I want you to know that I feel responsible," he started to say something before she stopped him.

"I don't blame you, Jake. Gage chose to go to Syria. He didn't include me in that decision, but I know my husband, he wouldn't have gone if he wasn't sure there was something he could do. I'm not mad at you or Reigh.

I'm angry at Gage for not discussing it with me first. We had just reconciled and before we had the opportunity to make plans for our future he was gone from my life. I wish we could've had more time, a few days or even just a few hours together before he left." She hesitated a moment and then realized Jake had stepped into Michael's old room; he seemed confused. "I was going to tell everyone tonight but I didn't want to interfere with your announcements. As you can see now, I have news too," she said, pointing to the baby furniture. "Gage and I are expecting a baby. It breaks my heart, Jake; he was gone before I even suspected. The baby is due a month after your little girl. I'm worried and a bit sad. I may have to raise our baby alone."

Morgan picked up one of the plush stuffed toys that had arrived for the baby today, it was an angel. Morgan held it in her hand and tried to say something so that Jake wouldn't feel any sense of guilt. "It's not your fault or Reigh's; it's really no one's fault that Gage isn't here. He did what he thought he had to do. He knew if he told me first I would have tried to stop him from going. I miss him, Jake, and I'm really worried that there hasn't been news."

"My raging hormones are no help to me right now; my feelings are amplified, whether good or bad."

Jake took her in his embrace and they cried together. He was glad she didn't hold him responsible. Someday he hoped he would be able to forgive himself. He had a bad feeling about the situation that Gage was in but until he had Intel he didn't want to speculate. He changed the subject to lighten the mood and Morgan was glad that he had. He asked what she thought of Reigh. She smiled and offered her honest opinion; Reigh was breathtakingly beautiful and seemed to have a wonderful persona.

He smiled and let her know what was happening at McCleary's. "Mom is already planning a wedding and a baby shower, all at once. You know how Mom is when she sets her mind to something. She is adamant. We need to be married properly, in a church in front of family and friends. She wants to invite Reigh's family over from England so that the families can meet before the wedding. I told Mom that I wanted to wait until there was news about Gage but she insisted it couldn't wait. I told her I wasn't comfortable going forward without Gage but she insisted, knowing you would want us to go ahead with the wedding. I want you to know that I'm comfortable waiting if that's what you want."

"Jake, mom is right; the world doesn't stop turning because Gage isn't here. You need to do this and I need to start making plans for my future as well. Gage will understand when *he does come home, if he comes home.* As a matter of fact, he would be happy knowing that I insisted you move forward with your plans. You'll see; it will all work out. I'm going to be fine, stop worrying about me," she said, as she linked her arm into his as they made their way to the door.

Morgan insisted that Jake leave, go back to McCleary's and rejoin his party. She said she had dishes to do and was feeling a little tired, that she needed to get some rest. "But I'd love to have you and Reigh over for lunch later on in the week if you'd like to come over?" Jake agreed and left to go back to join the rest of the family at McCleary's. Morgan washed the dishes by hand just to pass the time even though she had a like-new dishwasher. It was hard to accomplish anything lately when all she really wanted to do was curl up in bed, sleep and dream of Gage, to be with him wherever he was, even if only in her dreams. She found peace there; Gage would always be waiting for her, taking away any fear she had about him being hurt or even dead.

Since Reigh and Jake had come home, they had spent a lot of time with Morgan. It was almost time for Jake to go back to the Middle East. While he was home he had done a lot of planning for their future. He knew he could not leave the military for another six months but opening a private security firm sounded like a good idea and the family supported his idea. Jake was enjoying his time with the family but that would end soon, he had found Reigh an apartment so that she wouldn't have to rely on anyone else. The family offered to put her up but she adamantly refused. She and Jake found a two-bedroom apartment overlooking the ocean in Belle Harbor. It was perfect for them, at least until he came back home. In six months they would look at homes in the area. He and Reigh didn't want to rush into anything until they were sure about what they wanted.

While Jake was still home, Reigh's family flew in from England. They enjoyed all the festivities planned by the McCleary's in their honor. From the moment they arrived, schedules were jammed-packed. Ellie made plans for them to see the sights and arranged luncheons and dinner parties to meet their extended family members. Reigh had two siblings an older brother, Matt, and a younger sister, Jeannie. Her parents and grandparents were lovely people as well. Matt had a great time with the McCleary brothers; they made him feel right at home. Jeannie had just as much fun but she and her boyfriend, Thomas, couldn't wait to return to England. They missed their homeland often. Before leaving, her family promised to return as soon as Reigh's baby arrived.

Michaela Rose McCleary made her debut two weeks earlier than expected. Reigh's family returned as promised and everyone enjoyed seeing Michaela Rose for the first time. She was so precious. The McCleary boys already loved their new niece. Patti's kids offered to babysit and help Reigh while Jake was in the Middle East, an offer she couldn't turn down.

Chapter Thirteen

A few weeks later, Morgan woke feeling restless, rubbed her stomach and wondered why her son was being so active. As luck would have it, Joe was scheduled to stop by and take her to the doctor and then to their last Lamaze class. He was due to arrive any minute, with each passing second she was feeling more than a bit odd. She went into the kitchen and noticed the angel lying on the counter. She usually left it in her car but had taken it out the night before. *Is Michael trying to tell me something?* She picked up the medallion and held it in her hand… she couldn't remember why she felt such a need to bring it into the house. "What are you trying to tell me, Michael?" She waited for an answer, but of course she didn't expect one. There was a knock on the door and she opened it and she was happy to see Joe on the other side. He had arrived a little earlier than he was supposed to but by the look on her face he was glad. She looked like she was already in labor; perhaps they wouldn't be going anywhere except to the hospital. He had waited for this moment for months and he was sure he could handle it but her pain made him doubt himself. Joe could only think of one thing. Gage would want him to step up and be there for Morgan when he couldn't.

"Do you want me to call your mom and let her know?"

Morgan warned him not to with gritted teeth. She wanted the birthing to be private and quiet. She was more afraid of her own reaction to the birth than anything else. She knew not having Gage there would be hard enough but she was afraid that today was going to be more emotional than it would have been otherwise. She was glad to have Joe to lean on. She couldn't have imagined going through this with her brothers and she refused to ask Patti. Morgan wanted Joseph Gage Delaney to be brought into this world free of drugs or stress and Patti's three birthing experiences had been drug induced. Patti was better left out of this picture.

Immediately upon entering the hospital, she was placed in a wheelchair and pushed into the birthing room. Since Morgan had pre-registered and called ahead, per her Lamaze instructor, the hospital had been expecting her. The hospital staff called her doctor immediately and he said he'd meet her at the hospital very shortly. After changing and climbing into the birthing bed, she and Joe were shocked when the doctor informed Morgan she was already dilated eight centimeters with contractions coming every two minutes. Dr. Cohen informed her that her son was growing impatient. Immediately, she thought, *"Gage, your son will be here within the next few hours and everything will be different for us." I'm about to become a mother again.* Lying there, she thought about a few recent events like the scare she'd had two and half months earlier when it was reported that a body had been found in the Syrian desert. They'd identified the body as belonging to someone of Greek decent but it didn't stop Morgan from panicking as she waited for news about Gage. The news of another mutilated tortured body, shortly after that, almost drove Morgan into premature labor. It was reported that body parts were found the night before Jake arrived. She hadn't heard anything else since the discovery but she assumed no news was good news. Morgan promised herself not to watch the news or read newspapers until after her son was born. She couldn't help thinking about her dreams. Gage hadn't come to her in her dreams as of late. He had stopped coming to her in her dreams the day before the party for Jake. She didn't want to take any chances with their son's life by thinking that there might be a connection to the body that was discovered and Gage or that her last dream was a warning of some kind. She knew she had to try to remain calm during the birthing of their son.

Morgan and Joe were watching the clock and counting the minutes in between contractions. Things began to move quickly, much faster than they anticipated. When Morgan became anxious, thinking that Gage wasn't coming home and that he would never see his son, Joe was able to keep her focused on the birthing of their child. The next time the doctor checked on her she was ten centimeters' and she was ready to push. Within ten minutes, Joseph Gage Delaney was born with ten fingers, ten toes, the blackest hair and bluest eyes she could have imagined. He weighed 7lbs. 13oz. and was 22inches long. The minute she gazed into his beautiful soulful eyes, it was like looking at a reflection of Gage and Michael together. Morgan's eyes welled up. Joe allowed her time to feel the pain of all the losses in her life because he knew it wouldn't be long before her agony turned to joy. She smiled at the little boy looking into her tear-filled eyes.

"Should I make the calls?" Joe congratulated Morgan and kissed the baby's forehead. "He's beautiful, Morgan. You're little guy is already precious."

"You may as well call everyone. The family will know something is up when they try to contact me at the house and don't get a response. Besides, I don't think my father would be too happy if he were to miss the first hour after his grandson's birth. Just ask them to give me a little time with the baby before they head up." She didn't notice Joe leaving the room as she continued to fuss over her beautiful little boy. She was so preoccupied that she hadn't even been paying attention to the nurses who had been asking to take the baby from her to clean him up and have the pediatrician look him over.

Morgan was tired but she didn't want her son to be taken away from her just yet, not even to be cleaned up. She was afraid Gage might be gone and having her son next to her helped her get through an unbearable ache she was feeling. Joe came back into the room to let her know her family would be arriving momentarily. "They were all excited when I told them the news, your mom, especially. She sends her love and said she can't wait to meet her grandson." Joe asked if he could hold the baby for a little while before the nurse took him away. Morgan shook her head slightly; Joe could see she was exhausted. He told her to relax and rest. He handed the baby to the nurse who said that Dr. Shaw, the pediatrician Morgan chose, was in the nursery and wanted to check on baby Delaney herself. Joe suggested Morgan let her family pick up the slack for a while. He knew they would love to help her.

Joe felt honored when Morgan announced that she had named the baby after her father, Gage's grandfather and him. She told Joe that she and Gage appreciated him and couldn't thank him enough for all he'd done. He was instrumental in pulling her out of the black-hole she had been in after she and Gage separated. Joseph Gage Delaney was named to honor the men who meant so much to her. Her Dad who was her pillar of strength, Gage's grandfather who passed away when Gage was just a young boy. His grandfather was the only role model in Gage's life; Gage said he owed him a debt of gratitude because it was his grandfather who helped mold the man he was today and Joe who had become more than a friend to them both.

Chapter Fourteen

"Where do you people think you're going with all those packages?" the charge nurse asked as she reprimanded the group she saw descending on her unit. Birthing rooms were not large and she was certain the family who stood in front of her more than exceeded the capacity of the room. Logan was the first to speak. He charmed Nurse Ann McPhilips so quickly; he had her helping them into Morgan's room and staying to socialize. The other nurses came into the room after Nurse McPhilips left for the night and thanked Logan for accomplishing something no one had ever been able to do in all the years they had known her.

Morgan couldn't believe her eyes, gifts, flowers and balloons filled the room to bursting. Logan even thought to bring food for her because he knew she hated hospital food. He brought enough to feed the night nursing staff as well, just to grease the wheel. Everyone took turns holding baby Joey as he was referred to. She laughed as each of her brothers' whispered the same thing in his little ears, "I'm the best-looking uncle in the family and I know you'll take after me just like your big brother Michael did. The time she spent watching them hold little Joey was bitter sweet. She knew Gage would have been such a proud father if he could be there. Michael would have been such a gloating big brother but he would never have the opportunity. Gage would have reveled in the idea of handing out cigars as he celebrated his son's birth and Michael would've loved having a sibling. Her mom watched her as she watched her brothers and knew what was running through her daughter's head. Ellie hoped and prayed that the angels above knew what they had in heaven with Michael. *Maybe Gage is there as well but I hope that's not the case. Everyone in this room misses them both very much.*

"Morgan, he's beautiful," her mom said as she held her grandson in her arms. "He looks just like Michael, may God bless him. Was the delivery very difficult?" she asked, trying to nudge her daughter away from the place her thoughts were taking her. Joe chimed in immediately, letting her know that the delivery went perfectly from start to finish. Joe beamed, he felt so thankful to have had the opportunity to witness such an event. Having shared this most intimate moment with Morgan brought them that much closer. He had a newfound respect for mothers and what they went through during childbirth. He and Neil had decided not to have children. Although Joey's birth was extraordinary he knew they had made the right choice. They had lived a very narcissistic lifestyle and for the most part they enjoyed it. But being part of a family was truly enjoyable. *Who am I kidding?* He loved the traveling and all the material things having money afforded them. Standing there, he decided they would live vicariously through Morgan and his new namesake. He watched as the family handed Morgan gifts. He and Neil would make sure their gift to this little man was special, but he needed time to think about what that gift might be.

Patti and Reigh sighed excitedly as she began to open the boxes. She held up each of the outfits' for everyone to see, each one seemed more beautiful than the prior one.

"Who gave you that?" Reigh asked as she and Patti admired the little baseball mitt and soft baseball in the cutest little wooden box, along with an authentic baseball signed by Derek Jeter and encased in an acrylic dome. She recognized the ball right away. Her father had given it to Michael after Jeter signed it for him at a game they attended when Michael was just three-years-old. Gage had returned the ball to her dad when he had cleaned out Michael's room. Her Dad told her Gage thought he should have it, as a remembrance of the time he had spent with Michael.

Morgan cried as she read the note her father had attached to the gift. It was a private letter to her, letting her know how much he cherished the time he'd had with Michael.

Dearest Morgan,

Congratulations on the birth of your son, what a blessing for all. When I was told that Joe was born, my first thoughts were of Michael. Our little man is watching over all of us, I'm sure of it. I'm sure he would be happy to see you smile again. I wanted to give Joe something special today and Michael's baseball was the first thing to come to mind. A simple ball, but the memories it awakens, are my most treasured moments with Michael. Michael would want his brother to have his ball and he would want us to make new memories with Joe.

Not a day goes by, Morgan, that I don't think about Michael. I miss him terribly; I miss his smile, his laugh and the way he would look when he was deep in thought. He reminded me of Gage, when he did that. Gage was always thinking of the outcome before he acted. Michael lives in our hearts and memories; when we remember him it should be with a smile. Be happy Morgan, you have a beautiful baby boy to live for. We are all here for you if you need us; Gage will return to us, I believe that.

Love,
Dad

Her dad had the knack for saying just what she needed to hear at just the right time. Their memories of Michael should always be cherished with a smile, he said, but now was the time to make happy memories with Joey. Morgan looked at her *dad; I can't imagine not having him in my life.* She had the best father a girl could ask for and she was grateful he was there to get her through this difficult time. He understood the pain and loneliness she felt because he felt it too. She would keep his note and read it whenever she needed his strength. Her dad chose that moment to kiss her forehead. His first-born grandson had meant the world to him; he missed him more than he cared to admit. They had bonded strongly. Sometimes when he was alone, he found himself going to that same dark place, the same place Morgan visited all too frequently. The only thing that brought him back was the realization that his little girl needed him to stay in the present and remain strong for her. Sometimes he thought Michael was pulling him back, begging him to be strong for his mother. Even though Michael had been young when he passed on, he was an old soul at heart. Joe remembered what he asked of him before he died, "Grandpa, you need to be strong for my Mom and Dad when the end comes because they need you." Joe would go over to their house and spend his free time with Michael, often surprised at the level of conversation that came from such a young man. Joe smiled at the thought as he stepped back from Morgan.

Patti and Reigh took a moment to give Joe a big hug. Though they didn't say anything, they understood his need to protect Morgan, to try to make this day special for her. There was no jealousy in the McCleary family. At some point in each of their lives, everyone had felt their parents' unwavering love when they had needed it most. They owed their parents a great deal and Morgan hoped she had acquired their parenting skills in order to raise Joey properly.

The phone began to ring and Logan picked it up. It was Jake; he was calling from the Middle East. He congratulated her and told her he wished he could be there, that he would be home soon and check on her then. Jake said John used his connections to make sure the news was relayed to him right away. Morgan assured him that she and little Joey were doing just fine and there was no need for him to worry.

After hanging up the phone, while everyone was busy talking about Joey, Morgan thought about Gage and the man he had become, in spite of the appalling life he had been forced to live as a child. His grandfather had tried to save him from his drug addicted parents but his illness hindered him from doing what he wanted for the grandson he loved so much. He had tried to take Gage away from his parents legally, the parents who didn't really want him in the first place. But his grandfather became too ill to care for the boy he had been raising any longer. He succumbed long before the paperwork was approved. Gage was left with his addicted parents until he was finally taken away and put into foster care. Gage rarely talked about foster care to anyone, and seldom with Morgan. She recalled one conversation about another boy in foster care but couldn't remember his name. He and Gage had been very close but lost touch after the military or so she thought. Gage said he had his reasons for not speaking much about his foster brother but she never pressed him about what he meant by that. She often wondered what happened to the other boy. She also remembered Gage telling her he never forgot certain values his grandfather had taught him. Gage had tried to instill those same values in his boyhood friend while in foster care. Suddenly, Morgan looked around the room and once again she was thankful for her family and now, for baby Joey as well. He would be on the receiving end of all this love and devotion; for that she was indebted to her family.

"Okay, all of you out," the night nurse ordered. *"I've let you stay much longer than I should have.* I expect all of you to follow the rules next time. Today was a gift from Nurse McPhilips," she said, winking at Logan. "She will not be so generous tomorrow."

John taunted Logan on the way out the door but not before each of them wished Morgan well and offered to come by tomorrow if she would have them. Ellie made an announcement that they all should stay home tomorrow and let Morgan rest. She said she would be stopping by the hospital tomorrow *alone* and she would bring Morgan anything she needed.

Morgan was glad when they all left. Her mom offered to spend the night but Morgan requested she leave as well. Joe had already agreed to stay. Joe had left the room to make some calls and was just returning as the clan was leaving. He promised Ellie he would look after Morgan and Joey until she returned in the morning.

Joe asked Morgan if she felt like getting a little exercise and offered to take her for a spin around the maternity ward. Morgan moved slowly and grabbed her robe. She thought she should take advantage of the opportunity since the baby nurse had just taken Joey to the nursery. They chatted about anything and everything as they walked down the hall. She told Joe she had never had a friend like him and wanted him to know she loved him.

"I'll always be here for you, if you need me. Besides, Neil is on call all night. He's staying at the hospital tonight. Your son has good timing; he gave us both something to do. The nurse already told me the chair in your room becomes a cot. It's all set up, so I may as well stay, right?"

"I'm glad for your company, partner," holding his hand a little tighter.

The months were passing quickly; Joe and Neil were spending a lot of time with Morgan and Joey. They often dropped by and would end up spending the night so Morgan could get some much needed sleep. As time passed, Joe was becoming concerned for Morgan, as was the rest of her family, but no one knew what to do. They had just put Joey down for his nap when Joe heard Morgan cry out in her sleep, as he had numerous times. Apparently she had been dreaming about Gage. It broke Joe's heart, watching his friend in so much pain at a time when she should be celebrating. He worried about her since Gage had been missing for over a year. Even Joe doubted the possibility of receiving good news since so much time had passed. If constant reports of beheadings in Syria frightened him, he could only imagine how scared Morgan was on a daily basis.

The body they had found so long ago was still unidentifiable. DNA results were inconclusive. Since teeth were missing they had nothing to compare dental records with. Fingertips had been removed. There was no one available for DNA comparison since Gage hadn't any family, until Joey was born. John didn't want to approach Morgan about allowing anyone to take samples from Joey. He did that on his own. He took a hair sample from Joey and dropped it off at the lab himself.

Joe and Neil wished there was something they could do for their friend. "Maybe we should wake her up?" they asked each other at the same time. Morgan needed sleep more than anything. Neil went to the foot of the bed and rubbed her leg, hoping to sooth her and push her nightmares away. Neil knew Gage was in her dreams and from the sounds she made, he knew her dreams weren't sweet and soothing.

Chapter Fifteen

Morgan dressed Joey for their morning walk on the beach. The time was flying by even faster after bringing Joey home from the hospital. The family had been busy celebrating one important event after another. The first party was Jake's homecoming, the next his wedding, followed by baby showers and christenings. Everything took place in just a few months.

It had been over a year now since they had heard anything about Gage. John and Jake constantly tried to find out what they could, but to no avail. She suspected John knew more than he was letting on but she didn't press him. Morgan tried to keep upbeat and, for the most part, she was able to keep up the façade for her parent's sake. But when she went home at night, after putting Joey to bed, her tears were her only company; she cried until she fell asleep. Gage was there each night in her dreams and he would brush those tears away, promising her that things would get better. Sometimes, she thought she was going insane because her dreams seemed so real. She didn't want to give up the dream time she spent with Gage, even if she knew in her heart he was trying to say good bye. He told her often it was time for him to go home.

Morgan was spending a lot of time with Reigh since Jake had gone back to the Middle East. She knew he had been in Syria searching for any sign of Gage. His unit was given details about where Gage might be but Jake hadn't found him yet. Morgan and her new sister-in-law had a common bond these days. It was great to have someone to talk to who would understand her situation and not judge her. Watching the babies babbling together was an extra bonus; they were too young to realize the joy they brought to Reigh and Morgan as they helped to relieve their daily tensions.

Reigh told Morgan that Jake had promised her that he would not take any unnecessary risks in Syria, but she suspected he would do what he had to in order to accomplish his mission. Morgan knew Jake had less than a month before he would be returning home, hopefully with news about Gage.

Jake's security firm was already up and running, thanks to the family. Reigh believed he would have a lot more work than he could actually handle. Jake had gone into business with Patrick Dorman; a retired police captain he had known from the neighborhood. Patrick had already hired ten new employees in addition to the fifteen they started with. The recent hires, retired police officers and ex-military men and women, were enjoying their new employment and the camaraderie that they each shared. Reigh was excited for Jake, knowing he would be happy that the company was growing so fast. He had been concerned about starting a company while he was still in the military but it seemed he had chosen wisely. His business partner had seen to it that the business flourished during his absence. The question on everyone's mind was when is Jake coming back? Alas, the answer was anyone's guess.

"Hey, little guy. I love you. Do you want to go and see grandma now?" Morgan asked as she bundled Joey up and headed to her parents' house. She loved the way her four-month-old boy looked at her with so much trust and adoration. Morgan hadn't thought it was possible to love a child again after losing Michael, but loving Joey came easy to her. She talked to Joey about Michael and his dad almost every day. Sometimes it looked like he knew what she was talking about. She would check the baby monitor often and see Joey cooing and smiling, as if he saw someone standing next to his crib.

She prayed to Michael often, to ask the angels to keep Joey healthy and keep Gage safe. She knew Michael was with her, she could feel his presence. But it always felt as if there was an adult presence as well. She thought she could feel the feather of a touch of a larger hand on her face or her shoulder, usually when she was feeling vulnerable or scared. It was easier to talk about Michael and Gage. Morgan chalked that up to a feeling she had, knowing Michael was there with her and Joey, even if only in spirit.

"I want Daddy to come home, Michael. Please find him and keep him safe, my little angel," she whispered as if he was really there. Suddenly, she felt as if someone had covered her hand with his or her own. It was strange; she had never felt anything as clearly as that before. Then the weirdest thing happened, she felt the touch of this larger hand on her cheek.

As tears flowed and her heart broke, she whispered, *"Gage, I know it's you. I can feel you. You promised to come home to us. If I feel you it means only one thing, you're not coming home, are you?"* She wanted to believe that Gage was still alive and trying to reach out to her, but this felt different.

"I don't know what to do, Gage. I miss you so much and I worry that I'm not dealing with everything the way I should. I'm ready to make a life for me and Joey and I know now it will have to be without you." She wiped the tears from her eyes, picked her little boy up and hugged him a little closer. Morgan put Joey in his car seat and buckled him in tight before grabbing his diaper bag and heading to the car. After placing him in the backseat and assuring he was nestled in, she sat in the driver's seat and continued her conversation with Gage, "People must think I'm crazy when I talk to you, Gage. I need to hear something, anything. The unknown is worse than anything I've ever imagined."

The trip to her mom's this morning seemed longer and Morgan thought a walk on the beach might help to relieve her of the sudden anxiety she was feeling. She didn't know what had brought it on, except that perhaps it had something to do with fact that Gage hadn't appeared in her dreams since he had told her it was time for him to go home. She wondered if it was an omen but she didn't want to think about it. She had never felt his touch on her face before when she was fully awake. His touch made her wonder if he was no longer present in this world. *Could he be with Michael?* She was afraid for Gage, for the first time in a long time she was losing faith. *Maybe a walk on the beach will help me to clear my head, anything to get rid of this feeling of hopelessness.* She parked the car in the driveway and her mother came rushing out of the house to greet them and help her.

"Mom, would you mind keeping an eye on Joey for about half an hour? I want to go for a walk on the beach. I need to clear my head," touching her brow, knowing her mother would take the baby.

"You know, Morgan, you're not in this alone. It's been over a year and although I know you don't want to hear it, you may have to prepare yourself for the worst, if not for your sake, then for Joey. In time, it will get easier. Every time you look into Joey's eyes you'll remember Gage and Michael. Sweetie, they'll be happy memories, I promise," she said taking the baby from Morgan. "If you need anything at all, we're always here for you."

"I always believed if he was dead I would know it somehow, in here," indicating the spot in her heart where she kept him alive. She followed her mother into the house, dropped her bags on the table, unbuttoned Joey's coat and placed him in the crib. Joey instantly began to play with the soft hanging toys swinging just above him. She thanked her mother again for taking Joey, left the house and headed for the beach. Morgan made her way down to the water's edge and picked up a few shells along the way. She and Gage had walked this beach on numerous occasions, too many to count. It had been one of their favorite things to do. They felt close to Michael on the beach. Morgan looked at the seagulls and watched as they glided through the air. She wanted to believe when everyone said the pain would get easier to bear for her it would but somehow she doubted it ever would. Michael was gone and now she wondered whether Gage had joined Michael as well.

One night while at her sister's house, after Gage had been missing a year, it was suggested that she start dating again but Morgan got irate and stormed out of the house. Gage wasn't dead, she would never believe that. That had been two months ago and now Morgan admitted to herself that she was losing her faith in him returning. She loved Gage with all her heart and didn't want to give up on him because, truth be told, he had never given up on her, though many thought he had. Wherever he was, she was sure he was trying to make it back to her and she would be here waiting for him when he did. But she couldn't stop thinking the same thing over and over. *Why didn't Gage come to me in my dreams? Is he in trouble?* Morgan was sure he would have found a way into her dreams if he could. Then there was the touch that she had felt. It was all so very confusing. She had been walking back to the house when she plopped down on the sand and stared at the ocean. After a few minutes, she closed her eyes and was able to relax. Suddenly, she heard a familiar voice, she turned she couldn't believe her eyes. Gage looked different. *Why does he look that way?* He smiled and asked her if she'd like to take a walk.

"Sure, does anyone else know you're here?" They continued walking down the empty shoreline.

"I stopped in and saw Joey. He's beautiful, Morgan. I'm so glad you have him. I need you to do something important for me. Ask John to get in contact with a friend of mine, Nick Manetti; he may go by the name Pete Scali. He was C.I.A., I'm not sure if he still is but I need you to find him." Gage smiled as he brushed the hair from her face. "I want you to remember that I love you more than anything in this world. I am so grateful for all the time we've had together. We've shared a lifetime of love, Morgan. Remember that. Forever and Always, always and forever, remember me."

Morgan grew concerned, *Why, is he saying these things to me?* "Who is Nick Manetti? Why is it so important that John find him?"

"I asked Nick to do something for me and I don't think he'll forgive me or himself for asking it of him. I know he did what I asked and I want you to thank him for me, tell him not to feel guilty. There is nothing to feel guilty about. Can you remember all that?" Gage was being mysterious; Morgan was fighting to understand why. As they turned and headed back toward home, Gage whispered something in her ear and Morgan became startled. It was something he always said to her when he was leaving. "*Forever and always,*" he whispered again. She usually responded, *always and forever.*

"…Hey, you! Morgan heard a voice from a few feet away. She was startled. *Did I fall asleep?* She turned and noticed that Logan had joined them on the beach. "Mom said I would find you down here. Do you want some company?"

"Can you believe it?" she joked, pointing to Gage. The love of her life had come back to her. Only Gage wasn't there now. He had disappeared. *Where did he go? Did I imagine he was there?* Morgan was scared. Her heart began to beat heavily against her chest. Suddenly, she put it all together. Gage was gone for sure. She knew she had fallen asleep and he was saying good bye to her the only way he knew how. She had just had a conversation with her dead husband. She didn't know why or how Gage had died but she knew, in her heart for sure, that he was gone.

"Can I believe what?"

"Nothing, I was just thinking out loud," she said, tears just beneath the surface. She had to figure out why it was so important to Gage that she locate Nick what's-his-name and tell him Gage forgave him. But forgave him, for what? As soon as she went back to the house, she would have to write down the two names Gage given her. Nick Manetti and Pete Scali. Who was Nick Manetti and what did he have to do with Gage? For now, this would have to remain her secret. *I can't even tell Logan.*

"Mom was worried about you. Are you sure you're ok?" He was puzzled by the look on her face. They walked a little further in silence until Logan picked up a seashell and flung it into the water, watching as it skimmed along the surface. They did this as kids just to see whose shell would stay on top the longest.

"Still the champion, I see." Morgan didn't want to think about the reality of the situation any longer. She had a son and if what she suspected was true, she'd be raising him alone. She was sure she had seen Gage for the last time. She would attend to his last wishes.

Logan knew something was different today. There hadn't been word about Gage in a long time and he had a bad feeling; Morgan was acting very different today. "Joey is getting so big. I can't believe how fast the time has gone. Remember when Mom and Dad would say time flies faster the older you get? Well, I'm beginning to believe it. It seems like only yesterday that I might have had to make a trip to Hollywood to defend your honor."

Logan laughed, put his hand under her chin and raised her head so he could look into her eyes. "Are you *really sure everything is ok? I'm here for you; if you want to scream,* we have the whole beach to ourselves."

Morgan didn't want to share with him what just happened to her, not yet. She needed to make sense of what had just happened first and then speak to John. She needed to see if Nick Manetti existed, find out who he was and what connection he had with Gage.

"I'm fine, let's head back. I'm sure Mom is worried." When they reached the house, Joey was busy playing with his toys and her dad and mom were preparing lunch in the kitchen. Logan reached over his dad's shoulder and took the sandwich he had just prepared. Logan took a bite and told him that it was good before trying to hand it back.

"Keep it," their father said before turning to Morgan.

"Morgan, would you like a sandwich? I'll make it for you while I make another for myself," her Dad teased him as he smacked the back of Logan's head.

"No, I'm not hungry. Is John working today, do you know?"

"I believe he's home today…" Just as Joe McCleary was finishing his sentence, John came walking through the front door.

"Lunch, good, I'm starving," he said as he kissed his mother, then Morgan and shook his dad's hand before hugging him. "What's going on?" he said while he sat in a chair opposite Logan.

No one said anything but he could tell something was up. Their mom and dad spoke simultaneously as they told John Morgan had been asking for him. He turned to Morgan. She told him she wanted to talk to him in private.

"Let's go to Dad's office," he said curiously. John knew Morgan had a close relationship with Logan and he was surprised to see that Logan didn't have a clue.

John closed the door and he and Morgan sat on the couch. "I'm not sure where to start. You're going to think I'm crazy but I need to ask you to do a favor for me. Can you use your connections to find someone for me?"

I wonder what this is all about. "Who do you want me to find and why?"

"His name is Nick Manetti. He went by the name Pete Scali, he was C.I.A." John would surely want to know the reason she wanted him to find Nick Manetti but how could she answer that question. My husband, oh, by the way, I know you haven't found him yet but I know Gage is dead. He asked me to do this one last favor for him. *How crazy does that sound?*

"How do know Nick Manetti?"

"John, I've never asked you to do anything for me before. Please, do not ask me why I need to find Nick Manetti. I'm not sure you would understand my reason for looking for him." Morgan watched John mull over what she had just said. His face told her that he chose to trust her for now. He would find out what he could today and get back to her. If Nick Manetti was out there, he would find him. He had only recently given them Joey's DNA. John was hoping staff would process it quickly to see if it matched the DNA from the unidentified remains from Syria. And if it was Gage, and he hoped it wasn't, they would know.

John chose to keep this to himself as he said, "I'm going into the office this afternoon to check on something. While I'm there I'll look up Nick Manetti and see what I come up with. I'll come by tonight if I find anything." John wondered if the time had come to give Gage's letter to Morgan. He was to give it to her if anything went wrong and it seemed that Gage was running out of time. He would return tonight with the letter and hopefully the information she asked him for.

John and Morgan joined the others in the kitchen. While everyone enjoyed small talk and lunch, Ellie could see her daughter was preoccupied. She prayed every night for news about Gage. Even if the news was bad, it could and would be dealt with. Constantly living in limbo was not good for Morgan. When everyone was finished, Morgan announced she needed to get Joey home and had other things to do.

Logan asked if he could hang out later and Morgan agreed. She had shared a lot with Logan and she had to admit he never judged her, not even when she told him about her Gage dreams. She had always thought Gage would find his way home to her. After today's dream on the beach, she seriously doubted her conviction.

Things were complicated enough without trying to explain some of the things she had shared with Logan to anyone else, especially the family. They would never believe her if she told them she believed the bond she and Gage shared was so strong that he would find a way to communicate with her *even if he had indeed passed on. Just thinking about that, it even sounds crazy to me! No one will believe me, not even Logan.* She would have to decide what to tell Logan later. She didn't feel like she was going crazy. Knowing she had a name, Nick Manetti, made Gage's appearance to her more real. Joey needed her to be stable and somehow she had to do that and still keep her promise to Gage.

Logan came by as promised just as she put Joey to bed. She invited him in and they went directly to the deck overlooking the ocean. They set the table for dinner and Logan poured wine. The surf was unusually calm; they both sat and reveled in its beauty, talking about the house, Gage and happier times. While they talked, Morgan's agonized. *How should I begin this conversation with Logan? I know he's worried about me.*

"I'm fine Logan. I know you're wondering what I was thinking about today on the beach," she said, as her voice quavered slightly. "I was thinking about my future. I've decided to go back to the office two days a week. Perhaps for no other reason than to keep myself busy. If I spent two days a week helping Alex, maybe I could get my imagination revved up enough to begin to write again. I've had a mental writing block lately. Maybe I could write at night after I put Joey to bed. I'm sure Alex has had his hands full for the past few months without me. I bet he could use the help."

Logan listened patiently. *I think that's a good idea.* But he was glad Alex hired new help rather than expecting anything from Morgan after the baby was born, as he had originally planned. He had heard that Alex had been interviewing potential prospects for the assistant's job but he hadn't followed up with him to see if he had found anyone yet. Logan knew Alex kept in touch with Morgan but didn't know if he had mentioned looking for an assistant.

Logan wracked his brain to try to think of ways to help Morgan with her issues. He knew the secret she was hiding from the rest of the family. He knew Morgan believed Gage came to her in her dreams and that he had found a way to keep in touch with her. *For the time being, I won't let them know her secret but if things get out of hand I will insist that she seek professional help.*

They talked some more and slowly the conversation drifted toward more pressing matters…Somehow, she was going to have to cope with her black hole. All she asked in return was that Logan supports her and not gives up on her. She promised that if she needed help she would get it, but then she asked that he trust her judgment. *Maybe there is some merit to what she believes. If she believes Gage comes to her in her dreams, who am I to doubt her. If there is a way for that to happen, I'm sure Gage can make it happen.* It's a crazy notion, but if it helps my sister cope, so be it. He was perplexed. *How will this story end?* But for now he would support Morgan's theory, *even if she decided not to tell him about it.*

Logan decided to talk about lighter fare. "Mom tells me your agent called with news that your last book made the top ten on the Bestseller list. You must be ecstatic. Do you think they'll make this one into a movie?" Logan asked to lighten the mood. He had read Morgan's books and saw the first movie, although he usually didn't care for romances. He was into Sci-fi mostly but he wanted to support her. *But I do think Morgan's novels are intriguing.* He envied the way her mind worked and how she was able to tell stories with multiple plotlines and still keep it all flowing. It was amazing, how she strung all those thoughts together without getting mixed up. He certainly couldn't have done it. He was really happy that she had found her niche.

"I believe Michele mentioned that there was a strong possibility that this book would become a movie, too. She's in negotiations right now but until she gets the number she feels I deserve, she's keeping our options open. So far, she hasn't done wrong by me. Michele Ruggerio turned out to be the best agent I could've asked for. I trust her completely. She's negotiating with the same producer I worked with on my last project. He's very interested in buying the rights to my latest book to create a screenplay and he wants me to be on set to help ensure authenticity, just like the last time. It's really very exciting." When Michele had first told her the news, she wasn't sure she could attempt anything of that magnitude again, but it would certainly take her mind off Gage, if only for a little while. She told Michele she would have to think about it, now that she had Joey. Arrangements would have to be made for Joey's care while she was on set and she wasn't sure yet how she felt about spending so much time away from him. The producer was offering a lot of money and perks so she didn't know what to do. Her saving grace was that the movie would be filmed in New York City, so she could commute from home. He had even agreed to have a car take her to and from her home each day.

"I think you should take it. It's an added bonus, knowing that you would be in New York for the filming, and besides, you know we could all help out. What reason could you possibly come up with not to do this?" he pleaded with her as he waited for her reply.

There was no reason for her to turn down the offer. It would certainly help advance her career, if she decided to accept. The producer had already been in touch with her personally to go over some of his ideas, who he thought best to play the main characters and what he might change to bring the story to the big screen. Morgan had to admit that Wesley Jordan had a gift; she believed in him and his vision. He could definitely bring her ideas to fruition on the big screen. With another one of her books being turned into a movie, her future as a writer would be assured. Wesley had a way of maintaining the authenticity of her work. For that, she was grateful. She had always said she would work with him again if given the opportunity.

"Maybe you're right, Logan. It would help if I was to keep busy. Between the baby, the movie and helping out at the office I think I might be kept busy enough. Don't you agree?" she asked, adding, "By the way, you would be thrilled to know Wesley is thinking about allowing Callie Hayden to play the lead." Morgan smiled, as she glanced at the shocked look on Logan's face. Everyone knew Logan had the biggest crush on Callie Hayden and for the longest time. The family had teased him often enough and told him to get over her, he hadn't a chance of meeting her, let alone wooing her.

"Don't go there, Morgan, but if you can swing an introduction, it would be greatly appreciated." Logan gave Morgan a playful come hither look. She laughed and told Logan he was quite the womanizer.

She added, "If you're searching for a good woman, look close by, right under your nose."

"What do you mean?" he asked, extremely confused by her last statement.

Morgan didn't want to tell Logan anything about Lizzy, his chef. What Lizzy felt for Logan was private and she had asked Morgan not to say anything to him. Morgan promised herself she would only interfere if it took Logan too long to figure things out for himself. She knew Lizzy had completed law school and she certainly didn't need to work nights at McCleary's. Lizzy was patiently waiting for Logan to come to his senses.

In the meantime, it was good to have Logan around for moral support. She would call Michele and tell her to take Jordan's offer and would let Alex know she had decided not to come back to the office.

Morgan decided to call Alex right away while it was on her mind. Logan waited patiently while she was on the phone with him. She had no idea until she called Alex that he had already hired a personal assistant. Jordan Winters was working out better than he thought because it freed him to do a lot of the field work he enjoyed most about his job. He told Morgan that when Gage returned, he would suggest Jordan Winters stay on permanently. Hopefully he would be an asset to Gage and with Jordan's help; he and Gage could have personal lives of their own. Jordan was more than willing to stay on, he loved it and he was learning a lot. He told Alex he had heard about Gage and was looking forward to meeting and working with him. Morgan ended her conversation with Alex feeling better than she expected. *Gage always told me I shouldn't sweat the small stuff worrying about work.*

"What did you mean on the beach today when you came out with that weird statement?" Logan finally asked.

"I know this is going to sound insane, Logan. I want you to know up front that I am perfectly capable of thinking coherently. I was just going down to the beach to clear my head. You know how I tell you I see Gage in my dreams?" Logan acknowledged that she had indeed told him as much. "I didn't dream about Gage last night. I woke with the oddest feeling of loss and emptiness. I can't prove it, Logan, but now I believe Gage is gone. I think he came to me in my prior dreams because he didn't want me to fall apart and I believe he had something to do with the coroner not being able to identify that body until he felt I was ready to hear the news. I know that sounds crazy but I can't help this feeling I get. I believe Gage has been dead for a long time. He stayed with me in the only way he knew wouldn't frighten me, in my dreams. I believe he stayed for as long as I needed him to stay," she said with such conviction.

Logan continued to listen and said nothing. He didn't know what to say to her. He wasn't a shrink but this whole situation was getting weird. He knew there was more to her story and that she was holding back for one reason or the other. "I know there's more, spit it out. There is *nothing you could say that would be any weirder than what you've already told me.*"

"I saw Gage in a dream at the beach today. I think it was his way of saying good-bye. But, what was really strange was what he asked me to do." Logan stared at his sister in shock. Whatever it was she thought she saw, obviously she believed it. "He gave me the name of an agent he worked with, asked me to find him and tell him he forgave him since he only did what Gage had asked him to do. I don't know what he meant by that but I asked John to find the agent for me; he said he would and try to get back to me tonight."

He doubted that John was told the whole story. John would've called a family meeting so they could get together and get Morgan some help. His phone was ringing, interrupting his thoughts. It was John and he sounded weird.

"Logan, are you with Morgan?" John sounded panicked.

"Yes, what's up?" He told Morgan he was going to continue the call in the other room. He told Morgan there was a problem at McCleary's. He didn't want to frighten her. "What's going on?" Logan asked John in a whisper.

John thought about the report he had just received from Quantico. He couldn't imagine the night he and Logan were about to face. "Do you remember the body that was found mutilated in the desert? They suspected the person had been tortured to death?" There was silence for a good twenty-five seconds while John found his voice. "It was Gage. How the hell are we going to tell Morgan? We sent her husband to his death, Logan. I feel responsible for his torture. How the hell do I live with that?" Logan stood in shock as tears streamed down his face. Gage was like a brother and if everything that John was telling him was true, Gage had suffered a horrific death because they asked him to search for Jake. John repeated what the report told him, trying to form the words as his throat was constricted with grief. The sad news cut them both to the core.

"They cut him into pieces, Logan. The bastards made sure he suffered every last second of his life. The report said he was shot in the head right between the eyes but the body had too much damage and there wasn't much left to know if the bullet was fired before or after the torture. They assume after. Whoever did this to him wanted to inflict the most pain possible. How do we tell her? How do we tell, Jake?" he asked in a whimper.

Chapter Sixteen

Morgan wondered what was taking Logan so long. As soon as she saw Logan with tears streaming down his face, she knew she had been right all along. She knew he had just found out what Gage had confirmed to her earlier in the day. He was gone. *Now what do I do?* Gage was the love of her life and now he was gone. *How do I go on?* She didn't need Logan to say anything. She didn't want him to speak. Morgan walked out of the house and down to the beach. She knew Logan would respect her need to be alone, he would stay with Joey. The night was closing in, the sun was down on the horizon; the beach would be empty even if she needed to scream.

"What do I do now, Gage?" she asked him aloud. Suddenly, off in the distance, she saw a male figure heading her way and with him, a young boy. The young boy was running towards her. *Am I going crazy?* As the two got closer, she saw that it was Gage and a healthier more energetic Michael. Gage smiled as they approached. He knew she understood what seeing him and Michael together meant. He also knew she would find comfort and peace when she heard about his death officially, knowing he was with Michael.

"*You know you have to go on without us, don't you? Joey needs you. Michael and I have been with you for long enough; it's time for us to go. I need you to be strong babe. Joey needs you to be strong.*" She felt Gage's touch against her skin as he kissed her cheek. "*...Forever and always.* "He whispered.

Michael couldn't wait to talk to her. He tried to tell her about how healthy he felt and the people he had gotten to know and now that he had his Dad with him heaven was an even better place. He told her that all the pain was gone; he had no trouble running anymore. He never felt out of breath even. "I miss you, Mom. Dad says we'll see you again someday. He said Joey needs you now and we have to go back. Be happy, Mommy. I like when you smile at Joey." Michael looked happy.

"Morgan, I want you to be happy. I want you to live." Gage put Michael up on his shoulders and they began to walk away, but not before Gage uttered one last plea to her. "Don't forget to find Nick. Tell him I said thank you and there's nothing to forgive. He needs to hear that from you."

Morgan stared at the empty beach. She knew she would have to go back into the house and face Logan. By now she knew the family had been told and would be circling, but in a good way. *I wonder if anyone has been in touch with Jake yet.* He would be devastated by the news. She had to be strong for everyone because she had a distinct feeling that Jake, John and Logan were each going to blame themselves for Gage's death. Gage didn't blame *them and he certainly wanted Nick to know he forgave him. But for what, I wonder?*

As Morgan entered the house again she witnessed the tremendous amounts of pain and grief. John, Alex, Logan her Mom and Dad, as well as Patti and Bill and Reigh had all arrived to be there for her. She felt defeated, exhausted but somehow a little relieved as well. It was over; Gage was with Michael and that knowledge helped to soften the blow of Gage's death. As hard as going on without him was going to be, she had to find a way to pick up the pieces and go on. She had her son to think about and somehow she knew she was going to have to get through this. Just put one foot in front of the other, wasn't that what everyone always said. She heard a car slam on its brakes close to the front door and within seconds Joe came running through the door. He took one look at her and paused.

Joe looked around the room and thought the rest of the family seemed be dealing with the news a little differently than Morgan. She seemed almost too complacent. *What's going on?* He saw John in the dining room and he looked as though he was talking to Jake through via Skype. Joe was trying to take in everything around him and still stay focused on Morgan. He could hear Jake's torment through the computer. Jake let John know he would be home as soon as he could. He heard him ask about Morgan, John said he hadn't had a chance to talk to her yet.

He glanced over to Morgan again and was concerned by her seeming indifference. He couldn't talk to her with her family there but he knew he needed to get her alone. Joe stepped towards her and held out his arms. "I don't know what to say to you. How can I make it better for you?"

Morgan stepped toward him. "You can't. No one can, Joe. This is my new reality. I can't believe he's gone. One afternoon Joe, that's all I had with him, just one. Why didn't he stay?" She felt safe in his embrace and she knew Gage did what he did so Jake could live. *That's the kind of man Gage was.*

The next few days were a blur but somehow she made it through. She had been notified that there would be a star added to the wall in the lobby of C.I.A. headquarters for Gage Delaney. No fuss, no names, but she would know that one of stars belonged to Gage and someday she would take Joey to see it. The details about Gage's death were divulged slowly, a little at a time, and it hurt to know how much he had suffered at the end of his life. It was unimaginable that anyone would go to such lengths to make a person suffer. Morgan felt numb as they lowered Gage's coffin into the ground. It seemed ridiculous to have a coffin when there was so little left of him to bury. But Morgan went through the motions because it made it easier knowing he was with Michael. The funeral services were difficult for the rest of the family. She tried as hard as she could to relieve her brothers of the guilt they felt but she didn't think it was working.

After the funeral everyone went back to McCleary's. Joe insisted the staff talk to him about all the expenses. He didn't want any of the bills to go to Logan. He handled everything with Lizzy. Joe told her to spend whatever she needed. It was the least he could do, he said. All the friends, family and co-workers who attended Gage's farewell shindig filled McCleary's to bursting capacity. Even special agents attended. Joe wondered if they should even be there but they respected Gage Delaney too much not to risk attending. The family was numb; but after all the small talk and the stories it did lift their spirits somewhat. He worried most about the woman who was trying to be strong for them all.

Joe thought back to the eulogies that Jake and John delivered at the mass. They had repeated over and over again, through their tears, that Gage had been too young to die. His, life had been cut short too soon. Gage Delaney was a man who had so much to give and now we all will have to learn how to go on without him.

"Gage is with his son now," John said, and he hoped that offered some solace to Morgan during this awful time. John told stories, little snippets of the greatest love story he had ever known, the love story between his sister, Morgan, and her hero husband, Gage Delaney. He had never seen two people who loved each other more than they did. Throughout everything that happened in their lives they never lost sight of the love they shared with each other. Sometimes life was pretty cruel to them but their love never faltered.

Jake's eulogy was more of the same, although he added how much he and his unit learned from the man they had once referred to as a super soldier.

Logan stood up unexpectedly, after Jake was finished, and asked if he could say a few words. He lightened the mood with funny lighthearted stories of Gage, the man who would want them to remember him and smile. "He would want all of us to celebrate his life. Think of something that Gage did that made you smile or laugh. I'm sure everyone can think of at least one thing. This is what Gage would want you to do as we say good-bye to him. Smile and remember my friend, my brother. Gage Delaney will always hold a place in our hearts and when we recall a memory of him, let it be with a smile. This is who Gage was." Logan hesitated and smiled, recalling a memory of Gage he held close to his heart before returning to his seat.

Morgan smiled at Logan and mouthed the words, *Thank you* to him. *Logan is right; this is the way Gage would have wanted to go out, with funny stories and memories shared by all who attended and a party to celebrate his life. Gage had led a very fruitful life so there were a lot of stories and tributes told throughout the day.* Morgan loved it. As the crowd began to dissipate, Morgan looked for John. She still had one promise to fulfill and she was going to do everything in her power to do it as quickly as possible.

John was sitting in a corner wishing there was something he could say to Morgan to make this day a little easier for her, but he was at a loss for words. John thought about Gage being honored with a star on the wall at C.I.A. headquarters but no one would see it or know why he received such a distinction. He thought about the men and women who had died in service to their country, the men and women no one heard about because their identity had to be kept secret for the safety of others. John stood off to the side and lifted his glass in salutation to the brother he loved. He and Gage had always had a strange relationship. John was always waiting for Gage to hurt Morgan but he never did. He had to admit he had never seen any man love a woman as much as Gage loved Morgan. As John looked up, he saw Morgan coming toward him and froze.

"It's been a tough day for everyone," she said as she sat down beside him. "Do you remember that favor I asked?" Morgan watched John wipe a tear from his eye as he tried to regain his composure. Being the person Morgan was, she ignored the tear. John was always the controlled one. He wouldn't want anyone to see him lose his cool or be compassionate. It soothed her weary soul knowing how he really felt about Gage.

"Yes, as a matter of fact, I just got word from Gage's handler that Nick Manetti was an agent up until about six months ago. He said when things went south with Gage, Pete Scali a.k.a. Nick Manetti, held it together for about six months after Gage died. But he fell apart and couldn't do the job any longer. Apparently, they were close and Gage's death hit him real hard. He lost his edge, in his line of work that's very dangerous, so he resigned. No one has heard from him since. The handler said Nick and Gage were like brothers. Did you know that? One of their mutual friends said that when Gage died, Nick just lost it. What makes you ask about him anyway? I didn't know Gage spoke to you about other agents."

Why am I really asking? But she knew she had to see this promise through to the end. Gage had his reasons for wanting her to contact this man and she hoped she would find out what they were, and soon. She would ask John for one more favor. She had to locate Nick Manetti.

"I need to find him, John." She could see by the look on his face that he wasn't comfortable doing what she was asking him to do without knowing why. He needed to hear the whole story and whether he believed her or not, she would have to convince him that it was what Gage had wanted.

Joe, Logan and Jake sat together, watching the conversation taking place between John and Morgan, wondering why John had an extreme look of bewilderment on his face. John didn't believe in ghosts or spirits but there was no other way to explain how Morgan knew about Agent Manetti. Absolutely no one was privy to that information. Apparently Gage's handler had given him his undercover name, Pete Scali. John had his doubts whether he could find him but he owed Gage that much at least. "I'll put in a call tomorrow and find out his last known address; maybe we'll get lucky. What are you going to say to him if and when we do find him?"

Morgan had no idea how Nick Manetti would respond what to she had to say to him. She would find him and perhaps he could clarify things for her. It wasn't much for John to go on but Morgan hoped it was enough. Nick Manetti had answers and she wanted them.

John reached into his pocket and took out the letter Gage had asked him to hold for her. He was to give it to her when all hope was gone. "Gage asked me to give this to you when we were certain he wasn't coming home. If you want I'll leave you alone to read it." Morgan looked down at the envelope and pulled it up to her chest and took a deep breath. This letter contained Gage's last words to her.

Dearest Morgan,

You were and always will be my Forever & Always. If you are reading this letter, I will never get the chance to tell you in person how much I love you. I will never be able to tell you what our last moments together meant to me. Holding you in my arms and making love to you made me feel whole again. I have loved you from the first moment I set eyes on you and time didn't change that. If anything I loved you more. I didn't believe in love until you walked into my life. It was as if my soul had been searching for you and gave a sigh of relief when our eyes met. We had that forever kind of love Morgan. It's rare to find your soul mate but we managed to do it. If you're reading this though, it means that I won't be coming home. I made the decision to go to Syria and I don't want you or anyone else to feel any guilt for the decision I made. I knew the risk. I want you to be happy Morgan. Don't give up on life. Be happy, live for us both. Find solace that I'm with Michael. Until we meet again, I want you to be happy.

Forever & Always,

Gage

Morgan had tears in her eyes as she pressed the letter to her chest again. It was weird but she felt at peace. She knew that Gage had come to her so that he could soften the blow of his death. Seeing him and Michael together was comforting and it made hearing the news of his death easier to deal with. Michael had Gage to look after him now and that was comforting. She would cherish this letter from Gage forever and would be grateful for their time together.

John put feelers out as soon as he arrived at the office. He ran Nick Manetti's name through every search engine available but whoever Nick Manetti was, he didn't want to be found. He had to be going under an alias; that would make it difficult to find him. John knew Nick Manetti was a professional spy and if he didn't want to be found he would be impossible to locate. John tried everything; he even called in all favors owed him. Before you could say Nick Manetti, everyone was looking for him as a favor to John McCleary. There wasn't a soul in law enforcement or the military who didn't know who Gage Delaney was and what he gave for this country so everyone was more than willing to do this favor for John.

Chapter Seventeen

Morgan had just attended the last party for the debut of the movie based on her last book. It had been a year for highs and lows and she was glad the year was finally coming to a close. Joey was growing by leaps and bounds and he was super healthy. She had come to terms with the way her life had turned out. Even though she felt guilty about not being able to fulfill her promise to Gage, she was content for the first time in a long time. She may never find Nick Manetti but it wasn't from lack of trying. Hoping on the off chance that she would get lucky, she had looked for him in every town and city she had visited this past year.

Morgan surprised everyone when she accepted Logan's invitation to spend New Year's Eve at the McCleary's annual gala. Joe and Neil agreed to attend the party as well. Ellie McCleary was thrilled to babysit for all the grandchildren if it meant Morgan might finally get out and enjoy herself. She and Joe would plan the night for all the kids; it would be something they would remember forever. This was a celebration for everyone and a new beginning for others.

Joe and Neil took one look at the woman coming down the staircase and started to howl. She was beautiful. Morgan looked radiant in the black number she was calling a dress. "Wow!" they said simultaneously. "I don't think you'll be alone at midnight."

Morgan laughed; it felt good to laugh for a change. She didn't know if going to McCleary's was a good idea but she was ready to start over, she had been ready for a while. Gage was with Michael and she was content with that. Tonight would mark the beginning of her new life.

Nick Manetti bought two tickets to McCleary's New Year's Eve celebration so he could find out who was searching for him. He had been living in the Colorado Mountains for one and half years with his closest neighbors being a hundred miles away. To say he lived a secluded life was an understatement.

It had been two years since Gage had died and he still felt haunted by the memory of seeing what happened to Gage. The guilt was still tearing him apart and he didn't know if he would ever get over what Gage had asked him to do. Gage had asked him to shadow him on his latest mission. If he signaled him, he was to take the shot. Gage had said 'ask no questions, just shoot'. Nick stuck around for longer than he should have after firing the kill shot. He watched in horror, stricken to the core by what they had done to his mentor, his friend and his brother. Nick had never been squeamish in his life but he threw up that day. Gage had been right. Isis had wanted to torture him and if they were able to capture him alive that was what he knew they would've done. They had him and were prepared to take their time as they tortured him. Gage had taken that pleasure away from them by having Nick do the unthinkable.

Who are the McCleary family and what do they want from me? He no longer went by the name Nick Manetti or Pete Scali. He was greeted at the door by a bouncer who checked his ticket and asked him where his girlfriend was. At first Nick didn't know what he was talking about, but then he remembered he had purchased two tickets for the night's festivities. He had forgotten about that. He didn't want anyone to be suspicious about why he had arrived in town and he knew his story would be a little more believable if he'd had a lady friend. He told the bouncer to give the other ticket away since he didn't have a significant other, not anymore. The bouncer handed him a funny hat, a horn and wished him well. "There are a lot of single ladies to choose from," he stated with a grin. *Could things be any crazier?*

He found himself a stool at the end of the bar and ordered a drink. He decided to keep tabs on the people coming and going and get a better feel for the McCleary's. The guy behind the bar looks like he's in charge of the place. He watched the man greet a few of the patrons, take note who was who in this one group then move on to another. He tried not to make eye contact, especially with the woman sitting across the bar. He thought she was trying to make eye contact with him. He studied her on the sly, and obviously she was checking him. He knew he had to stay focused on the mission. *She's hot and her friends aren't too bad either.* The idea being part of a couple made him laugh.

Nick Manetti didn't think he was a one woman man but then he didn't think Gage had been one either. For a moment; he allowed his mind to wonder. *When we were younger we were a force to be reckoned with. Women weren't safe around us.* At least their virtues weren't safe. He and Gage were more the 'love them and leave them' sort of guys. Nothing distracted them from their end game. They were going to be the best in their fields and they had accomplished that. They'd had no time to have a family. *We were each other's family.* He hadn't met Gage's wife and he hoped he never would. *I know Gage loved the woman almost to the point of obsession.* Nick had been happy for Gage. *Maybe someday I'll find a woman who will rock my world, just as Gage had.*

He didn't like where his thoughts were taking him. Gage's wife was out there somewhere and she was a widow because he put a bullet between her husband's eyes from a distance, killing him with one shot. He was a trained sniper, one of the best. But no matter how he tried to rationalize what he did, Nick couldn't forgive himself for killing the one person he loved like a brother. He had killed his brother. He had killed many men and women but his last shot would live with him forever. *Why didn't Gage ask me to kill the other men there?* I might have been able to kill the leader and three of the other men before they realized what was happening. But Gage assured him that if he gave the signal, it was because there was no other way. He had wanted him to take the shot and just walk away, not hang around.

"Mom, are you sure you're able to handle all the kids?" Morgan asked, as she joined Joe and Neil. "I'll stay home if you want?"

"Don't be silly. The girls are old enough to watch themselves and your little guy is already in bed for the night. How much easier can you make it for us?" Ellie McCleary was looking forward to a quiet night, making popcorn and watching movies with the girls. Jake had Reigh's family in town so her mother was taking care of Michaela while Jake and Reigh took her younger brother, Matt to McCleary's. It was going to be a nice evening for everyone.

"Go and enjoy yourselves. I don't want hear another word. …Out the door now, all of you. Morgan, take care of yourself and sleep in tomorrow before you come here for Joey."

"Your Mother is quite the character," Neil teased. "I'm glad we decided to attend the McCleary's shindig tonight. It'll be fun; I'm looking forward to it."

Logan was talking to Alex about all the plans Lizzy had to enhance business. *Lizzy is the best thing that has happened to me in a long time.* McCleary's was doing better than he hoped, thanks to Lizzy's suggestions. He was even thinking about buying the building next door and expanding. He had talked to Alex about the expansion and he was looking forward to handling it for Logan. Alex glanced over at Lizzy. *She's beautiful, that red dress is smoking hot. Why hadn't he noticed Lizzy before?* Alex turned to Logan and saw the way Logan was looking at Lizzy; suddenly Alex realized his big brother was thinking the same thing. *It's funny, but she was always right under his nose and just now was he was taking an interest. Obviously Lizzy only had eyes for Logan because she was oblivious to the eyes on her at the moment.* "Weird… I never noticed the attraction between you two until now."

"What did you say?" Alex didn't answer him because Logan wasn't paying attention to him at the moment. His attention was focused on Lizzy. He wasn't focused on business right now.

Why does Lizzy give so much of her time to McCleary's when she has a great career at a Manhattan law firm? He recalled Morgan mentioning something similar to him just the other day. *Could Lizzy really be interested in me?* Logan felt as if he'd just been smacked in the back of his head. *Why didn't I see it before?*

McCleary's New Year's Eve celebration had been her idea. He had decided to close the restaurant and host the biggest bash McCleary's had ever had. They were packed and there was not a ticket to be found. He looked around the room and then back to Lizzy, they both smiled at each other from a distance. Tonight was obviously going well and he had her to thank for it. He tried to make his way to Lizzy but he was stopped with every step he took. He was seeing Lizzy in a different light and he had to admit he liked what he saw. It wasn't the dress, although she looked amazing in it. Lizzy seemed different, she had an air of confidence about her that he hadn't noticed before. He could see that by the way she was handling herself. *Maybe I should reevaluate my relationship with Lizzy.*

Nick Manetti also took notice of the puzzled look on Logan McCleary's face as he looked at the woman who had just walked through the doors. It was apparent to him that the two shared some chemistry. So far he's managed to observe Logan McCleary and the younger McCleary brother, Alex. His research had uncovered two more brothers, John and Jake. He wondered if they would be in attendance this evening. Jake was military, a Special Forces commander; the other brother was F.B.I. He believed John McCleary had started the investigation, but he hadn't come up with a plausible reason why he would want to find him. There were two sisters; both married, he never bothered to look at them; he assumed one of the brothers was the key to the puzzle.

Nick watched the door; two men came barreling through it with a woman following behind them. Nick felt as if he'd just been punched in the solar plexus. Whoever she was, she was beautiful. He couldn't help staring at her. He was good at his job and although he was watching her, he couldn't possibly let her know it. Yet, he knew she felt his eyes on her. She looked up and scanned the room as if she was searching for the cause of her anxiety.

"I'm glad you were able to make it, Sis," Alex said as he greeted Morgan. "Look toward the end of the bar. I think another McCleary has jumped ship." Logan and Lizzy were deep in conversation and Morgan couldn't help but think it was about time.

"It's about time," she said, before asking if John or Jake had arrived.

"John said he was parking his car and Jake should be here in a few minutes." Alex asked what she was drinking. Joe and Neil had already made their way to the bar and were coming back with drinks for everyone before Morgan had a chance to answer Alex.

Joe handed Morgan a drink, then Alex. Alex took the drink and thanked him. Joe wasn't surprised that Alex had been doing such a great job running the company in Gage's absence. He had kept his eye on things so that he could offer Alex support but he was handling himself very well. Joe had been concerned that the barracudas would be circling. What he lacked in experience he made up for; he had balls. Alex was making a name for himself in the business world and Joe was proud of him. Joe knew Morgan trusted Alex explicitly.

John walked into the bar and wondered if he had made a mistake as soon as he saw Morgan. He would have to face her without having the answers she wanted so desperately. *Who is Nick Manetti and why is it impossible for me to find him?* Even if it killed John, he promised himself he would find this guy. Morgan was talking to Alex as he made his way over to them. He noticed their attention on Logan. Logan was focused on Lizzy, wow did she look different. *What's happened to little Lizzy?* Now there was a woman in her place and John understood the reason behind Alex and Morgan's fascination with Logan's newfound interest in Lizzy.

"Mind if I say a big wow? Where has Lizzy been hiding?" He and Alex laughed while waiting for Morgan to tell them to control themselves, but she didn't. She seemed to be looking around the room, as if searching for something. "Can I help? Are you looking for someone in particular?" John asked.

"No, I just had such a weird feeling. I'm glad you made it. John, relax tonight, okay? I know we need to move on. Not just me, but all of us." Morgan knew John still felt guilty. As a family, they had to heal. Gage would want that. Although Morgan still felt guilty for not being able to follow through on her promise to Gage, she promised herself that she would find Nick Manetti and she hoped it would be soon.

"Jake and Reigh will be here soon, along with her brother, Matt. Remember Matt? He loves Rockaway; he is looking forward to a night on the town with all of us. I don't think he realizes we are all getting older. Those late nights are becoming harder and harder to recuperate from," John added taking a swig of his beer.

"So true," Morgan looked over at Logan and saw how enamored he was with Lizzy. *I think he's officially taking himself off the market tonight.* Jake and Reigh joined them. After greeting everyone, Jake took notice of his missing brother. Little Lizzy didn't look very virtuous to him at the moment. He knew Lizzy was an attorney but he had to admit before tonight he saw her the way he thought Logan had. She was like a little sister to them but he could see that Lizzy would play a very different role in Logan's life.

Reigh put her arms around her husband, asking him what she had missed. When Jake blurted out their theory, Reigh looked over at the couple and smiled, agreeing wholeheartedly.

Just then, Logan told Lizzy they needed to finish their conversation later because they had guests to attend to. They both needed to mingle and make sure that everyone was having a good time. Lizzy went to one side of the room, Logan the other. Lizzy approached the man sitting at the other end of the bar, alone. She wondered why such a good-looking guy was not with anyone. He assured her that he was very comfortable and thanked her for her concern. Manetti told Lizzy he was new to the neighborhood and bought the tickets as a way to meet people.

"Everyone here is very friendly, you'll see. I'm sorry, but I didn't introduce myself. My name is Lizzy and I'm a friend of the owner, Logan McCleary," holding out her hand.

"Alex Summers, it's a pleasure to meet you," shaking her hand. *Why did I just use Gage's undercover name. It's the only name that came to my head and it was stupid of me.* He didn't make mistakes like this. The woman who had walked in with the two men had his brain in a flux. If John McCleary was searching for him, he now felt as though there was an arrow pointing straight at him.

The next few hours went along without a hitch. Midnight was coming and Morgan wondered what she was going to do when all the couples in the room began kissing their significant others. *Maybe I can sneak away and step outside just before the ball drops.* It was a possibility. She decided that now would be a good time to check out the buffet table Lizzy had set up. She had been so busy talking to their friends, people she hadn't seen in such a long time; she had forgotten to eat and the alcohol she had consumed was beginning to affect her.

Chapter Eighteen

Nick Manetti watched as she made her way to the buffet table. Perhaps, he might kill two birds with one stone. He was attracted to this lovely creature and she was noticeably familiar with the McCleary clan, so... Maybe she had the answers to his questions and wasn't aware of it. Nick made his way to the table, reached for a plate and followed her down the line. When she reached for slice of meat, he did too. The touch of his hand sent quivers down her spine. There had been only one man who was able to do that to her. "It seems we have the same taste," he said as she turned to look at the man who had her feeling this way.

This man is beautiful. Are men beautiful? Where have my words gone? Why am I finding it difficult to have a conversation with him? She could tell just by looking at him that his demeanor screamed trouble. *Why am I so attracted to him?* She needed to walk away and she needed to do it immediately. She knew she wasn't ready for someone like him. She tried to seem uninterested but when he reached for her plate and offered to take it to her table she was nervous, so she accepted.

Morgan took a deep breath. "Do I know you?"

"No, I just moved to town recently. I don't really know anyone. I'm Jack; I was told your name is Morgan, am I correct?" he asked as they ate. After sharing some small talk, Nick realized Morgan was one of the sisters. She hadn't said her last name but she said she was single. His information was usually spot-on but it was apparent he had gotten the wrong information, at least about one of the sisters. His information said both sisters were married. As midnight approached, Morgan excused herself, and Nick watched as she stepped out the front door of the bar, heading to the street. He decided, against his better judgment, to follow her. He could hear voices coming from inside as they began the countdown. She knew he followed her but she didn't know why. He frightened her, just the way Gage had when they'd first met, but she wasn't that innocent kid anymore.

The countdown hit two just as Nick moved into her guarded space. One, he heard, as he lifted her chin and kissed her softly on her lips. He hadn't meant to be so forward, not to her, but he couldn't help himself. He could tell she had such kissable lips. He deepened the kiss and she realized she wasn't fighting him any longer. She was an experienced lover; he could see that even from her kiss. She was definitely stunning and he was deeply attracted to her. *There, is definitely another side to my Morgan.* He was amused that he had just *thought of her as his* Morgan. She acted every bit the proper lady but he could see something inside her burning to be freed. He didn't know if it was the alcohol but she was absolutely turned on by him and he was turned on by her.

"Morgan, honey, I don't think you want to do this here. If we don't put a stop to this right now I'm going to be very embarrassed. Do you live close by?" He wanted her and he didn't want to think about her family and why they were looking for him, especially not right now.

"I can't leave with you no matter how tempting you are, Jack. I don't know you and I don't go home with strangers." He admired her tenacity and her strength. *Morgan, what are you doing to me?* He laughed at the irony of it all. Her brother or brothers, for all he knew, wanted him dead. In his business he had made a lot of enemies and the time and energy they were spending trying to find him made him think it wasn't just to say hello. There were reasons people searched for someone for a long time and none of them could be good at least not in his situation.

"Let's go back inside, maybe you and I should get to know one another a little better." Nick had almost dismissed his reason for coming to McCleary's; he was more interested in getting to know Morgan.

The two of them entered the bar and were immediately joined by her family. The men were very interested in the new man in town and what he wanted with their sister. Lizzy started the introductions.

"Alex, I'd like you to meet Morgan's over protective family. Let me introduce you; this is John, Logan, Alex, Patti, Bill, Jake, Reigh, and her very dear friends, Joe and Neil." Nick shook hands with the entire family but he couldn't help but notice the blank look on Morgan's face. She looked confused as he realized Lizzy had just introduced him to the family as Alex while he had introduced himself to her as Jack, it was *another stupid mistake. One Nick had never made before.* Nick didn't know what he was going to do to make it right but apparently she wasn't correcting the mistake and she wasn't going to give up his secret just yet. He knew he had some explaining to do and he needed to come up with something plausible. He didn't want to lie to her but he had no idea what kind of situation he was walking into. He could tell she felt betrayed but he didn't know why it bothered him so much. Nick was used to being deceptive. It was how he made his living and stayed alive, until a year and half ago.

It was another hour before Nick could get Morgan alone to talk to her and when he did he begged her to let him explain. Morgan didn't know why she trusted this stranger, but she did. It went against everything she believed in yet she was perfectly willing to give Jack or Alex or whatever his name was the benefit of the doubt. *I hope I don't regret this later.* He asked if they could talk privately and she agreed. They stepped outside into the cool fresh sea air and Nick thought about where to begin.

"I know you're probably wondering why I told Lizzy my name was Alex and I told you Jack, right? I don't want to seem cocky but I didn't care if Lizzy was introducing herself or one of her friends to me. I'm a private investigator and I am here representing a client. The woman I represent was sure her husband was here, or supposed to be here, with another woman. I didn't mean to deceive you, Morgan. I'm sorry." Nick watched her eyes as Morgan processed the information. Her reaction was telling. She was concerned but she believed him so for a second time he lied to her. Nick was having a hard time lying to this woman. He had only just met her but what she thought of him really mattered.

"Did you find him?"

"No, he isn't here. I watched everyone who walked into the place, but other than thinking your brothers might be the man I was looking for, I didn't see him." John and Jake looked a lot like the cheating husband, he said, but now he knew they couldn't be him. Morgan laughed, John wasn't married; she assured him. "John is a law enforcement agent and he's single. He is too involved in his job to be married and Jake is a retired Navy Seal, recently married, so you can count him out too."

"So is it Alex or Jack, or do you go by another name?" She could tell he was lying to her by the way he looked away from her when he spoke. Gage had taught her the signals to look for when someone was lying to you. "Why are you lying to me, Alex or Jack or whoever you really are?" she asked as her voice rose in a disappointed sigh.

Nick Manetti didn't know why but he was about to put his life in danger for this beautiful woman standing before him. "My name isn't Alex, Jack or Pete. My birth name is Nick. Morgan, my real name is Nick Manetti. I don't know why your family is looking for me and that is why I kept my true identity a secret. I still need to know why your brothers are searching for me." Nick saw a shocked look on her face. She was stunned for what seemed like ages before she uttered a word.

"Nick Manetti," she whispered. "I've been searching for you for two years, not my family, just me. I have a message for you from someone but I don't want you to think I'm crazy when I tell you what I have to say. I don't even know where to start…" Morgan tried to gain her composure. *I can't believe I've finally found him after all this time. But I haven't felt this way about anyone since Gage and I don't want him to disappear when I tell him what I have to say. What should I do or say?*

"You have a message from whom?" Nick wondered if he was still in danger.

"I'm afraid I don't know where to start. My husband was killed in Syria two years ago by Isis. I don't know what you had to do with my husband but the message…" she paused as Nick moved toward her, held her shoulders and asked her to stop, in a whisper.

"I'm sorry, I'm so sorry for whatever pain I may have caused you. I didn't think I had a choice," he mumbled but continued, almost babbling. Morgan tried to stop him but he kept talking as he told her that life was in the past and he had been trying to put it all behind him. He told her that two years ago he'd had to do something that he hasn't been able to live with and that was the reason he walked away from the C.I.A. She was trying to let him vent but she knew she needed to talk to him about Gage.

"Stop Nick, I wanted to give you a message from Gage." That was all that left her mouth when he froze. She said she had a message from Gage and of course he knew Gage was dead.

"What, but Gage is dead," he said in a defeated voice.

"I want you to listen to me. Don't interrupt me, no matter how insane this sounds. Promise me?" He took in a breath and for the first time things were making sense. He now realized the woman who was able to get Gage Delaney to settle down was standing right in front of him. This Morgan was the Morgan Delaney. He wasn't surprised that Gage had fallen so hard. *She'd had the same effect on me!* She still hadn't mentioned her last name but he was convinced that Morgan had been Gage's wife.

"Gage and I had a connection that few couples have ever experienced. We felt things, almost like twins do. The moment Gage stopped breathing, I knew it. He came to me in my dreams." Her eyes began to well up as she continued to tell him this unbelievable story. "He stayed with me for much longer than he should have but when it was time for him to go I watched him pass from this world into the next, along with our son. I know that sounds crazy, I even thought I had lost my mind." She was sobbing and although Nick wanted more than anything to hold her and console her, he didn't. "Gage asked me to find you. He said I had to find Nick Manetti and that he may go by the name of Pete Scali. He told me to find you and tell you he forgives you. He said you did what he asked you to do and that you needed to forgive yourself. He made me promise to find you. He said you needed to hear this from me and only me," Morgan could see that the ex C.I.A. agent was visibly shaken.

Nick had always considered himself a man's man. Yet, he was falling apart at the seams and he didn't want her to see him like this. *Is this a joke? How did Gage's widow know anything about what I'd done?* No one knew what I had done. He and Gage hadn't even told their superiors what they were up to. At C.I.A. headquarters they had believed he quit his job because he'd lost his edge. No one had any idea that the guilt he felt by causing Gage's death was the catalyst behind his withdrawal. *How does Morgan know anything and what does she know?*

John had been worried about Morgan and went looking for her. She had left McCleary's over twenty minutes ago with a stranger and they had just met. *Who is he and where are they?* He decided to see for himself and told Jake where he was going. Jake decided to join him. If Morgan needed them, they would be there for her. When John and Jake walked outside, they were confused by what they saw. Morgan was in tears and Alex, or whoever he was seemed just as rattled as she was. "What the heck is going on?" Morgan looked up as her brothers approached.

"I'm fine. John and Jake, I'd like you to meet Nick Manetti. We were just talking and if you could give us some privacy, we will finish our conversation." John knew his sister wasn't asking, she was telling them to leave. Neither man knew who Nick Manetti was but they were pretty sure she was in no immediate danger.

Once the two men disappeared Nick bucked up to prepare himself for the most difficult conversation he'd ever had in his life. "We need to talk, Morgan. What I need to say to you is just as important as what you just shared with me. You may never want to see me again after you hear what I have to say. You may hate me for what I have to tell you, but I ask you for the same patience you asked of me. Say nothing until I explain everything fully." He waited for her to respond, she agreed. He wanted her to understand what happened in Syria, how much he loved Gage and how hard it had been for him to do what he had to do.

"I was still an active agent when I got a call from Gage a little over two years ago. Gage taught me everything I know. He was my mentor, my friend, and my brother. Gage and I were in a foster home together as kids. I often think that had I never met Gage I would have been dead long before now or a thug living on the streets. Gage was determined to succeed and he made sure he took me along for the ride. I wasn't a Seal, like Gage. I was a Ranger but we stayed in contact and re-connected years later when Gage joined the C.I.A. He recruited me shortly thereafter. We were both good at our jobs. He spoke about you to me whenever we arranged to see each other. But the golden rule was to keep our private lives private and that included from each other. So, even though I knew of you, that was all

I knew, no details. So two years ago, Gage called me. He asked me to shadow him on a mission that he knew was extremely dangerous. He didn't want anyone to know I was there. It was a mission he didn't believe he would return from."

Morgan was listening intently. Gage knew how much danger he would be in while trying to save Jake but he went anyway. He'd done that for her, she knew that. The tears began to surface as she listened to Nick. There were times when she wanted to beg him to stop but she knew she couldn't. It had to be endured by both of them until the end. Nick took off his jacket and wrapped it around Morgan.

"Gage had been sanctioned by the C.I.A. to attempt to gain the release of the British journalist in Syria. I thought it was odd that he had come out of retirement for this but I never questioned him. I would have followed him anywhere. I owed him that much. After he had gained the release of the soldier and the journalist, he sent them on their way and I continued to shadow him so he could leave the country safely. He told me it would be difficult, especially with a bounty on his head, and he didn't have much hope of getting out alive. I had to shadow him for one purpose, one purpose only. I was to take a kill shot if he gave me the signal. Nick could see that Morgan understood what he had implied. He killed Gage. Nick had never cried but tears ran down the side of his face as he explained why he took the life of the man they both loved.

"It took all of my willpower I possessed not to approach them as I saw men take Gage into a dilapidated building. I watched as they tied him up and beat him mercilessly. Through my scope, I could see he was ordering me to stay put via our prearranged signals. He ordered me to do absolutely nothing. I saw the one in charge walk into the room and film what they were doing to Gage. I knew, and so did Gage, that he wasn't getting out of that room alive. We both knew there was nothing I could do to save him. Gage knew the man with the machete in his hand was going to torture him before killing him. Gage looked up and gave the signal and, God forgive me, I took the shot. I'm so sorry, Morgan. We both knew we had no other choice." Nick stared at Morgan and willed her to say something, say anything. She seemed to be in shock. He didn't know whether he should share anything else. What he had just revealed to her, even their government hadn't been privy to.

Morgan recalled what the officials had told her. They had said Gage could've been alive as each of his limbs was severed from his body. Nick Manetti was offering her some solace, knowing Gage hadn't been alive when those horrible men did what they did to him. Isis wanted our government to believe Gage was alive, but he wasn't. Gage, in his dying moments, had taken that power from them. *Do they know about Nick Manetti?* She still had questions.

"Why didn't the C.I.A. know about you?" she whispered.

"I wasn't there, officially. I was there for Gage. The C.I.A. never would've condoned being on the same op with him. He was sanctioned but they had no idea I was in that part of the world. I was in China, allegedly. If the op went terribly wrong it would've been on Gage's head. They would have blamed it on a rogue agent. The only way I could help Gage was to remain hidden in the background. The agency thought that someone else might have been there but it was never proven. They knew he was shot with a bullet to the head but without additional proof, they couldn't tell where the kill shot came from or who fired it. I don't know if it helps you to know he didn't suffer, but I assure you he was not alive when they did what they did to him,"

Morgan knew that Gage's death had deeply affected Nick and now she understood why Gage had appeared to her. He wanted to relieve them of that shared guilt and what better way to do that than to have them meet. It was obvious that Nick had stayed around after the kill shot and bore witness to the horrific event that took place afterwards.

"You need to talk about what you saw, Nick. You know that, don't you? I know what they did to him and hearing your version makes it easier for me to live with. I loved Gage with all my heart. What he did was courageous and for that my family will always be grateful to him. I knew, after he came to me that day at the beach, that he was with our son. As difficult as this might be for you to understand, I want to thank you for taking that shot. Gage didn't deserve to suffer and you made sure that didn't happen. I'd like you to stay on, if you can. My family would love to meet you and I know two men *who really need to meet you.* Jake and John have never forgiven themselves for Gage's death. If they met you and everyone talked, it would be beneficial to the healing process." She waited, at first she didn't think Nick would accept her offer, but he did. Now, they had to go inside and convince her family to wait with their questions until the morning. *This is too much for one night.*

Chapter Nineteen

Ellie had just put her new grandson down for a nap when she heard a large commotion outside. She went to the window and saw her sons heading toward the house, as if on a mission. *Am I seeing things?* She rubbed her eyes. She had thought she had seen Gage and Michael standing on the other side of the street, watching what was happening. She looked closer as they smiled at her and then, in an instant, they were gone. Ellie was stunned. She had never experienced anything like that before. She saw her sons approaching and decided to keep her apparitions to herself, at least for now.

"My God, what are all of you doing here; you all look like you're on a mission?" she asked, trying to forget about ghosts.

"Mom, where is Morgan? Did she bring Nick Manetti here?" John asked.

"Morgan hasn't come by yet," Ellie had said, understanding her daughter's need to be alone. "I'll call her if you want but if you wait I'm sure she'll be here soon. Joey is waiting patiently for her." She wanted her sons' to give Morgan some breathing room. Alex decided to mention that Morgan had found Nick Manetti herself yesterday; they were all supposed to meet here to talk to him.

I wonder if seeing Gage and Michael had anything to do with this Nick Manetti. Gage seemed contented and it appeared to her that Gage was saying good bye, that he would not be coming back. Ellie didn't know what her son-in-law was trying to say but she was curious to meet Nick Manetti.

Morgan had hoped that her walk on the beach this morning would give her answers she craved but there were none forthcoming. She thought if she and Nick were together, Gage would appear but he didn't. They walked for hours watching the water as it crashed against the shoreline. Morgan hadn't felt Gage's presence at all; she wondered if that meant something. *Will I ever see him again? Maybe he wants me to go on without him but can I?* Forever and always, always and forever, that's what they had always promised each other. She glanced over at Nick; he was studying her. She could see he knew she was having second thoughts, wondering if what was happening between them was a good thing, or not.

She definitely had a physical attraction toward Nick but could this ever develop into something more? *Am I ready for this?* I have so many questions.

"Nick, I don't feel him anymore. I always felt him when I came here, to the beach. It was the one place I felt he was still with me. Do you think he's angry, that I spent the night with you?"

"Please, don't do this to yourself." Nick lifted her chin, looked into her eyes and said just what she needed to hear. "I know Gage and I know he would be happy for you. He would be happy for us. We were both in a dark place when you and I met and he brought us together. Gage led us through the darkness and into the light," holding her hand in his and bringing it to his lips. "Don't demean what we shared last night. I don't want this to end. I agree that maybe we need to slow down. We can date the proper way and see where it goes. If we get to know one another, what might happen is anyone's guess. This is an opportunity for us to start over, like a new beginning."

Nick had never felt this connected to any woman before and he wasn't about to let go of it. He'd never had time to have a relationship in the past and truth be told he'd never wanted to be tied down. He had never stayed in one place long enough to establish any kind of relationship and in his line of work any serious relationship wasn't ever in the cards. The job was just too dangerous. He felt at peace in his heart when he was with Morgan and he couldn't explain it, not even to himself. Gage always told him that when the right woman came along, he'd know. Nick never thought they'd have a bond with the same woman. He wanted Morgan to give them time to get to know each other and see where the relationship would lead. After a time, if she decided he wasn't right for her, he would accept it and move on. But he was hoping it would be forever and always. He and Gage had always said they would be there for each other, forever and always, always and forever. As lame as it sounded, it meant everything to two young boys who lived through hell in their early years. They'd always had each other, through all the abuse they went through in foster care.

Morgan began to question the decisions she was making. *I don't want to lose Gage forever.* She decided to go back to the house and introduce Nick to her brothers, as planned. She knew they had a lot of questions but after that she needed some time alone. She didn't want to hear any more news about terrorists, killings or torture. She had heard and lived through enough bad news for a lifetime. Once Nick met with her family and had the conversation as promised, she wanted to put all of this behind her.

"Gage, your death was devastating to me. I love you, I always will; Forever and always, as promised. No one will ever be equal to what you meant to me. You're not here anymore and I know that. I'm glad you're with Michael. Take care, my forever love, until we meet again," she said silently while staring at the place where Gage had stood and talked to her. He had his reasons for leaving and knowing him the way she did he would want her to move on and not hold back, otherwise relying on her memory of him as a substitute for her happiness.

Chapter Twenty

SPRING

Morgan sat on the back deck and looked out at the ocean. She pulled her knees to her chest and shivered a little as the cold ocean breeze hit her body. It was invigorating, being able to take in a breath and enjoy the home she and Gage had built together. She was happy with the life that Gage left for her and Joey. She had come to terms with his death and finally felt peace, knowing he hadn't suffered during the last moments of his life. Nick had done what Gage wanted him to do and she hoped he had forgiven himself. The alternative was something she didn't dare think about. *Nick, I forgive you.* She whispered her thoughts into the air and hoped with all her heart that he had finally forgiven himself. Morgan was in a better place these days, more like her old self than ever before. She knew Gage had worried about her and hoped he was witnessing the person she was today. Her writing career was soaring and Gage's construction business was doing great, thanks to Alex. She let her thoughts roam. She was thinking about Nick a lot. She couldn't get him out of her mind.

After the family had met with Nick in January, they genuinely liked the man he was. Her brothers felt they owed Nick a chance for everything he had been called upon to do. They asked him to stay on, Nick jumped at the chance. He wanted to get to know Morgan and the opportunity was being placed in his lap. Alex offered him a job with the company and it worked. He was happy there and he loved being a part of a family. He knew now why Gage was so content. It was the first time he'd ever bonded with anyone other than Gage. Logan offered him an apartment above the restaurant and he settled in quite easily. Not a day went by that he didn't thank Gage for what he'd done for him. The cloak and dagger life he'd led before was practically a distant memory these days.

Alex couldn't believe the rapport Nick developed with his men. Work got done faster and mostly without incident. Nick understood unions and he handled the problems that came up without much grief. He always repeated what Gage would have said in the same situation. Most men and women wanted a decent wage and safety on the job; if you give that to them they'd give you an honest day's work and never let you down. Nick and Morgan saw each other for a few months and everything seemed to be going well. He even attended Sunday dinners at the McCleary's. He was fitting in with the brothers nicely. Jake had finally found a home for himself, Reigh and their little girl. Nick even helped him move in.

Logan and Lizzy were a couple these days. Although she worked less at McCleary's, they were adjusting well to this new relationship. *Everyone was waiting for the announcement.*

In less than a year, two brothers are in committed relationships. I never saw this coming, Gage.

Morgan smiled, stood up and leaned against the rail staring out at the ocean. She couldn't help talking to Gage about the night she asked Nick to leave. She knew now, it had been a mistake. She recalled their conversation with such vividness.

"Why, we're good together? Aren't you happy?"

She hadn't doubted herself before but after encountering Laura Peters at C.I.A. headquarters she had decided to reassess their relationship. Morgan had gone to C.I.A. headquarters with her family to pay homage to Gage by touching the star given in his honor. Nick was with them along with a few of the agents Gage had known from the past. As Nick made the rounds and introduced the family to people he knew, Morgan was approached by a woman who, up to this point, had stayed in the background.

"Mrs. Delaney, my name is Laura Peters. I knew your husband and wanted to offer my condolences personally. We met when he was searching for Nick. I was Nick's handler, very briefly I might add. Nick and I were in a relationship at the time and for my safety he asked for another handler. I know Nick has been having a difficult time adjusting to civilian life. He has recently requested reassignment to active status. It seems he's missed *the life and us*," referring to the relationship between Nick and herself, which she made abundantly clear. "I think he stayed with your family as long as he did out of loyalty to Gage. He did tell you that he and Gage were practically brothers, I assume?" Nick had a weird look on his face as he joined them and asked Morgan if everything was okay.

Suddenly, she realized that Nick wasn't falling in love with her but he felt obligated to her. She might've acted completely out of character by sleeping with him that first night but perhaps it had more to do with the loss they both felt. Morgan couldn't help feeling foolish but she also felt a sense of responsibility to Nick. She had allowed their relationship to continue without making sure it was what Nick wanted. *Maybe his guilt made him feel that we were his responsibility?* She couldn't allow him to believe that. She would find a way to set him free, to let him live the life he wanted, not only as an agent but a life with Laura too. It broke her heart knowing that he wanted this woman. Laura Peters was everything she wasn't. The woman was beautiful in an exotic sort of way. She on the other hand, was the girl you took home to mom.

"Nick, you're such a worrier. Everything is fine. Isn't that right, Mrs. Delaney?" Laura had stated.

"Sure, everything is fine."

Nick didn't know what had just transpired between the two women but he was sure Laura had something to do with Morgan's sudden change of attitude. He would make damn sure Laura didn't hurt her. It was just like Laura to insinuate anything, whether about him or Gage. Laura still held a grudge ever since he had called things off between them and asked for a new handler. It was dangerous enough for him in the field without having a handler to worry about, one who was one step away from being committed. The woman was insane. Gage had told him to get rid of her. He didn't know if it was the job or what, but the woman was downright crazy. He had wanted nothing to do with her but he didn't want to see her lose her job so he didn't let the company know how nuts she was. He often wondered if that had been a mistake.

Morgan enjoyed the rest of that afternoon with the family and Nick took them site seeing. Throughout the day, Morgan couldn't help thinking about what Laura had insinuated. Nick had immersed himself in her family and she knew it would be hard to ask him to leave. Her brothers would miss him. She began comparing herself to Laura and she always came up short, in her mind. It was like comparing a starlet to the girl next door.

She decided the only way to know for sure where she stood with Nick was to let him go. Gage once said that if you love someone, you need to let them go. If he or she comes back to you, they were always yours in the first place. Morgan knew Nick wouldn't go without a fight. She had to find a way to convince him that she needed time alone. That had been six months ago; it was tough at first.

Alex kept in touch with Nick during the past six months. He would drop an occasional hint to Morgan about how he was doing. Alex told her he had kept Nick on the payroll. Contrary to what Laura said, he wanted to keep his job with the company and Alex agreed to keep him on. Nick was becoming a vital part of the company. Even though he lived in Colorado, he and Alex were still a great team. It felt like old times for Alex. Working with Nick was just like working with Gage. Nick was handling all the overseas work, the work Alex found himself missing.

There was a knock on her door; it was Alex. She poured him a drink and asked if he wanted to stay for lunch. Alex had a gift in his hand, he handed it to her. "What's this? My birthday isn't until next week."

"Aren't you going to open it?" Morgan looked at the box, she was curious as she opened it. The beautiful gold necklace had an Irish inscription on the back of its hanging pendant. *Mo Anam Cara.* She was Irish but she had no idea what it meant. *Perhaps Mom will know or better yet I can look it up on the computer.*

"Who is it from?"

"I was under the impression you two weren't talking to each other?"

Morgan knew that the gift was from Nick. "We haven't been lately. He's probably just being nice. You know I'm Gage's widow and all."

Alex watched her fumble with the necklace. It was clear that Nick still rattled his sister. "How are things at the office?" she asked, to change the subject.

Alex smiled to himself; he knew Morgan got reports from the accounting department every month. She knew Gage's company was growing faster than anyone could've imagined. Alex had all the paperwork revised so that the company now belonged fully to Morgan, under her maiden name. The company would never be connected to Gage; should there be any fallout from past C.I.A. missions. Alex knew Gage would've wanted him to do this and he was very happy with the salary Morgan insisted on paying him. It more than compensated for the time he put in and she would've gladly paid him more if he wanted it.

Alex was happy with the choices he had made and continued to make. They spent the next hour avoiding the elephant until Alex picked up the necklace to admire it.

"What does it mean?" When he realized she didn't know, he fished his phone from his coat pocket and typed in the words. He smiled when he read its meaning. "My soul-mate," he told her.

Morgan was shocked. *Did Laura lie to me? I think I just wasted six months of our lives.* "I guess Nick feels a little more for you than you thought he did."

Alex decided to let Morgan think about what the necklace meant. "What time are you going to McCleary's Friday night?" As soon as he said it, he regretted it. Lizzy would kill him. She'd been planning this surprise birthday party for weeks with Reigh's help. "Damn, I'm such an idiot, pretend you heard nothing."

Morgan grinned, now she had something to hold over Alex's head. "I hate being the center of attention. Why didn't you talk them out of this? I appreciate it, but you know I hate the fuss."

"It's only one night. Besides, your birthday gives everyone something to celebrate." Alex walked over to where Joey was busy playing with his trucks. "Hey, my little man. Give me a hug. I have to go and meet Uncle John over at Grandma's."

"What's John up to?" she asked, following him into the living room.

"Nothing much, he wanted me to come with him to look at a few houses. It seems another brother has decided to remain in Rockaway. He wants to make sure the house he buys is in good shape."

"Wow! John, a homeowner! Is he seeing anyone?" Perhaps John was looking to settle down for another reason. Alex shook his head, as if he didn't know. "Good luck with the house hunting. Let me know if you guys find anything. Tell John, if he needs anything I'm here."

After Alex left, Morgan looked at the necklace and decided calling Nick would be too impersonal. So she called and made arrangements for a flight to Colorado. Then she called her mother and asked if Joey could stay with her for a couple of days. As soon as Ellie heard the reason Morgan needed a sitter, she was only too happy to oblige. She knew her daughter and Nick had made a connection. *I think Morgan and I need to have a little chat; I can't wait to see her and Joey.*

Morgan called Joe Kirby and after telling him about the necklace, she asked him if he'd give her a ride to the airport.

"You don't have to ask me twice. I always liked that guy. I told you there was absolutely nothing between him and that woman. I spoke to her for less than ten minutes and I already knew she was nothing but a conniving bitch. Pack something sexy. I have a feeling your real birthday gift is waiting in Colorado." It made Joe smile to hear how happy she sounded and as he thought it about it a bit more, he was glad that Morgan had taken the past six months to grieve Gage properly. When she and Nick got together this time, he knew there wouldn't be a third person in the relationship. Morgan was a healthier person now and he was happy for her.

Ellie McCleary greeted Morgan and Joey at the door. Right away, Morgan knew there was something her mother couldn't wait to tell her. "Mom, you have an odd look on your face; I've seen it before and you're scaring me. What do you want to say?" she asked nervously.

"I don't know if you'll think I've lost my mind but do you remember the morning after you met Nick?" Her mother continued her story. "I went out to the street because I had heard a commotion. Then I saw your brothers getting out of a car and walking toward the house. Suddenly, my attention was drawn to a figure standing across the street, a silhouette of a man with a boy on his shoulders. I couldn't believe what I saw, Morgan. As clear as day, I saw Gage with Michael on his shoulders step out of the shadows. They smiled at me; Gage looked as though he was saying goodbye and I think he wanted me to know he and Michael were going to be okay and you didn't need him anymore. He looked contented. I don't know how I knew it but I did, I'm sure of it. I wanted to tell you sooner but you didn't seem ready to hear it. Do you think I'm crazy?"

Morgan was stunned but now she knew why Gage hadn't appeared to her since that day on the beach. "Mom, thanks for telling me this today. I needed to hear that and I hope it's not too late for me and Nick. I know I hurt him when I asked him to leave. He sent me this today." She pointed to the necklace and pendant around her neck. "Do you know what it means?" It was a rhetorical question, but she had a feeling her mother knew what it meant.

"Mo Anam Cara…of course, it's Gaelic; *it means my soul-mate*. It seems my future son-in-law knows what it means to fall in love. Go to him, Morgan. You've both been through more than you should for such young people and you both deserve to be happy." Ellie McCleary could see that Joey always put a smile on her daughter's face but Nick Manetti was the man to help her to enjoy life again. She would surely give thanks at church this week for all the good fortune coming to her family.

Chapter Twenty-One

Nick had been out on a run and heading back to his cabin, as he approached, he sensed someone there. He slowed down and waited to see if they would show themselves. He knew it was a friendly, the racket they were making made it obvious. As he got closer he saw Morgan standing by the window. *She looks more beautiful every time I see her.* He hoped he knew the reason she'd come to see him but he had to leave the next move up to her.

"Nick, I've been such a fool. I received your gift today. It's beautiful, by the way. I needed to know if you mean it."

"I meant every word of it...Forever and Always, Morgan Delaney. I'm in love with you. I've loved you from the moment I first laid eyes on you when you walked through the door at McCleary's on New Year's Eve. I knew I had just spied on my soul-mate. How could I and the only other person I ever loved on this earth possibly love the same woman? I can't even begin to explain how much Gage meant to me. Gage was my lifeline while growing up. He gave me hope when I had none. Gage believed we could do great things and I believed him because Gage had never let me down. I have to admit that knowing I could take care of you and Joey for him comforted me but don't doubt for one second that my feelings for you have anything to do with Gage."

Nick moved closer to Morgan; he could see her breathing was becoming labored. His future was excited to see him and he knew he could make her uneasy the closer he got to her. *She can't hide what she is feeling from me.* He lifted her into his embrace. "I've waited all my life for you. If you doubt how I feel about you, let me take you inside and show you just what you do to me," he said as he lifted her over his shoulder and carried her into his home. No one had ever seen the inside of his place, not even the delivery people. They would always leave packages on the front porch.

Morgan was quite surprised when he put her down. Nick's cabin was very homey, not at all what she expected. She thought, given the life he'd led that she would be walking into a bachelor pad. It was small with a beautiful updated kitchen and an open concept living room with a strikingly exquisite fireplace. Off to the side she could see a half bath. But what drew her attention mostly was the room to the back of the cabin, probably the master suite. She wanted to run to it.

"You look like you're dying to explore so let's go, pronto. Welcome to our suite for the night, my lady. I hope it meets your expectations." Nick knew she loved what she was seeing.

The king-size bed was definitely inviting. She couldn't help herself as she fell into the bed; it drew her in like a magnet. He told Morgan to get comfortable and he would join her after taking a quick shower. Nick turned on the water and lathered up hoping she might join him and she didn't let him down. They made love in the shower until their skin began to wrinkle and the water turned cold. *So this is what it feels like to be content. We are finally where we're meant to be and it can't get any better than this!*

They talked all night about the past, the present and their future. Nick insisted they stop in Las Vegas on the way home. He wanted Morgan to become his wife and he didn't want to wait another minute. Neither one needed or wanted the fanfare of a large wedding. If the McCleary's chose to celebrate the event, they would do so at the restaurant Friday night during Morgan's birthday celebration. He asked her if she wanted to have other children. Her response made him very happy. He knew he would love Joey as if he was his own. Maybe someday Joey would look after his child the same way Gage looked after him while growing up. Gage protected him when they were younger and often took beatings that were meant for him. He would be forever in Gage's debt.

He watched Morgan looking at the few pictures he had situated around the room. She wore his tee shirt to cover her naked body. As he stared, his body gave his feelings away. Morgan picked up a picture of him and Gage when they were young kids. Right next to it was a shot of them both meeting at an airport. The last framed picture Nick had was the last picture they took together, when they met to discuss the infamous kill shot.

"Is that hard for you to look at?"

"No, I loved Gage and I have nothing but great memories of the time we shared but you, Nick Manetti, are my future. I love you; besides, if anyone would be happy to see us together, it would be Gage. Never doubt that I love you and the fact that Gage brought us together makes our union that much more meaningful. Now, didn't you promise me a massage?" she teased as she lifted his tee shirt over her head, exposing her body to him.

"What are you doing to me, Morgan Delaney, or should I say Morgan Manetti? I never asked you, but I would be honored if you would allow me to adopt Joey. It's up to you and I'll fully understand if you don't want me to. I have been giving this a lot of thought and I have to tell you if you didn't come here, I was coming to McCleary's on Friday night. You don't have to worry, Joey will always know who his father is and I'll tell him everything I know about him. You'll have to tell me and Joey all about his older brother, Michael." Suddenly, he realized Morgan had tears in her eyes, but they looked like good tears. He smiled as his future wife jumped into his arms.

"Yes, now let's get busy starting that family you were talking about."

Nick knew he had met his match, that he'd never grow tired of the woman in his arms. He had to pinch himself to make sure it was real. He had been so used to living lies that this life with Morgan was something he always thought would be out of reach for him.

Ellie McCleary was excited but promised to keep their secret until Friday night. She couldn't wait for the rest of the family to hear the news, including Logan's announcement. Logan and Lizzy were going to announce their intentions to marry on Friday as well. Mrs. Nick Manetti, it had a nice ring to it. She wished they had waited for the family but she understood the urgency to move on with their lives.

Ellie McCleary stared out her kitchen window while doing dishes; she had a big smile on her face. John and Alex, maybe next year will be their year. Life was good for the McCleary's. The family was continuing to grow and each of her scoundrels was finding a woman who would conquer their wandering souls.

THE END